The Shingle Bar Sea Monster and Other Stories
Laura Solomon
Proverse Hong Kong

THE SHINGLE BAR SEA MONSTER AND OTHER STORIES uses surrealism and black humour to explore human predicaments, emotions and aspirations, and to suggest solutions to life's challenges. The situations are extraordinary, the aspirations and emotions are common, and the solutions debatable. A young woman is taken to a sea monster's underwater palace and helps the mermaids preserve seaweed. A girl finds that her right hand can no longer feel. Another girl becomes her younger sister's guardian angel. Two men of different tastes and habits struggle to co-exist after the head of one is grafted to the body of the other. An executive experiences uncontrollable anger after undergoing open-brain surgery. Two sisters continue their childhood rivalry after being reminded of a favourite TV programme. A male scientist is forced to give up the child that he himself gave birth to. On the verge of burnout, a jaded London lawyer heads out to the Mojave desert to set up a new life for herself. Ghosts visit two sisters. A girl hears her dead grandmother speak. A modern day Lady Bluebeard lures men to grisly deaths, but adores her seventh husband and cannot bring herself to kill him. A young woman defends her passion for writing. A blind man in love carries a magical cane that makes flowers bloom on the pavement. An amnesiac builds a new life for himself. During the progress of a new relationship, secrets are revealed. A wife suspects her husband of having an affair with a group of mannequins. A woman flies to New Zealand to begin a new life as a romance novelist. Another woman buys a lighthouse through the encouragement of a friend. A schoolboy learns to levitate and is stoned and drowned by jealous classmates. A man finds the button for rewinding his life. Conjoined twins learn to survive and even thrive in the world. The purchase of a duvet leads to estrangement between an established couple, caused by the woman's extraordinary metamorphosis into a feathered winged creature. Always interesting, these stories – with their often bizarre realities – prompt us to see our own lives from the perspective of others. Do we also live in a somewhat off-centre world?

LAURA SOLOMON has an honours degree in English Literature (Victoria University, 1997) and a Master's degree in Computer Science (University of London, 2003). Her published books include *Black Light*, *Nothing Lasting*, *Alternative Medicine*, *An Imitation of Life*, *Instant Messages*, *Hilary and David*, and the poetry collection, *In Vitro*. She has won prizes in the Bridport, Edwin Morgan, Ware Poets, Willesden Herald, Proverse Prize, and Essex Poetry Festival competitions.

The Shingle Bar
Sea Monster

and Other Stories

Laura Solomon

Proverse Hong Kong

The Shingle Bar Sea Monster and Other Stories
by Laura Solomon.
Alternate pbk edition published in Hong Kong by Proverse Hong Kong,
December 2016.
ISBN: 978-988-8228-08-9
Copyright © Laura Solomon 2016
Available from: https://www.createspace.com/6762085

First published in Hong Kong by Proverse Hong Kong, 20 November 2012.
Copyright © Laura Solomon 2012.
ISBN 978-988-8167-35-7

Enquiries: Proverse Hong Kong, P. O. Box 259, Tung Chung Post Office,
Tung Chung, Lantau Island, New Territories, Hong Kong SAR, China.
Email: proverse@netvigator.com Web: www.proversepublishing.com

The right of Laura Solomon to be identified as the author of this work has been
asserted by her in accordance with the Copyright, Designs and Patents Act
1988.

Cover photograph of, "The Spirit and Movement of the Girl", courtesy of the
artist, Li Hongbo, and the Schoeni Art Gallery, 21-31 Old Bailey Street (Main)
and 27 Hollywood Road (Branch), Central, Hong Kong,
www.schoeniartgallery.com.
Cover design, Proverse Hong Kong and Artist Hong Kong Company.
Page design by Proverse Hong Kong.

Proverse Hong Kong

British Library Cataloguing in Publication Data (for 1st pbk
edition)

Solomon, Laura, 1974-
The Shingle Bar sea monster and other stories.
I. Title
823.9'2-dc23

ISBN-13: 9789888167357

Acknowledgements

The photograph, "The Spirit and Movement of the Girl", is used for the front cover courtesy of the artist, Li Hongbo, and the Schoeni Art Gallery, 21-31 Old Bailey Street (Main) and 27 Hollywood Road (Branch), Central, Hong Kong, www.schoeniartgallery.com.

Prior Publication Acknowledgements

The following short stories have previously been published as shown below:

Anesthesia, *Inscribed*, US, May 2009.
Braille, *Southern Ocean Review*, NZ, 2008.
Braille, *First Edition Magazine*, UK, March 2009.
The Head (then called "Cerberus"), *Frost Writing*, 2009, Sweden; *Bravado*, NZ, 2009.
Cognition, *Dublin International Quarterly*, UK, July 2009.
Count Homogenised, *The View From Here*, UK, 2009.
Dummies, *Southern Ocean Review*, NZ, 2008.
The Faker, *Sentinel*, UK, 2009, *LinQ*, Australia, 2009.
Lady Bluebeard, Random Acts of Writing Submission, UK, February 2010.
The Latest Lighthouse Keeper, Biscuit Prize Winners 2010.
The Lighthouse (3000 word version), *Takahe*, 2008, NZ.
The Lighthouse (5,000 word version) – *First Edition Magazine*, UK, March 2009.
Sprout, first published in the 2004 Bridport Poetry Anthology and later in Laura Solomon's first short story collection, *Alternative Medicine* (2008), by Flame Books, UK. Translated into Czech by Olga Walló, 'Sprout' appeared in *Krásná*, summer issue, 2011.
Twins, *Gravity Publishing*, 2010, UK (audio); *Blue Crow Magazine*, Australia, 2010; *Litro Magazine*, UK, 2010.

The Shingle Bar Sea Monster
and other Stories

Table Of Contents

The Shingle Bar Sea Monster

My cousin Stella was always telling me tales about the Shingle Bar Sea Monster. He was three metres long and had suckers the size of bread-and-butter plates on his tentacles. He could eat you whole, devour you in a single gulp; you'd be rotting in his belly as he ploughed through the ocean waves. She'd only seen him once, off the coast of the shingle bar, but she said she'd always remember the sight. The rest of us thought that Stella was a liar, making up tales in order to get attention for herself.

Stella and her family lived in the house next door to mine. We were always hanging out together, bouncing on the trampoline or running under the sprinkler or taunting the neighbour's Alsatian with a piece of steak impaled on the end of a stick. We were good mates; there was only ever the occasional fight – Stella and my brother throwing gravel at each other in the driveway. Petty arguments about this, that, or the other.

I was the same age as Stella, twelve years old. We had recently discovered cigarettes. Stella had even figured out how to blow smoke rings. She thought it made her look sophisticated. She taught me how to French kiss too, we practised on our teddy-bears, the ones we ought to have outgrown by the age of twelve, but somehow hadn't. We were half-women, half-girls, in betweens, we hadn't quite hit adolescence, hadn't started menstruating, hadn't sprouted breasts.

Stella was a leader and I was a follower. She was far more gregarious than I was, always climbing trees and sailing down rivers on makeshift rafts. I sat on the sidelines and watched.

I was a clingy, anxious child often to be found hiding behind my mother's skirts. The world, for me, was a frightening and dangerous place, filled with muggers and rapists and thieves. Even the school playground held its fair share of turmoil; kids getting their ears twisted, kids getting shoved off the jungle gym to land on the hard bark beneath, kids booting other kids in the shins and running off laughing. Even home, with its domestic arguments, was sometimes unsafe – Mum and Dad rowing about whose turn it was to put out the rubbish or who should remember to feed the cat.

*

Stella usually talked about the sea monster at night. What with us being neighbours and all, I often stayed over at her place, two or three times a week, more if my parents were going through one of their rough patches where they rowed all the time and I needed somewhere to escape to. Stella and I would lie in our separate beds in the same room and she would start up with the sea monster talk.

"He eats all kinds of things," she would say. "Not just fish but seaweed too. And humans, given half a chance. You wouldn't want to go in swimming if the sea monster was in the water. Dry land's the place when the monster's about."

Stella was obsessed with the sea monster and I wasn't quite sure why. Her own family life was harmonious, perfect. Her parents never fought. She was an only child and rather spoilt. She had all kinds of toys; three bikes, piles of dolls she was rapidly out-growing, a mini-tramp, three hula-hoops. She had pets too; hamsters and goldfish, cats and mice. She had everything. My parents were more austere, tighter with the purse-strings. Stella's mother bought Stella all her clothing from high-end fashion boutiques, my mother either bought my clothes from charity shops or sewed them on her old Singer sewing-machine. In comparison with Stella's, my backyard was barren, empty. No mini-tramp, no spa, just dry brown grass and scorched earth in the summer and a lush green covering in winter.

Sometimes when Stella talked about the sea monster I would accuse her outright of being a liar.

"You're making up stories," I would say. "You're pulling my leg. There is no sea monster – it's all in your mind."

And maybe it *was* all in Stella's mind, the sea monster nothing other than a figment of her over-active imagination, a monster conjured from the depths of her subconscious.

I wondered for about six months whether the sea monster was real or not and then one day I decided to see for myself. I stole

10

Stella's bike and my father's binoculars and made my way down to the shingle bar. It was a cloudy sort of day with a light rain falling. I parked the bike up against a wooden bench and walked down to the water's edge. I held the binoculars to my eyes and scanned the surface of the ocean. Nothing out of the ordinary, just the choppy ocean waves and the odd seagull soaring and diving overhead. I would have to be patient, I told myself. I would have to learn to wait. Keeping the binoculars fixed to my eyes, I sat down on the stones and waited and watched. And waited. And watched. Until finally, finally, could it be, there in the distance, a tentacle flicking up out of the water? I adjusted the focus on my binoculars. Yes, it was, making its way towards me, the sea monster, ploughing through the ocean waves, heading my way.

I kicked myself for not bringing my camera. Photos would be evidence, photographs would silence all the critics, those naysayers who denied the sea monster's existence. In he came, closer and closer to the shore, looming larger and larger in my field of vision. He was almost at the beach now, then suddenly *schlup*, one tentacle came shooting out of the water, wrapped itself around my waist and dragged me out to sea. I was going for a ride with the Shingle Bay Sea Monster! The excitement, the dread! He was very considerate, I must say – a gentleman. He kept me up above the surface of the water so that I didn't drown, although my legs dragged through the briny drink. Out we went, out, out to sea, further and further, the feeling in my gut part terror, part excitement. What if he ate me, devoured me whole, in a single bite? What if I slipped from his grasp and drowned? I was full of unanswered questions. And all the time, further and further we went, the sea monster seeming to move faster and faster, gathering speed.

And then he dived, with me still on his back, held fast there with a tentacle. The sea monster flicked the end of another tentacle into my mouth. Oxygen was flowing out the end of it. I inhaled deeply. Down we went, down, down to the ocean depths, where the pink coral blooms and strange creatures with extra fins and eyes lurk and swim about in the dusky gloom.

I saw then ahead of me a glittering gold palace. The sea monster made straight for the open palace door. Inside, on maroon chairs sat a plethora of mermaids, swishing their fishy tails and combing their long tresses. At one end of the table sat King Neptune, trident in hand. The chair at the other end of the table sat empty. The sea monster swum with me over to the table and placed me gently in the empty chair. There was a crown before me on the table. He used one tentacle to place it on my head, making me, I suppose, Queen of the Mermaids. Hostile looks flashed across the faces of the other mermaids. Perhaps I was usurping somebody else's place, perhaps one or all of these mermaids had been hoping to be made Queen. I would have to earn their respect, I decided. It would be no good simply to be *placed* at the head of the table – I would need to earn the right to be there. Somebody struck a dinner gong and six waiters came gliding in as smoothly as if they had wheels attached to their feet. Boiled seaweed was dished up onto every plate, including mine. I would have to eat it, if I wanted to be accepted here. I lifted up my fork, impaled some of the slimy weed upon my prongs, pushed it into my mouth. I chewed and swallowed. It tasted of sea water and not much else. There was plenty of seaweed on everybody's plate.

"It's not always this way," said one of the mermaids with a flick of her tail. "There's always plenty of seaweed in the winter months but when summer comes around we tend to starve."

Now here was a problem I could solve, thus endearing myself to the mermaid community. I racked my brains for a solution to the problem.

Salt water – the perfect solution. If I could only get myself back onto dry land I could distil sea water and preserve the seaweed. I tapped the sea monster on the shoulder and motioned to him that we should head back up through the ocean currents to the shore. He wrapped one tentacle around my waist and carried me up towards the surface. Once on dry land the sea monster handed me a conch with which I was to summon him when I wanted to return to the palace under the sea. I biked home to collect my Bunsen burner and a pot in which to distil the salt water I would use to preserve the seaweed. Back at home I noted that the calendar on the wall now read Wednesday – it had been Saturday when I left. I lit the Bunsen burner and placed the pot on top of it, placing the seaweed inside the pot. I boiled and distilled until it seemed to me that the seaweed was sufficiently preserved and then I put the seaweed in a plastic bag and biked back to the beach. I raised the conch to my lips and blew. There was an interval of a few minutes and then I saw the sea monster surface way off in the distance and come swimming in across the ocean waves. It wrapped one tentacle around my waist and we took a dive down, down to the underwater palace. I gave one of the mermaids the preserved seaweed and told her that more would be on the way.

Over the next few days I repeated my regime – scooping up handfuls of seaweed, preserving them in the salt water. The mermaid would take me swimming with her, and we would explore the coral reefs and rocky outcrops that lay on the bottom of the ocean.

I took to spending two weeks under the sea with the mermaids and then resurfacing to spend two weeks at home with my family. For a year I led this strange double life. I had two personas; that which I donned when with the mermaids and the mask I wore when with my family. When with my family I was conservative, straight-laced, it was only when with the mermaid community that I let my hair down. Boy did those mermaids know how to party! They had their own special hooch that they brewed down there in the ocean depths, seaweed based, strong as anything – a couple of glassfuls of the stuff and you'd be knocked out. I spent more than one night on the hooch with the maids, awakening in the morning with a thumping headache, feeling as if a team of mountaineers were hacking at my temples with ice picks. Hilary would come to soothe me with a cold facecloth and a cup of chamomile tea. And everywhere I went the sea monster had to go too, one oxygen-exuding tentacle jabbed intermittently into my mouth so that I could breathe underwater.

One morning I awoke to find one of the mermaids, Hilary standing at the side of my bed, clutching a cup of tea and looking serious.

"What's up?" I asked her, taking the cup of tea from her hands.

"There's something I want to discuss with you," she said.

"What is it?"

"King Neptune is looking for a wife for his son Orion. He sent the sea monster to get him a human female – you."

"Can I meet Orion?"

"Yes, I'll take you now. Follow me."

She led me through the palace rooms to the room where Orion sat – his study. She knocked on the door. A voice within replied that we could enter. The bookshelves of the study were lined with leather-bound books. Orion swung round on his chair to face us.

"How can I help?" he asked.

"This is your wife to be," said Hilary, without offering my name.

"Well, I'm very pleased to meet you," said Orion, springing to his feet and shaking my hand.

"Likewise," I said.

*

Both Neptune and Orion were human yet they seemed to have no problem breathing underwater.

"How do Neptune and Orion breathe?" I asked Hilary later.

"They have gills as well as lungs," replied Hilary. "Inside their clothes where you can't see them. Hidden away."

*

Even though the mermaids were my adopted family, I came to think of them as my real family and my real family as being a group of people that I had adopted. The time difference between the world under the sea and the world at home was something I couldn't fathom. It was like Narnia, I supposed, where the world through the wardrobe has its own temporal scheme which is quite separate and distinct from that of the real world.

Since I had solved their seaweed-preserving problem for them, the mermaids had been nothing but welcoming to me. It was the first time in my life that I had felt truly accepted. The last time I had been home my parents had been in the middle of a blazing row. I had no idea what they were arguing about, but it must have been something that got them both hopping mad, because they were screaming and yelling. Mum even picked up a stack of plates from out of the kitchen cupboard and threw them to the floor where they smashed into shards and splinters of various shapes and sizes. Until now, my parents hadn't commented on my absences, those times when I had been away under the sea, with the mermaids. But now, angry as she was with Dad about something or other, Mum turned to me and yelled, "Where the hell have you been? I've been dead worried about you."

"I've been with the sea monster and my mermaid friends," I glibly replied. "Down in the depths of the ocean."

"What the hell? You've made friends with a sea monster?"

"Yes, the Shingle Bay Sea Monster. He's not a bad sort once you get past the gruff exterior. And King Neptune wants me to marry his son, Orion."

Telling porkies. Maybe, I thought, this friendship with the sea monster and this potential marriage were best kept to myself. Maybe they were things it was best not to share with others, especially if they would be disinclined to believe me.

Twice a week I went home to my family and on one of these occasions I would visit Stella. Stella was jealous of my time with the sea monster.

"I wish I had a monster I could go diving with," she said softly.

"You could come down to the underwater palace with me and the sea monster," I suggested. "I guess he can take two of us at once – a tentacle each."

"Really? Yes, I'd like that. Can we go now or shall we go later?"

"Let's go now."

*

We walked down to the edge of the ocean and Stella summoned the sea monster with the conch. He came in across the ocean waves, tentacles flailing above the water's surface. The sea monster wrapped one tentacle around Stella's waist and another around mine, put one oxygen-exuding tentacle into Stella's mouth and another into mine and took us out, out to sea and then dived with us down to the underwater palace. The mermaids welcomed Stella to their community with a special song and dance routine; a fin-waggling salute and then dished up a plate of seaweed each. Stella ate hers, pulling a face. Hilary came up to where I sat at the table and tapped me on the shoulder.

"Word in your ear," she said, beckoning for me to follow her.

I rose from the table and followed Hilary to the far corner of the hall, the sea monster trailing along beside me so that I could breathe.

"What is it?" I asked.

"Well, it's King Neptune's latest plan. He's intending to kill the sea monster to get his gills for you, so that you can marry Orion and stay down under the water forever."

The sea monster curled up his tentacles.

"I'm not sure how I feel about that," I said. "I mean, the sea monster's been a good friend to me so far. And what exactly do you mean by 'get his gills for you'?"

"Neptune's planning to do a graft – to graft the sea monster's gills into your chest so you can breathe underwater."

"But what about the sea monster?"

"He dies so you can live down here."

"Seems a little harsh – for him, I mean."

"Neptune really wants you for Orion's wife. You don't know this, but a month or so prior to you coming down here Neptune went up onto the land, looking for a wife for Orion. He spied on you, scoped you out. It wasn't just a fluke that you were brought down here, you were specially selected."

"Why me?"

"Neptune overheard your parents rowing, sensed that you were dissatisfied with your life above ground and might therefore be happy to begin a new life with us, down here under the sea."

Neptune had been right; I *had* been dissatisfied with my life up on dry land. But would life under the sea be any better?

That night I went to bed thinking of the sea monster. Could I stand to see him killed so I could have a new life as Orion's wife? And Orion? I didn't really know him – what would marriage to him be like? Liberation or just another kind of trap?

I slept on it overnight and when I awoke in the morning I had reached my conclusion. I couldn't bear to have the sea monster killed. I would have to return to my former life, with the parents that rowed and with Stella telling me tales about the sea monster whom I had once thought was fiction and whom I now knew was fact.

I summoned the sea monster and motioned to him that we should head back up to the beach. We surfaced through the ocean depths. Back home to the family. Pulling into the driveway, I heard the same familiar shouts, my parents rowing again. The same old rat race to run. So I turned my back on a life under the ocean and resumed a life on land. At night I would dream of it; the sea monster's gills grafted onto my chest, my underwater life, a life lived down deep where the fishes swim, my back turned to my family forever.

Anaesthesia

On the eve of her fifteenth birthday, Deborah Jacobs discovered that her right hand felt no pain. The painlessness wasn't possible with the left hand, only the right. The discovery had come quite by accident; a burning log had rolled from the fireplace onto the hearth and, lacking a poker, she'd thought, *perhaps if I just try and flick it back on.* With the palm of her hand flat on the log, she'd pushed it back into the flames. She'd felt nothing. It hadn't hurt a bit. She had no blisters, no burns. How very strange. She was immune to fire. To test her new hypothesis, she plucked a combusting pine cone from the flames and held it steadily, unblinking, unflinching, in her right hand, for a full three minutes. Transferring the cone to her left hand she yelped in fright, quickly returning the burning article to the conflagration.

Nobody had cautioned her about this. They'd warned her about sprouting breasts and annoying periods and pesky boys who were only after one thing, but nobody had mentioned being insusceptible to flame. How could she possibly discuss this issue with her parents or friends? They would think she was crazy, they would turn her into a freak show, charging people to see her hold burning objects for hours at a time; jealous, they would turn on her with lancing words and glaring glances. There was only Nancy, who had been born fifteen minutes before Deborah herself, Nancy with whom she shared everything, Nancy, who was psychic when it came to her twin. As younger kids, the two of them had practised ESP. One would hide an object somewhere in the house and then send telepathic signals to the other, who would "tune in" to the signal being transmitted. They called it their "messaging system", as if it was software that they'd developed. They'd excelled at it. Nothing remained hidden for more than a minute. Sometimes, they'd signal at the dining room table at teatime. – *Pass me the peas please.* – As they'd grown older, fearful of being discovered indulging in an activity which they thought of as illicit, they'd stopped

18

practising, and then they'd got rusty. Deborah could feel it sometimes, the edge of a message prickling at the corner of her consciousness, but it had become hard to hear what was being said; there was too much crackling and static these days, as if her antennae had died. The twins were identical; people always struggled to tell them apart. One of their favourite tricks was swapping identity. A couple of years ago, their favourite books had been the *Sweet Valley High* series, with the popular, blonde, blue-eyed twins; but they'd outgrown those now. Nancy and Debbie weren't blonde or blue-eyed; they were dark, part Spanish, in fact, with long straight black hair that hung almost to the waist. Nancy was the more emotional of the pair; Debbie could be very cold and clinical, logical, swift and ruthless. She didn't suffer fools. Nancy cried at soppy movies and was often telephoned by friends when they needed support or advice. When Nancy wanted to break up with a boy, she would send Debbie out on a date with him, so that Debbie would break the news.

Be gentle, she would say. *Don't crush the guy.*

Gentle wasn't in Debbie's nature – she was brutal, forthright, straight to the point.

Listen, she would say (sometimes adding *Listen, buddy*, if the guy was a tough customer), *Whatever we had, it's over between us now.*

If she got one of those clingy, needy guys she would say, *I'm seeing somebody else.*

Debbie/Nancy (or Nebbie or Dancy as they sometimes called themselves) was a lethal combination. Nancy would lure them in and start chewing and Debbie would spit them out.

She found Nancy in the family's inflatable rowboat, out on the pond, rowing in circles, feeding the ducks from a plastic bag full of crusts. A thin layer of ice coated the surface of the pond. Nancy must be freezing, thought Deborah, she wasn't dressed properly; she wore only a T-shirt and jeans. Nancy was a wildlife freak – she was forever rescuing stranded chicks, bringing them inside the house to feed them on bread softened by warm milk, taking in stray kittens and puppies that she found meowing and barking around some grubby, dark alley in town, leaving plates of food out for the foxes who sniffed around their property, their

19

own habitat having been so brutally encroached upon. Their parents had tried to make a rule – *no more animals* – but Nancy hadn't listened, though she housed none of her finds inside the house; instead she kept a veritable menagerie out in the shed, where she visited them several times a day, bringing gifts of food and affection. Deborah sat down in the long grass, pulled her knees up to her chest and waited.

Nancy hadn't seen her, but she paused, cocked her head to one side as if listening to something nobody else could hear, and then began rowing over to the edge of the pond where Deborah crouched. Perhaps their days of telepathy weren't over.

"What's up?" Nancy asked when she docked.

"Something strange," said Deborah.

Deborah's history was a series of strange events. Disaster seemed to yap at her heels but, curiously, she was never affected – she merely felt the brush of tragedy's cloak as he whisked by. She'd been caught in an earthquake when visiting the nearby city of Upton (she'd been in a Habitat store at the time and she'd crouched in a doorway as all around her plates and teapots and vases hurled themselves to the ground and shattered into a million fragments). She'd been sunbathing at a beach in Thailand, on holiday with a friend's family, when a minor tsunami had struck (she'd managed to outrun the wave and watched from the safety of a nearby hill as others struggled and drowned). She'd been involved in three car accidents; miraculously, she had escaped the prangs unharmed – others had suffered gaping wounds, whiplash, broken bones.

"Something strange, eh? Sounds like you. What is it?"

"I know this is going to sound crazy, even for me, but my right hand won't burn."

"Won't *burn?*"

"It can't feel anything. I held a burning pine cone for three minutes."

"Maybe the nerve endings are dead."

"Come on, I'll show you."

They left the rowboat on the side of the pond and headed towards the house. The fire still burned, its orange flames licking at the logs.

"Watch."

Deborah picked up a medium-sized log and held it in her right hand, smiling. Nancy stared, mouth agape.

"Spooky," she said. "Maybe you're part witch."

"Oh, don't say that."

"Perhaps we should take you to Doctor Grant then. See what he has to say about it."

Doctor Grant was their family GP; he was shifty-eyed, he wouldn't look at you when he diagnosed, giving you the impression that he was simply making things up, lying to you, that he'd bought his qualifications cheap over the internet.

"No, no. I guess I just have to accept it."

The birthday itself was a disappointment. The girls' father had left over a decade previously, just buggered off one morning without warning; he'd left no note, no phone number, no forwarding address. He paid not a penny of maintenance. He'd departed in the morning to go to his usual place of work (he was a sales rep for a local IT firm), but that evening he didn't come home. Nor did he return on any subsequent evening. Their mother had telephoned his company to be told that he'd handed in his notice a week ago, and nobody had seen hide nor hair of him since.

For the past three months Nancy had been dating Jacob Mortimer, a boy two years her senior. Debbie and Nancy (who had nicknames for almost everybody) called him 'The Brain'. Jacob, now in his final year of high school, was top of almost every subject; calculus, biology, Japanese. He could converse fluently with the many Japanese tourists who swarmed through their town in the summer months. He was sporty as well; basketball, football, cricket – he was proficient in them all. On the looks front, he'd been blessed with a strong, masculine jawline, dark green eyes – cat's eyes – full lips. He wasn't so bad as long as you ignored one feature. The ears. They stuck out from the side of his head like open car doors, as if they were antennae, as if Jacob could tune in to various short wave broadcasts.

"Why don't you have them pinned?" Debbie had asked when she'd first met him. (Nancy was far too tactful ever to have asked a question such as that.)

Jacob wasn't phased. He eyed Deborah coolly and said, "This is how God intended for me to be."

He'd been raised a Christian and still went to church every Sunday. He was forever trying to get Nancy to convert, to turn to the church.

"Just come along to my church group on Thursday night," he'd say. "There's plenty of girls there your age – I think you'd like it."

Nancy would screw up her nose and shake her head. Now she wanted to get rid of him. She'd had enough of the ears and the attempts at conversion. Her mother tried to convince her otherwise.

"That boy's a catch," she said. "The cleverest boy at your school – he could be a doctor or a lawyer or anything. Kid's a keeper. For God's sake, Nancy, don't be breaking up with him over a trivial thing like *ears*."

"It's not just the ears Mum. It's the religion as well."

Debbie knew her services were going to be called for. Nancy and Debbie shared a room – a two bedroom house was all their mother could afford to rent. The room was tiny – their twin single beds were positioned two feet from one another; if they'd reached out they could've held hands in the darkness.

"Hey Debs," said Nancy, calling out from her bed. "Would you do the honours with Jacob? He's starting to get on my nerves. It's all the God talk."

The girls had been raised atheists – God was for people who couldn't think for themselves, who needed a heavenly guide to tell them what to say and do, God was for those who still had the ability to trust, who wanted to have faith in some higher power. The moon's silver illumination shone in through the window. These were the things you could rely on, thought Deborah, the sun, the moon, death, taxes. Everything else was shifting and unstable and could be snatched away without so much as a second's notice. There was no God to depend upon.

"Are you sure?" asked Debbie, who thought that Nancy could do a lot worse than Jacob.

There were so many drongos out there, *mongs* as the girls sometimes called them. Mongs and mingers. Debbie herself never dated anybody; she had her small circle of girlfriends with whom she had more fun than she ever could have had with any stupid *boy*. They went to the cinema and to the beach, they went shopping and roller-blading. They gossiped on the phone for hours.

"Yeah, I'm sure," said Nancy. "It's time to move on. To get some closure."

She'd taken to recording Oprah Winfrey every day and watching it after school. People spilling their guts out for the edification of an audience. It was a modern day confessional, that's what it was. A priest had been replaced by millions of viewers. It was a purging, catharsis.

"Alright then," said Debbie. "If that's what you want to do. When were you going to see him next?"

"Saturday. His parents are going out. We were going to watch videos at his house, order in some pizza."

"Alright. Consider it done. Though you really should learn some of these skills yourself. One day I might not be around to do your dirty work for you."

"Just one more time okay? I promise after Jacob I'll do the dumping myself."

As was usual when they swapped identities, Deborah dressed up in Nancy's clothes; a short denim mini, a hot pink jersey, knee-high brown leather boots, hot pink plastic earrings. She tied her hair back with a matching pink hair band as Nancy was wont to do.

"How do I look?"

"Just like me."

"Good, good."

"*I* can't even tell the difference."

Jacob's house was a fifteen minute walk from their own. She trotted along, clack, clack, clack, the boots making her sound and feel like an adult.

Jacob had hired *Alien versus Predator – Requiem*. She'd assumed he'd be into something more highbrow but maybe after all that calculus he liked to unwind with mindless twaddle. He dialled Dominos and hit "play" on the DVD player. She wasn't going to let him know that things had come to an end straight away. Why not just see how the evening would progress? They were just at the part where a Predator-Alien hybrid first bursts from a dead person's chest when Jacob bent across to kiss her. It felt lovely. Gosh, his eyes were an unusual colour. He bent down to unzip one of her boots and then sat up suddenly, as if slapped.

"Hey that's not right."

"What's not right?"

"This patch of freckles. That wasn't there before."

"Course it was. You just never noticed it."

"No, no. You've worn these boots before. I've *unzipped* these boots before. Those freckles were never there."

He looked at her in horror and disgust.

"You're not Nancy are you? You're, you're...*the other one.*"

The "other one", yes, she was indeed the "other one".

"Whatever," said Deborah. "Anyway buddy, you're dumped."

"You can't dump me. You're just a stand in. If I'm going to be dumped by anybody I'm going to be dumped by Nancy. Your voice is slightly different too, by the way. Higher pitched. More squeaky."

Squeaky? He made her sound like some sort of rodent. She got up to leave, but he grabbed her by the wrist.

"Listen, you tell that coward formerly known as my girlfriend, that if she's such a wuss she has to send her sister to break up with me, then *I'm* breaking up with *her*. I got in first, alright, just let it be known. Sheesh! What a family."

Deborah shot him a filthy look and strutted out through the front door.

Nancy was furious.

"Oh my God, do you mean he sussed us out, how embarrassing. It'll be all round school on Monday. People will think of us as deceitful little swine."

"Hey, it was your idea. I wanted you to go in and face up to him."

"I'll apologise to him when I see him."

"Good idea. Try and prevent him from talking about us behind our backs."

That was the night her left hand went numb. It started with a feeling like pins and needles in the tips of her fingers, and then spread up through the palm of her hand towards the wrist. She was lying down watching television at the time, with her chin resting in her hands. She thought that the pins and needles were occurring because the circulation had been cut off due to her pose, but when she sat upright and shook out her hands, sensation did not return to the left one.

Here we go, she thought. *Get that drawing pin, let's do a few more tests.*

She stabbed the pin into the palm of her left hand. A complete absence of pain. She took a pine cone from the fire and grasped it. Nothing. She walked into the bedroom where Nancy lay on her back reading A.S. Byatt's *Little Black Book of Stories.*

"Hey Nance," she said. "The other hand's gone."

"Gone? Whatcha mean *gone.*"

"Gone numb."

Nancy stared at her.

"This is getting creepy now," she said. "My twin's ceasing to be fully human – she's becoming robotic, an automaton."

"*You're* getting creeped out. How do you think *I* feel?"

"Hey maybe your life is imitating art."

She flicked her eyes toward the book she was reading.

"There's a story here about a woman who turns to stone."

"Well, how does she survive?"

"It doesn't happen all at once. It happens piece by piece. Not just any old stone either – precious stones, rubies and opals and stuff. She *sprouts* stone."

"That's just fiction. This is really happening, happening to *me*. This is real life, not just some story."

"You'll be alright. Maybe you'll thaw, like a frozen girl coming back to life."

"Pigs might fly. This stuff is gonna be permanent I can feel it in my bones, in my waters."

Debbie didn't usually speak like that – she was far too logical to believe in intuition, in the value of *feelings*. She was a creature ruled by reason.

It must have been a month later that their father telephoned. It was Debbie who answered the phone; nobody else was home – Nancy and their mother had gone to the Asian Food Market to pick up some cheap noodles and fish balls for dinner. She didn't recognise his voice – well, how could she have, she'd been five when he'd left, barely out of infancy. All she knew of him was his absence, the hole where he should have been, the space that he left in his wake. It was a space that their mother had tried to fill; she'd done her best to be two parents instead of just one, she'd made them sit with her when she did her tax return so they'd know how to do it, she'd taken them fishing and hiking and taught them how to stand up for themselves, never to let anybody else push them around.

"Hi," said the voice on the other end of the line. "That you, Nancy?"

"No, it's Debbie. Who is this?"

A pause.

"It's your father."

"I don't have a father."

"Come on love, don't be like that."

"Who is this *really?*"

"I told you, it's your father. I'm in town over the weekend. I was hoping I could take you girls out – maybe to a basketball game."

"We hate basketball."

"Just to meet up, then."

Just to meet up? For ten years the creep had vanished, contributed nothing to their lives, not a penny of maintenance, not an ounce of fatherly guidance, and now he thought he could just pick up the telephone and waltz back in as casually as if he'd never been away.

"That'll be the sunny Friday," said Debbie, and hung up the phone.

He didn't call back. She didn't tell anyone about the phone call, not even Nancy, with whom she shared almost everything. It was like a Sopranos episode – *You're dead to me.*

It was three days later that the left hand side of her face froze. She was standing in the bathroom, brushing her hair in front of the mirror, pulling faces at herself out of boredom when she noticed that only one side of her face was moving. Nancy, also in the bathroom, cleaning her teeth, paused in her ablutions and stared at her twin's reflection in the mirror.

"Hey Debs, it's affecting your face now."

Deborah said nothing. The left half of her face felt as if it belonged to a stranger. She willed it to move, prayed for it to function, but it was as still as if it had turned to stone.

"Right," said Nancy. "This has gone too far. We're taking you to the doctor; I don't care what you say. Come on, we'll get Mum to drive us."

"No, we can't tell her what's going on. She'll freak out. She's got enough on her plate. Haven't you seen how exhausted she looks lately?"

"We'll take the bikes then. Come on."

"Okay, but we're not gonna tell him about the hands."

"Bell's Palsy," said the doctor. "It often passes of its own accord. You'll wake up one day and you'll be back to normal."

I don't even know what normal is anymore, thought Deborah.

"It won't inhibit your functioning. You'll be able to do everything just as you did before."

"But what caused it?"

"There's no specific cause. Most likely you'll find that it passes of its own accord. There are very few cases that result in a permanent disability."

He prescribed anti-inflammatory and anti-viral drugs. Eye drops for her left eye so that it wouldn't dry up, since she was having trouble closing it. Her face never did unfreeze though.

The Angels

I was five years old when I saw my first angel. My twin sister Melanie had drowned that summer and I was missing her terribly, although I was too young fully to understand what had happened. All I knew was that there was nobody there to help me dress up my dolls, or hit the notes on our brightly coloured xylophone, or to pull faces across the table at. Nobody there. I was a shy girl and I didn't make friends with other children easily, not at kindergarten, nor in the neighbourhood. Nor did I bond with the children of my parents' friends who sometimes came around for dinner. After Melanie drowned, I was a solo unit, a girl alone, soldiering bravely on through an indifferent universe.

The river in which Mel had drowned ran down from the hills behind our house, through the fields to the left of us and on down to the sea. Mel hadn't been in deep water; she had tripped and fallen and hit her head on a stone and been knocked unconscious and drowned in the river's shallows. We weren't meant to be there; we had snuck through a gap in the fence and picked our way down a steep hill, through waist-length grass until we reached the river. I was the only one with Melanie. I was too young to understand that she would die, face down in the water, and so I just stood there, terrified, calling her name over and over. For half an hour or so I stood calling her name and prodding her to try and get her to move, to turn over, to stand up, to do *something* and when it finally dawned on me that she wasn't going to respond, I ran back home to the house and alerted my mother, who sprinted, frantic, rushing back through the fields to where my sister's body lay. The sky was black that day and did not lighten for quite some time.

The angel appeared at the funeral. My father was giving a short speech when I felt a draught rush by my face and, turning, I saw her, standing by the door, wings down, a beatific look upon her face. She was so beautiful that I froze and could not turn my eyes away. My mother, seeing that my face was turned, turned too, but she saw nothing there for she swung back immediately and prodded me to do the same. I could not swing back around. I was mesmerised. The angel smiled, a small smile; the corners of her mouth just turned up a little at the edges. Then I blinked and she vanished, as if she had, quite simply, blended into the air. On the short drive home I was very quiet. I was quiet all that evening and for quite a few days and afternoons and evenings after that. I was thinking about what I had seen. I didn't know, of course, that it was an angel; my parents were not religious people and I had never heard of such things. All I knew was that I had seen a very beautiful woman with wings sprouting from her shoulders and that she had smiled at me. It wasn't until my mother and I were visiting my sister's grave and I saw a figure much like the one I had seen in the church, but made of stone, that I discovered what I had seen.

"Mummy," I said, pointing at the stone angel. "What's that?"

"That's an angel, darling," she said.

"What's an angel?"

"A heavenly being who serves God."

A heavenly being who serves God! It sounded so grand. *Imagine being an angel*, taking orders from God Himself.

"Sometimes angels have messages for people," my mother continued. "They can help out."

Even grander! Listening to God and relaying messages to the human race. I decided that it would be quite nice to be an angel and for several days after we had visited the cemetery I walked around flapping my arms like wings and delivering to my parents small notes written on pieces of paper, the subject matter of which was always my own name, which was the only word I could write.

For many years after that I did not see angels. My life was ordinary, dull even. I attended the local primary school, I played in the backyard. (Following my sister's drowning I was no longer allowed in the fields that bordered the river.) I begged my mother for another brother or sister. Katie came along shortly after I had celebrated my tenth birthday. I don't know whether or not my parents had been trying to have another child, but she was a welcome addition to our family. I sat her on my knee and tickled her and made her laugh. From an early age she was a great mimic; if you pulled faces at her she would imitate the face. The second angel appeared shortly after Katie's birth. I was standing beside Katie's cot, singing her a lullaby to help ease her passage into sleep when the angel materialised beside the window. This time it was as my mother had said; she had a message for me.

"I want you to promise to look after your younger sister," she said. "To protect her in any way you can. You are to be her guardian angel."

The angel's face was too bright to look into; she seemed to radiate. I averted my eyes, stared at the floor and nodded. Such responsibility, to become a guardian angel myself! Such an honour! I promised the angel that I would do all I could to look after Katie.

Katie needed a lot of looking after. She was accident-prone. I caught her in the cupboard beneath the kitchen sink, about to help herself to the Ajax and sternly reprimanded my mother, telling her that we needed kiddy fasteners on the cupboard doors. I found her at the top of the stairs, about to take a tumble and made my mother purchase a gate to keep Katie safe. Why was my mother so lapse? Mum was not a practical woman, she was a painter, a dreamer; she walked around with her head in the clouds. *Safety first*, I told her. *Our house needs to be child-proofed.* She didn't listen so I child-proofed the house myself.

When Katie started school I watched over her protectively. I walked with her every day to the school gate and made sure she ate her morning and afternoon teas and lunch, I walked her home again in the afternoon. She was a soft child, sensitive, skinless; she didn't like being around the other kids, she liked to be by herself, singing quietly, small songs, her own compositions. She often clutched at my hand or my leg, seeking reassurance. Her delicate psyche longed for something to cling to. I was it. I was her comfort blanket.

By the time Katie hit adolescence, I had left school and was at Oxford, studying law, learning about snails left in ginger beer bottles and other acts of negligence. My absence must have hit her hard, for when I returned home after my first term at university, she was very sullen and withdrawn and far moodier than she had ever been before. She barely said hello to me when I walked in through the front door, suitcase in tow. I had just completed three assignments in two weeks and was exhausted and didn't, initially, have time to focus on Katie and whatever problems she might be struggling with. It was my mother who took me aside, after I had eaten one of her home-cooked vegetarian meals, and told me that I should try to "get through" to Katie. She was going off the rails, said Mum. She'd taken up smoking and had come home drunk on more than one occasion and had got a tattoo of a dragon on her bum. Both she and Dad, said Mum, had made an effort with her, but it was as if she had built a brick wall around herself. They were worried, they said. God only knew what she would do next.

I remembered the promise that I had made to the blazing white angel; and, the following day, asked Katie if she wanted to come on a trip with me to the cemetery to visit Melanie's grave.

"I'd rather slit my wrists," she said, not very politely.

I sighed.

"Fancy a trip to the cinema then?"

"Don't reckon."

She was being impossible.

"Honestly Katie," I said, with exasperation. "Is there anything you'd like to do today? I'm only home for two weeks, so we might as well make the most of this short time together."

"The zoo then," she acquiesced. "I fancy a trip to the zoo."

Your wish is my command, m'lady. A trip to the zoo it was. Katie perked up a bit when she saw the monkeys chattering and gibbering together, but aside from that, she was as silent as a statue. When we'd seen all the animals that there were to see, I took her to the zoo café for lunch.

"Katie," I said. "I've never seen you like this. You really should tell me what's going on. That's what families are for."

She sighed heavily through her nose and turned her face away.

"Alright," she said. "I'm being bullied by a gang of bitches at school. They've really got it in for me."

"Verbal bullying or physical? Not that one is less bad than the other, of course..."

"Both, really. They wait for me outside the school gate and try to intimidate me by smacking their fists into their palms and yelling out shit like, 'there goes posh little Katie Davidson, oh la la.' They think I'm stuck up, up myself. A large part of the problem is that I haven't really made a gang of my own, you know, a group of girlfriends who could rally round and protect me, keep the bullies at bay. I'm a *target*. A sitting duck."

"Oh Katie."

I took her hand.

"That's terrible," I said. "You should've spoken up before now. Mum or Dad could've gone to see the principal."

"That'd only make it worse," she said. "Then they'd really have it in for me. Don't tell Mum and Dad this, but sometimes I just leave school at lunchtime and come home and smoke pot and listen to music. My grades are really starting to slip."

"Things'll improve," I said. "You'll see."

"Do you promise?"

She looked so small and fragile and pale.

"I promise," I said.

I paid for our lunches and we left the zoo, walking quietly, side by side, towards the bus stop.

That evening, I told Mum and Dad what Katie had told me. They both agreed that we, as a family, had to do something to stop her from being bullied further.

"She could change schools," suggested Mum. "Or we could go and speak to the principal."

"I don't think Katie wants you to do that," I quickly interjected. "She thinks that might make things worse."

"Well," said Mum. "I clearly remember seeing on the school's website that they have a zero tolerance policy on bullying."

"Changing schools might be best," I said. "Is there anywhere else she can go?"

"We're zoned for the school she's at, but we might be able to pretend she lives with Uncle Hugh and get her in at his local Girls' Grammar."

"Why don't we suggest that to her?"

I felt so old, so sensible, so protective. She was my charge and I would take care of her, make sure that she got on alright.

"Does she retaliate at all?" asked Dad. "When they threaten her?"

"I doubt it," I said.

I couldn't imagine Katie doing or saying anything threatening or mean. She was far more likely simply to withdraw, to retreat further and further into her shell, into an unreachable dark corner into which no light could shine. My torch-beam of love, I thought, would go in search of her, show her that when things seem impossible, there's often a way out, another road to take, an alternative route.

We spoke to Katie the following morning. Mum began very gently.

"Katie," she said, sipping her coffee rather nervously, "Liz tells me that you're being bullied at school and we want to help you."

"Help schmelp," came the sullen reply. "There's nothing you can do."

"That's where you're wrong. There's a lot we can do. For one thing, we could get you into a different school."

A gleam of hope flickered in my sister's eye.

"Do you think? How?"

"Well, we can make out that you're living at Uncle Hughie's and get you into the school that he's zoned for. It's a good college. You'd have a decent shot at getting into a top university from there, I'm sure of it."

Katie was a brain box, very bright, advanced for her age. She'd written me letters, telling me how she wanted to study medicine.

"I don't know," Katie stalled. "I wouldn't know anyone and..."

"You could make friends there. Get back to the old chatty Katie we know and love."

"Do you mean you don't love me like this?"

"Not at all. It's just that you're so *different* now. You're scaring us a little. Adolescence can be a tough time for anyone, but you don't have to go through it alone."

"Yeah, and other clichés."

I could see that Mum was starting to get exasperated. Dad stepped in.

"It really would be best, Kate, if you changed schools. I don't want you staying in an institution where you're being picked on. You'll damage your health and your grades."

Katie threw her hands up in the air.

"Okay, okay. You got me cornered. I'll change bloody schools."

"Good," said Dad. "Now come here and give me a hug."

Katie obeyed with reticence.

The following term there were letters from Kate saying how much she liked her new school. She was settling in and making friends and achieving A grades and all was "peachy" (her word). I was thrilled for her and my own studies were going well; I had received good grades for my tests and assignments and was set to make it into second year Law. I had dreams of becoming a high-flying corporate lawyer; dreams based mostly on *L.A. Law* – the drama, the glory, the shoulder pads. I would wear power suits and bright red lipstick and boss subservient men about and take three hour power lunches at the Ivy followed by dinner at the Oxo Tower. I would get my hair done professionally every month, cut and dyed in the latest style. I would shop at Dolce and Gabbana and Prada and buy exorbitantly expensive perfumes. I would look and smell like a million pounds. The angels would smile on me, blessing everything I did.

At the end of the second term, I returned home again for the holidays, as was my pattern. Katie's reports of her well-being appeared to be wildly exaggerated if not entirely fictional. She was as skinny as a stick, she'd dyed her pretty auburn hair jet black, and (I was shocked to see) she had scars all up her arms as if she had been cutting herself. I didn't really know how to tackle the problem that my younger sister had become. It was too big for me, too wild, too scary. She'd been such a good, shy kid; who could've predicted the problems that would erupt? I could tell that Mum and Dad, too, felt overwhelmed. She'd taken to skipping meals, they said, refusing to eat her dinner. They were worried sick. The school had turned out to be not better, but worse. They suspected that she was being bullied there as well, though she wouldn't talk about it. They hadn't wanted to bother me about Katie since I was busy studying.

I felt powerless, as if my hands had been severed. Several times during the course of that holiday I tried to talk to Kate, but she rebuffed my every approach, telling me to "get fucked" to "push off" and to "leave her the hell alone." It was like the scene in *Alien* where the demonic creature bursts from John Hurt's chest. My sister had vacated and some minor devil had taken her place. She had metamorphosed. At night I prayed to the angels to appear and guide me, but nobody ever showed up. They had abandoned me, here on earth, with a second sister who was drowning, albeit in a different manner to the first.

"She's been self-harming," I said to Mum. "Can you stop her?"

"We've tried, love, we've tried. I've hidden all the knives, but she has a secret stash of razors somewhere that I can't find. It's terrible. God, I've taken her to see the family GP, but he wasn't much help, just said it was depression and stuck her on Prozac. She's on a slippery slope, a slippery slope, indeed."

Worries about Kate distracted me during my final term at university; I could feel the course-work beginning to pile up, to get the better of me. I called her once a week, but never got more than a few perfunctory grunts from her, over the telephone, I wrote to her every fortnight but she stopped replying to my letters. After final exams, I returned home to find that Katie had gone into the hospital the previous week. I was terrified by the thought of paying her a visit. She'd been eating little more than a couple of potatoes and some muesli a week, my parents said. She'd dropped down to nearly six stone; the doctors were worried she'd have a heart attack or organ failure. They had her on a drip feed, seeing a psychotherapist every day and a shrink once a week.

"She just keeps repeating that she's too fat," my mother said, bursting into tears. "She won't *listen* to anything I tell her. She thinks we hate her and don't want her around, but it isn't true. All I want is for her to get better and come home."

It was all too much for me. I felt like I'd been hit in the guts with a wrecking ball. I had failed, failed the angel, failed my sister; I'd probably fail law too and be forced to take a job in a supermarket checkout.

For days I avoided the hospital. I just couldn't bring myself to face it. It was as if somebody was trying to get me to turn and stare into the midday sun or directly into the face of one of those angels that used to visit me. Eventually, after about five days, I summoned the courage to pay her a visit. Everything about this was painful, like walking across cut glass. Mum had offered to go with me, but I had told her that I should go alone. Katie was lying on her hospital bed reading a women's magazine. This, in itself, was unlike her; she read Tolstoy and Dostoyevsky and Chaucer, not *Woman's Day*. She pointed to a picture of Posh Spice looking skeletal.

"There," she said, without even so much as a preliminary greeting. "That's what I need to look like."

I was furious; with Katie, with Posh Spice, with those dumb angels that had abandoned me, with everything. I snatched the magazine from her.

"You do *not* need to look like Posh Spice," I snapped. "You need to get better. Better in the head. You have an illness Kate, and the doctors here can help you get well."

"They only put me in here 'cause they don't want me around," she replied.

"Who's *they?*"

"Mum and Dad."

"They do so want you around. I had a big conversation just the other day with Mum and how much she was looking forward to you getting well and coming back home."

"Whatever."

Her arms lay like twigs on the bed. I could see the bones through the skin.

"Look, this is awful, Katie. For everybody. For fuck's sake, you could die."

I know I shouldn't have spoken to her like that, but I wanted to snap her out of it, jolt her back to reality, wake her up, exorcise her demons for her. I didn't realise that she would have to do all that work herself, that nobody else could do it on her behalf.

"You don't understand anything," she said. "You're exactly like the rest."

What *rest*? The rest of the family? The rest of humanity? This was horrific and inexplicable. Was it really being bullied that had done this to her, make her internalise some external threat, some enemy, as if, were she to destroy herself, nobody else could destroy her? Or had she always been fragile, an accident waiting to happen, a girl walking the edges of high cliffs, humming to herself, needing only a slight gust of wind to push her over the edge? I was surrounded by questions that I had no answers for. In the end I just kissed her on the cheek and said, "I hope you get well soon and come back to us. In one piece."

She shrugged and turned her face to the wall.

That night I walked to the cemetery to visit Mel. What sort of person would she be by now, if she had lived? Would she be studying at university or would she have taken a job? Would she have a best friend, a boyfriend or a series of fickle lovers? Would she still be a virgin? And, if she'd lived, would I still have begged my mother for a sibling, or would the long-suffering Katie never have been born to her life of apparent martyrdom and remained, an egg in Mum's ovary, a sperm in Dad's testicles, two halves never made into a whole. Maybe, I thought, angels didn't visit adults, only children, who hadn't yet learned how to shut their eyes and ears, how to tune heavenly visitors out, who still knew how to listen.

She didn't return home that week or that month, nor the next, she didn't return home all that summer. I worked in Primark, saving money for the following university year. My grades were posted out; I passed with a B minus average. Not brilliant, but not dire either. I visited Katie once a week, but she didn't seem to be getting any better, if anything, she was looking thinner by the day. The doctor took me aside and told me she kept pulling her drip feed out. Mum was a wreck. She couldn't paint and was having trouble sleeping. She said that all she could think about was Katie and how on earth we could save her from this horrible illness. She was blaming herself.

"I should've done more with her as a kid," she kept saying. "I should've spent more time with her, been less wrapped up in myself, in painting."

I tried to reassure her that this wasn't her fault, but she wouldn't listen. Dad was being stoic but you could tell that he was affected too; he was far quieter than usual, barely smiling, moving through his days like a robot.

It was in November of my second year at law school that I got the call from Mum and Dad. I knew when I answered the phone that sat in the hall of my dingy student flat, that it must be bad news. They never called me; Dad emailed every other day with reports on Kate's progress which was minimal if not non-existent.

"She's escaped," Dad said. "Run away from the hospital. Nobody knows where the hell she is. She could be anywhere, living under a bridge or down at the wharf. God, it's bloody awful. We've alerted the cops."

"But didn't somebody see her? Wasn't she in a secure ward?"

"Only patients who are a danger to others are kept in secure wards, not those who are a danger to themselves."

"Oh God. Didn't somebody see her escaping?"

"Apparently not. She must have timed it right, picked her escape route carefully. They reckon she went through the fire doors and down the fire escape at the side of the building."

"I'll come home, to support you and Mum."

"No, no love, don't do that. Stay and make sure you keep up with your studies. That's important. Remember *L.A. Law*."

Dad knew how much I loved that programme.

"Alright, but keep me posted."

I hung up, went to my room and cried for three hours straight, eventually falling asleep in my armchair, not bothering to go to bed.

The cops found her. Dad was right; she'd been living underneath a bridge, existing only on empty air, freezing to death. Her heart had given up the ghost. She looked so terrifying at her funeral, lying in her coffin, her gaunt face translucent, like the face of an angel or a saint.

The Head

It was beside him on the pillow when Blair awoke in the morning, grinning at him inanely.

"What are you doing on my pillow?" Blair asked.

It seemed a logical question. It turned to face him and said "What are *you* doing on *my* pillow?"

"Hey, I got here first."

"My dear, if you think that gives you extra rights, I think you'll soon find that you are mistaken. At any rate, it seems that the two of us may as well do our best to get along, seeing as we're *sharing* like this."

It spoke with an upper-class British accent; well-rounded vowels. It was a toff.

"We're not *sharing*. You're *encroaching*," said Blair huffily. "After all, it's my neck you're using."

"Just because you got here first doesn't necessarily mean it's yours. Anyway, it's not just your neck I intend to use, but your entire body. And I'll have you know that I paid good money for the use of that body. Nobody warned me that I was going to get stuck with a whinger."

"Paid good money? Whadda ya mean *paid good money*?"

A switch flicked on in Blair's mind and he groaned.

"Oh God, you're not one of those immortality freaks are you?"

"I may be a lot of things, but I most certainly am *not* a 'freak', as you put it. I paid three million pounds to be grafted onto you. And I'm grateful, I really am. I wouldn't be here otherwise. But you can benefit from me. You can learn. I'm older than you are. I have more experience."

"How old are you anyway?"

"What year are we?"

"2031."

"That makes me precisely one hundred and fifteen."

"I thought graftees were meant to be informed when they were being grafted onto? Isn't that the law?"

"They made an exception with you and me. I paid to be brought back as soon as the technology was available, and to be matched to the most suitable candidate, which happened to be you. In short, dear boy, my money over-powered your will."

"But that's terrible. You can't go around doing exactly what you want just because you're rich."

"Oh, don't be so naive. Don't worry, you'll adjust. You couldn't fix me a cup of Earl Grey, could you, that's my boy."

Blair hated being patronised.

"Fix your own bloody tea. And you can make me a cup while you're at it."

"Oh, I see. Like that is it. Very well then."

Through no volition of his own, Blair felt his legs fling over the edge of the bed and hit the floor. He fought the other mind, struggled to move his body in the opposite direction but, despite his age, the other man was stronger and was winning the fight to drag the two of them towards the doorway.

"Give up control," hissed the head. "Let me drive. We'll never get anywhere with two of us steering. This partnership looks like it's going to be worse than my fourth marriage."

"How do you think I feel?" spat back Blair. "I've been invaded in the most brutal manner."

"We're lucky we didn't bloody well bump you off," the head muttered as the two men, with the one body, made their clumsy way down the stairs. "You should thank your lucky stars you've got me onboard. With my financial expertise I could make you a very wealthy man. Even if I *have* been out of the game for nearly twenty years."

Blair made his mind inert and watched, partly in fascination, partly in terror as the older man took the jug to the sink, turned on the tap, filled the kettle and settled it in its electric cradle.

"So," said Blair, when the two men were seated at the kitchen table, sipping their tea. "How long have you been in nitrogen for then"?

"Oh, about ten years I was one of the first. A pioneer. I was completely *compos mentis* at a hundred and one, though I'd had two heart attacks and I knew my body was about to go. Rich as Croesus. That was in 2021, so yes, ten years. I'd had a good life, but I didn't want to go. Terrified of what lay beyond, you see.

Heaven, hell, purgatory or just a great nothingness. I had no idea. But I didn't want to find out. So they lopped off my head and whacked me on ice, bio-technology caught up with me in 2029 as you know, and *hey presto*, here I am. They should've brought me back sooner, but as I understand it, they were too busy trying out the technology on North Koreans first. It's not right, to treat a race as guinea pigs. All those abominations that were produced, all those failures. Still, their loss is my gain. I'm one of the first great successes m'boy. Cheers!"

And he clinked his mug of tea against Blair's.

"Please don't call me m'boy. I'm forty-two. I've got a good career as a financial analyst."

"And that's where I can be of invaluable assistance."

Blair ignored him.

"Just the one marriage – failed, but I'm not one of those who goes in for a whole string of wives, serial monogamy…"

"Oh, don't knock multiple marriages. Wives are like nappies. When you're done, chuck it away and get another. Best approach. It's the most sensible thing to do, you know. But don't over-exert yourself with too much thinking. You've just undergone a very major operation and you need to rest. For both of our sakes."

"But work," said Blair. "They'll be wondering where I am."

"Don't worry, my friend, that's all been taken care of. They have been informed that you will be out of action for at least two months."

"But what are they going to say, when they see me like this?"

"They'll think you're a hero. A *pioneer*, like me. We'll be the toast of the town. And wildly successful at that."

Blair eyed the head sceptically.

"If you say so," he said.

Blair paused.

"What was it like?" he asked eventually. "Being, you know…suspended?"

"Oh, I can't remember a thing. The last thing I recall is kissing my sixth wife goodbye and heading off to the hospital. Speaking of which, I wonder if she's still alive. She was a good deal younger than me."

The head wasn't the only one having problems remembering. Blair had no recollection of the operation. They had come for him at night-time, he could remember that much; his door being knocked down, the heavy feet up the stairs. They'd conked him out with a general anaesthetic and he'd woken, in his own bed, with this extra head. Such grafting was illegal, of course it was. He was the victim of somebody else's crime. The solution was simple. He would have to have the head removed at the soonest possible opportunity. He would not tell the head, of course. He would wait till it was asleep and then book himself in at the hospital.

For the rest of that day, Blair felt very tired, as if the head was draining him of energy. He supposed it took extra effort to keep two brains functioning and he resented the head for all it demanded from him. He didn't want to know its name. That would be getting too personal, and would make things more difficult when it came time to lop the head off.

The head was bossy. It wasn't content with the fact that it had been brought, Lazarus-style, back from the dead. It wanted to rule the roost. It wanted to have a say about everything, from what was cooked for dinner, to when the vacuuming was done, to the date when Blair would be ready to go back to work. It was a terrible nag. *Haven't you brought that washing in yet? Get out in that garden and give it a good weeding; your oxalis is going crazy. Remember to water the dahlias.*

Blair wanted to be rid of it as soon as possible. One night, about two weeks after the head had arrived, he waited till it was sleeping and then picked up the mobile and dialled the hospital.

"I want to book myself in for an operation," he whispered to the woman on reception.

"I'm sorry, I can't hear you."

"I want to book myself in for an operation," he repeated more loudly.

"Oh, well I'm afraid that patients can't actually book themselves in. A doctor has to do that."

"But I can't *get* to a doctor. It's complicated, please. Just get me an operating theatre and a good surgeon."

"I'm afraid we can't do that."

He hung up abruptly and sulked back down in the bed. The head was beginning to awaken.

"Did I hear you say something about an operating theatre?" it said sleepily.

"No, you were dreaming. Go back to sleep."

"Because I'm warning you, my boy, you don't want to mess with me. I have protection. I *know* people."

The head decided that it wanted to try and track down its sixth wife. It went online and searched the white pages for a Bessie Richardson. If it was the right Bessie, she was living nearby in Kensington. The head dialled her number and was overjoyed to find that he'd tracked his wife down. She hadn't remarried and she was very much looking forward to getting together with her husband. Blair heard the head inviting his wife over for dinner that evening. He'd never seen the head as happy as it was upon hanging up the phone.

"Oh, my darling wife," it sang. "Reunited again. Oh, she's alive, she's alive!"

It busied itself finding candles with which to decorate the table and searching through Blair's rather scant recipe collection in order to find something tasty to prepare.

"Coq au vin," it declared. "Just the ticket! She always used to love a good bit of chicken. Now, you will be a good boy and keep quiet for the evening, won't you? I don't want you doing or saying anything to put her off. It's been a while since we...you know."

The head had the audacity to wink.

"This is awful," said Blair. "I have to be party to you seducing your wife."

"It's not that bad. You can have your tea beforehand if you like; that way it won't be so torturous for you, watching us eat."

"It's not the food I'm worried about. It's the..."

"I'd do the same for you. Any time you want to have a lady over, just let me know and I shall vacate my mind. I'm quite good at it. You won't even know I'm there. That's what I expect you to do for me. Just put yourself elsewhere, on a beach in the Maldives or in some savannah. Think of England."

Blair was horrified. He mustered every ounce of his will and tried to fight the head as it set about preparing that evening's dinner, but he was overpowered at every turn. It was as if he was sitting at a chessboard, opposite some master, who could predict and counter his every move.

At quarter past seven the wife arrived. She wasn't Blair's cup of tea at all and the thought of having sex with her terrified him. She was one of those *artificial* women; fake, faintly claw-like nails, thick layers of make-up and coiffed blonde hair that looked like a wig. Blair had eaten a quick dinner of two toasted sandwiches. He hadn't felt that he could keep anything more substantial down.

"Darling!" she greeted her husband. "Oh, it's been forever."

She engulfed him in a bear hug, then stood back to survey Blair's toned body.

"My didn't you do well! Is he clever?"

"Above average but no great genius."

"It's not the brain that matters though is, it? I saw on the television that they were making advances in the area of research that would help bring you back to me, but I didn't dare to hope…"

"Sit down," said the head. "Sit down and let me bring you a wine."

She sat, he brought her a drink.

"So," said the head. "Tell me what you've been up to since I was put in nitrogen."

Blair did his best not to listen, but it was impossible. He listened to the wife rabbiting on about how difficult she'd found life without her husband, though he'd provided for her very well, materially, of course. She'd been so lonely, she said, no warm body to curl up to at night.

"But it's all been worth it, because now I have *this*," she said, squeezing Blair's bicep.

Blair, who was a regular attendee at the gym, found himself wishing that he'd run to flab instead, maybe then he would have held less appeal to the medical men who had considered him such a prime specimen. And less appeal to this ghastly woman who was squeezing his arm.

After the dinner was consumed, the head took his wife to bed. Blair hated every minute of it. He felt completely out of control and was disgusted by the grunts and groans of the couple. The

44

worst part was that it was *his* body that was being aroused, *his* flesh that was inside that hideous woman. He was being used.

In the morning, there was a champagne breakfast for the head and his wife and Blair was not invited, though the food went into his stomach of course. The two throats joined as one just below the voice box.

It is impossible, thought Blair, *to go on like this. I must rid myself of this abomination.* He would have to be careful of course. If he fed it poison, his own blood stream would be affected. If he attempted to sever it with an axe or a knife, Blair himself might bleed to death. He couldn't suffocate it because the two of them shared a set of lungs. He would have to do something that would kill off the brain, without killing his own body. It was impossible. He couldn't think of anything.

As it turned out, he didn't have to think for long. Somebody was kicking in the door. There was a brief struggle, an injection, and Blair's brain was shut down forever.

Cognition

It started with the headache. It wasn't dull and throbbing, it was a piercing brain-splitter; it threatened to cleave his mind in two. He was out playing golf at the time, with the CEO of a rival company, and he didn't want to admit weakness, so he played on, despite the team of ice pickers that were chipping away within his skull. He'd thought that the pain might fade when he returned home to his Kensington apartment and his immaculate trophy wife, with her designer clothing and her perfect blonde bob and her surgically constructed nose, but, if anything, the pain only intensified, until it was so fierce that he thought his mind might split in two. There was a ringing in his ears as if an angel was shrieking.

"What's the matter darling?" asked his wife, as he lay writhing on the sofa.

"It's the pain," he said. "Can you get me some Panadol?"

She walked swiftly to the bathroom and took a packet of painkillers from the medicine cabinet, stopped in at the kitchen for a glass of water and took him the pills and the glass. He swallowed the Panadol down, but they didn't do any good, the pain raged on like a blazing fire.

"Can you make me a doctor's appointment for tomorrow morning?" he asked. "Tell them it's urgent."

"Sure thing," she said. "You just lie back and take it easy."

She was a good wife. She had a maid to do the housework and a cook to do the cooking and she faithfully fulfilled her other duties.

"Are you sure?" she was saying into the phone. "It really is an emergency."

Pause.

"Okay then. That'll have to do."

She hung up.

"Nothing in the morning," she said. "It had to be in the afternoon."

"If that's all there is, then that's all there is."

He lay on the sofa, the pain so intense that he fought back the urge to vomit.

It raged, all through the night it raged. He barely got a wink of sleep, even though he took four more Panadol, exceeding the dose that was stated on the packet, and a Seconal. He rose in the morning, head still throbbing, forced himself to eat a breakfast of muesli and coffee and sat on the sofa reading *The Guardian.* At lunchtime, he cooked two eggs each on toast for his wife and himself, then waited for 2pm and his appointment. His wife drove him to the doctor's and sat outside in the car. The doctor listened carefully, then booked him in for a CAT scan in a month's time, such was the waiting list. Painkillers were prescribed. He took them daily. They did little to help. He staggered through each day – normally an abnormally proficient man, he struggled with his workload and had to cancel appointments he could no longer keep. Formerly a lusty man, he did not have sex with his wife over the course of the month. He felt like a walking corpse, the living dead, dragging heavy feet. – Leaden. – The pain was a cross to bear, an albatross strung around his neck.

The month was up. His time rolled around. He took his place in the hospital reception area, sat and waited. The doctor called his name.

"Mr Clifford?"

He followed the doctor through into the room where the CAT scan sat. At the doctor's request, he removed his belt and his watch and then lay down on the mattress, waiting to be zooted inside the vast steel machine, fighting back his claustrophobia.

"Are you ready, Mr Clifford?"

He nodded his assent. The mattress slid smoothly inside the machine. Surrounded by steel, beginning to panic, he forced himself to think of other things, filled his mind with visions of paradisiacal beaches, flower-filled fields, snow-capped mountains. When the scan was done, the doctor informed him that he would telephone him with the results in a few days time.

The days took an eternity to pass. He prayed that there wasn't anything seriously wrong with him, yet he suspected that there was. To drown his fear, he was drinking more than he should, two or three vodkas every night, with very little tonic and just a dash of lemon. Sometimes his hands shook uncontrollably during the day. When the phone call came, it was his wife who took it.

"Yes," she said. "He's right here. I'll just get him for you."

Trembling, Mr Clifford took the phone from his wife.

"Bad news, I'm afraid," said the doctor. "Do you want me to tell you over the phone or do you want to come into the surgery?"

"Over the phone will be fine."

"You've got a malignant brain tumour. A rather large one. About the size of a small grapefruit."

"Oh dear, I see."

Mr Clifford felt a tight knot of fear in his stomach. A *brain tumour* – however you twisted and turned the words, whichever way you looked at it, this could never be a good thing. The size of a small grapefruit! That was huge, in comparison to the size of the brain. A tumour could take over. It could metastasize, spread throughout his body, infect him. The tumour could eat him alive; he imagined it, the darkness spreading through him, patches of black amongst the red.

"So, what's in order?" he asked. "Chemo? Radiotherapy? An operation?"

"An operation," said the doctor. "We'll keep you awake during the surgery. The tumour's located right next to the area of the brain responsible for speech, so we'll have to be very careful. We'll discuss the operation in more detail next week, but basically what happens is; I'll show you pictures and you'll have to tell me what it is that you see. If you start to get muddled, I'll stop operating. It's the safest way. If we had you under general anaesthetic it would be much more difficult for me to tell where your brain ends and the tumour begins. Too easy for me to chop out something I shouldn't."

"What's the waiting list for the operation?"

"Six weeks."

"Do I have a choice?"

"Not if you want to live."

"Book me in then. Thanks for keeping me informed."

"You're welcome."

Every day of the six weeks dragged its feet reluctantly. At night, Mr Clifford dreamt of the tumour, expanding in his skull like a balloon that was being blown up, taking up more and more space, until it squashed his brain into one tiny corner, until his brain became minute, the size of a peanut, and the rest was just tumour, dark, evil tumour. He would awaken from these dreams panicked and sweating, his heart racing in his chest, galloping like an out-of-control pony, would reach out and grab hold of his wife for comfort, for reassurance, just to know that somebody was there. Then he would lie in the darkness, struggling to return to sleep. Some nights he felt that a great oppressive bird perched on his chest, threatening to peck his heart out.

The day rolled around, as all days eventually do. Mr Clifford rose in the morning, fixed breakfast for himself and his wife, kissed his wife on the cheek and headed out the door.

They gave him a general anaesthetic to open up his skull. When his skull was open, the surgeon began chopping out the tumour. Chop, chop, chop. A nurse stood in front of him, clutching a stack of pictures. *Can you tell me what this is?* she would ask. *A skier,* he would reply. *A totem pole. A teddy bear.* Chop, chop, chop. *How about this? Do you know what this is?* As soon as he began to grow muddled, the surgeon stopped operating, put him back under, stitched up his skull. He slipped into a coma shortly afterwards, lapsed into unconsciousness, sending both the surgeon and his wife into a spiral of worry. Was he going to pull through? Would he make it? He came round the next morning, rang for one of the nurses and asked for an orange juice. His wife came by at eleven. He was his old self, cracking jokes, clowning around. He squeezed his wife's hand and told her not to worry her pretty little head about anything; he would be home in a day or two. He spent the afternoon reading women's magazines; *Heat* and *Women's Day* and *Now*. The articles all seemed to be the same, from magazine to magazine. Brad and Angelina, Jen, Madonna. Babies born or adopted, properties purchased, tiffs and reconciliations. He consumed the curry that arrived on its plastic tray that evening, lay back and stared at the cracks in the ceiling. A daddy-long-legs and its young lurked in one corner.

That was good, that meant there were no white-tails around. Nothing to bite him in the night.

For two weeks, all seemed to be normal. The same old, same old, day in, day out, rising and going to his high-powered job, reigning over the minions, coming home to enjoy a quiet dinner with his wife, picking up *War and Peace* from wherever he'd left off – a spot of evening reading.

The first bout of anger came from out of the blue. His P.A. made a mistake in the letter she was typing for him and he blew like a geyser, went storming through into her office, which was next to his, threw the letter down on her desk.

"What the hell's this?" he raved, one finger jabbing at the typo.

Her eyes flicked over the error.

"Sorry," she said. "Sorry I made a mistake."

"A *mistake!*" he hollered. "Do you realise what could have happened if I'd sent that away to the client? They'd have thought I was a right royal idiot."

"It's just one letter," she replied. "A 'u' instead of an 'e'."

"One letter!" he fumed. "That letter could have cost me my reputation!"

She stared at him blankly. Later, she would call up one of her girlfriends and bitch and moan. *God, he just went crazy. Ballistic. Never seen anything like it. It's very odd. He's always been such a <u>mild</u> guy, well-mannered. God knows what's gotten into him. Maybe his wife's not putting out.*

What she said to him, her boss, was "I'll just put some Tipex on it."

"Oh no you won't," he replied. "You'll type the whole thing again."

She glared at him. Nobody spoke to *her* like that. Her resignation letter formed in her mind. With her typing speed, with her Word, Excel and Powerpoint skills she could easily find a job elsewhere in the city. She didn't have to put up with any crap. *And* she had a degree in English Literature. It was what she had promised herself, when choosing to be a P.A. rather than pursuing a more lowly-paid career (at least initially) as a journalist. *She wasn't going to take any crap.* She had friends who were berated by their bosses on a daily basis, treated as punching bags by power-tripping arseholes who compared Blackberry sizes (smaller was better) and cheated on their wives. She retyped the letter and then she typed her resignation. Took both letters into him; a month's notice period.

"Resign!" he scoffed. "You can't resign!"

"I think you'll find that I can," she said and swiftly exited the room.

What do I care, he thought to himself. *Women like her are hardly irreplaceable. I'll just get a new one. P.A.s are a dime a dozen.*

The second bout of rage occurred two days later when he was driving home through heavy traffic. Somebody tooted at him and he blew, wound down his window and yelled "Stop that bloody tooting!" When they leant harder on the horn, he threw his car into reverse and backed straight into the offensive tooter. That shut them up. Mr Clifford turned a corner and zoomed home, but not before the tooter had taken down his license plate number.

The third time he vented was three days later, at his wife. She had made *coq au vin* for dinner, forgetting that he had sworn off chicken for the time being. She had set the table with candles, and a blood red tablecloth.

"What the hell do you think you're playing at?" he ranted.

His wife stared at him blankly, as his secretary had done.

"I *told* you I was off chicken. Don't you ever listen to anything I say?"

He picked up the chicken dinner and walked through into the kitchen, threw it, plate and all, into the sink. The plate shattered. Another woman might have burst into tears but his wife just said icily, "Well, fix yourself something then. There's fish fingers in the freezer."

"I'll go out to the Chinese," he replied.

He slammed the door so hard behind him that the glass, with its frosted impression of a deer, shattered, just as the plate had done.

"Oh, Gary," he heard his wife say, but he ignored her and kept walking.

He returned with his duck pancakes and *hoi sin* sauce, his sweet and sour fish and his special fried rice and sat down at the kitchen table to eat.

"Perhaps the part of your brain that made you a reasonable man has been removed," quipped his wife.

He grunted at her and kept eating.

Later, in bed, she turned to him and said, "I'm not joking Gary. It's possible that the surgeon chopped out something that should have been left in. I think we should go to him and report these symptoms. See what he says."

"Don't be ridiculous. I'm the same man I've always been."

"Gary of old wouldn't have slammed the door so hard that the glass shattered."

"Whatever."

He reached up and switched off the overhead light, turned his back on his wife and fell into a deep and dreamless sleep.

The next day, as he was going through a list of CVs from potential P.A.s, he received a call from the cops regarding reversing into the tooter and decided that perhaps there was something in what his wife said after all. He rang the surgeon and asked to make an appointment.

"I would have thought it unlikely," said the surgeon, "that I could have, as your wife suggests, chopped out the part of your brain responsible for tempering your anger. And, in the unlikely event that this *is* the case, how could I possibly reverse the damage? It would not be possible for me to replace what has been taken away. No, I think it's probably just that you're under undue amounts of stress and these bursts of fury that you describe are your way of venting tension. Why don't you try meditation or yoga? Build relaxation time into each day; take time out, time to unwind. It's all too easy to get caught up in the stress of modern living. The pace of life in a big city like London can be intense."

"You don't understand," said Mr Clifford, "I never used to have these outbursts before the operation."

The surgeon waved his hand dismissively.

"Unrelated," he said, "Unrelated."

It was true. Prior to the operation, Mr Clifford had been a mild-mannered man, polite to a fault, friendly, kind. Something had altered. He was not the man that he had been before and yet, there was enough of the *nice* left in him that he did not want to become the kind of person who went through life making others pay, venting his fury willy-nilly, putting others in their place. He apologised to his wife. She accepted his apology but told him that he would have to organise to have the front door fixed, and that she wanted six new plates, as the plate he had smashed was part of a set. He apologised to his P.A. and she agreed to stay on a little longer on the understanding that if he mistreated her again, she would leave. Still the anger boiled in him, hot and black, a living, seething thing, creeping like a cancer, spreading like the tumour would have done, had it been left untreated. The anger was a horde of bees buzzing around his forehead, threatening to sting. The anger was a furious storm, blowing in his mind.

Like a woman, he turned his anger inwards. Mr Clifford, a forty-five year old man, married with no children, began self-harming. Such relief it gave him, to feel the tip of the razor slice the surface of the skin, to cut deeper, down through the layers of flesh. He favoured inner thighs, mostly, places his wife would never see. He loved the way the blood came pouring out, red, gushing, warm. He felt such satisfaction afterwards, as if the bees of his anger had come swarming out with the blood. He would wind a tourniquet around his leg and, when the blood had stopped flowing, would swap the tourniquet for a sticking plaster. He always slept soundly on the nights when he'd been self-harming, dreamt golden dreams, dreams of lounging on beaches with crystal clear water and golden sands, dreams of gliding effortlessly down mountains, barely noticing the skis that were strapped to his feet, dreams of relaxing in a spa pool, surrounded by nubile bikini-clad women. He awoke from these dreams refreshed, ready to face the new day. His wife noticed nothing. The day after lacerating he felt relaxed and happy, often humming to himself as he went about his work. The cutting made him a more pleasant person.

Six weeks after he'd first begun self-harming he gashed himself across the stomach. It bled and did not stop bleeding. He waited – half an hour, an hour, and then he panicked and called for his wife. She rushed into the bathroom, froze in the doorway when she saw him, said *Oh God Gary, what have you done?* and then ran back into the living room to phone for an ambulance. She rode in the ambulance with him, holding his hand. *Oh Gary, I didn't realise you were cutting. You could've talked to me; we could've got you some help.* Mr Clifford said nothing, just lay back in the ambulance, feeling drained. The bees buzzed on, not placated, as they usually were by his pain and his blood; they landed on his chest and his face, emitting their drone.

They stitched him up. Fourteen stitches, right across his belly. Black thread. Still the bees swarmed, refusing to be silenced. He dreamt of them at night, gigantic, each bee ten times the size of an ordinary bee, threatening him with their stings. His wife told him he needed counselling and booked him in with a local therapist. When he told the therapist about the bees she stared at him blankly, silently, leading him to wonder if he really was losing his mind. Invisible bees; it did sound slightly crazy. The therapist gave him a mood diary and told him to record his moods. She told him to think up an alternate activity to self-harming; such as taking a walk or phoning a friend. She asked him about his relationship with his wife – was he happy? *Happy*, scoffed Mr Clifford. Happiness was a mental state enjoyed by those in the lower echelons of IQ – clever men like himself became anguished neurotics or stressed executives; happiness was for idiots and dogs.

The anger hummed quietly in him; a dormant volcano, smouldering away. He did his best to keep a lid on it, to phone a friend rather than pick up a razorblade. He lived with the constant fear that his head was going to explode, skull fragments and grey matter splattered all over the walls. For three weeks he kept a lid on it, let life run over him, smooth, like a river, bothered by nothing at all. Then he blew.

His wife was late home from her shopping. She didn't work, she didn't have to – he provided everything for her, brought home the bacon.

"I'll be back at four," she'd said, as she headed out the door. "Just off to the mall with Shirley."

She wasn't home by four, she wasn't home by five and she wasn't home by six. She wasn't home by seven. For hours he waited for her, sculling red wine, feeling his fury grow. She walked in the door, hands full of bags, nonchalant as you like. She'd had her hair and her nails done. She was cheating on him, he knew it, felt it in his gut. Probably with that friend of hers, Karl, the one she was always going out to lunch with, the one she'd told him was gay. Half of him felt like punching her – that would teach her a lesson; half of him felt sickened by the thought of domestic violence.

"Where the hell have you been?" he hollered, hating himself for losing control, yet feeling unable to stop the flow of his rage.

She ignored him, went to the bedroom, shut the door. He heard her pull a chest of drawers across to block his entry into the room. Definitely guilty then – why else would she want to shut him out? He threw his bodyweight against the door, forced the chest of drawers back, thrust his way into the room. His wife was lying on the bed. Would he hit her, would he hit? He certainly felt like it. He furled his five fingers into a fist, pulled his arm back, ready to let fire. She looked up at him. *I've just been at the mall with Shirley. We had dinner in the food court; it's not such a crime, is it?* A pair of scissors sat on the dressing table. He wanted to stab her. Instead, he picked the scissors up, raised them in the air and brought them down into his wrist. He nicked an artery; the blood came out in spurts, shooting across the room, sprays of scarlet. He hadn't realised blood could shoot that far. He didn't try to put his finger over the wound or in any other way try to stop the blood from flowing.

His wife screamed and ran for the telephone. Mr Clifford walked calmly to the bathroom and put his wrist under the hot tap. The water swirled pink in the basin. The blood flowed and kept flowing. Mr Clifford knelt, keeping his hand in the sink. He could hear his wife calling his name and then he blacked out into a nothingness as dark as the depths of the ocean.

55

Count Homogenised

As a child, my favourite television programme was *A Haunting We Will Go*. *A Haunting We Will Go* was written and screened during the 1970s and '80s. The main character was a vampire called Count Homogenised. Normal vampires drink blood; Count Homogenised drank milk. Whenever he got thirsty, the Count would break into the fridge, steal all the milk and cackle to himself as he drank. The Count was invisible to adults, only children could see him. The Count always got away with his crimes and was never punished for his transgressions.

My older sister Margie and I used to play our own version of *A Haunting We Will Go*. Neither of us wanted to be the-kid-who-can-see-the-Count-but-isn't-believed; we always wanted to be the Count.

"I bags being the Count."

"No, I bags."

"I'm older than you," my sister would say. "I'm the one that gets to choose."

"You were the Count last time, it's my turn now."

And on it went. Truth be told, my sister was a better Count Homogenised than I was. The fake fangs we used sat in her mouth more comfortably, the cape fitted more neatly about her shoulders. My mouth was too small for the fangs, my shoulders too slender for the cape. She would steal milk from the fridge and tip it down her T-shirt. I was a petite blonde; Marge was brunette and more solidly built. Marge's Homogenised had a sinister edge; you got the feeling that any day soon he would tire of drinking milk and take to draining the blood of little girls. My Homogenised drank the milk and then apologized to the children who could see him for having done so. He felt guilty for his sins. My sister's Homogenised felt no remorse; the deed done, he was off to the next fridge.

I was a better victim though. I did bewildered well.

"Hey, who are you? What are you doing here?" I would ask, spinning on the spot like a cat that's having its tail pulled by teasing children.

(Here my sister's Count would give an evil cackle.) On I would drone. There was a pitiful element to my wailing.

"Quit stealing all the milk!"

"You are powerless to stop me," the Count would jeer.

More than once my mother, not realizing that we were merely playing a game, overheard my plaintive cries and came out into the backyard, where we would typically play.

"What's the matter love?"

"Nothing, Mum. Just a dumb game."

"Oh, that's alright then. For a minute there I thought you were genuinely upset."

I was also a better kid-who-can-see-the-Count-but-isn't-believed. Marge's kid was too demanding, overly concerned with facts and details, he wasn't melodramatic enough. He wanted to know precisely how many bottles of milk had been drunk, the exact time (down to the minute) when the Count had acted out his crime, the exact time (down to the minute) of the Count's departure. He wanted to interview all the other children who had seen the Count. *What did he look like when you saw him? What was he wearing? What ethnicity was he – Maori? Caucasian? Samoan? How tall? Over six foot? Fat, thin or in-between? Did he look nervous or was he calm and collected?* My sister's kid-who-isn't-believed wanted to build a psychological profile of the Count, so as to determine when he would be likely to strike again. No weeping or wailing for her – she was no nonsense. She just wanted to catch the villain, to get on with the job. She used a magnifying glass, like Sherlock Holmes and inspected the "bar" (our swing set) for fingerprints and other clues.

"Ah-ha!" she would cry victoriously. "A hair."

My Count Homogenised knew that her kid would track me down, sniff me out, drag me out from whatever rock I crouched sniveling under. Typically, my Homogenised would curl up in a ball and hide in the far corner of the garden, behind the foxgloves; and her kid would come marching over.

"Hullo, hullo, what have we here then? A nasty, milk-drinking, thief. He deserves a sound *smack*."

She'd whack me on the bum with a piece of wood. Sometimes at this stage, I would run crying to Mum.

"Mu-um, Marge hit me."

"Marge," Mum would reprimand. "Play nicely with Leah."

Sometimes I would hit her back and things would descend into a slapping match, till Mum came out to break up the fight.

"Break it up, somebody's gonna get hurt."

"Yeah, and it ain't gonna be me," my sister would sneer, giving me the finger behind Mum's back.

Today Marge and I are going out for lunch. My second marriage has "hit the skids" as Margie would say. Typical of me; I was always useless at picking decent men. I'm a sucker, a fool, easily duped. I pick guys who are all surface charm, but underneath it, *look out*, danger lurks. They are men with screws loose; they cheat on me, they snort coke, they find it hard to keep down a job. Marge's been married to the same man, Trevor, an electrical engineer, for eleven years now. No kids, but they're planning to have one soon. They own two houses; the one that they live in and a rental. I'm still renting; a small one bedroom flat I share with my second husband Will. Marge became an English teacher; I became a teacher too, but I'm still 'finding my feet' trying to get a career off the ground, bouncing round various temporary assignments, ricocheting from man to man like a squash ball.

The first thing she says when she sees me is, "You've dyed your hair."

"Yeah," I say. "Felt like being darker for a while."

She nods and we place our orders at the counter. You don't have to do that here, there's table service as well, but Marge is in a hurry, she has to get back to school in an hour. I'm between jobs; I've got all day. Marge orders a steak and Guinness pie with a side order of chips. I order a Caesar salad minus the dressing. We're halfway through our meal when Marge's arm shoots out.

"Look," she says, "It's Count Homogenised."

"Where?"

I look around.

"There, serving that table."

And so it is. He's minus his fangs and cape, of course, but it's definitely him. Marge kicks me under the table.

"Don't stare."

"You *pointed*. Pointing's worse than staring."

I turn my gaze back to my half-eaten Caesar salad. Count Homogenised walks past, hand raised in a salute, swinging his legs high in the air as he walks. A black moustache bristles on his upper lip.

"What's with his funny moustache?" I ask. "And that walk?"

"He's pretending to be Basil Fawlty," she says, pointing to the blackboard on the wall which reads *Tuesday, Thursday, Friday – Fawlty Towers Themed Lunch. Come dine with the crew from one of television's most popular series.*

"Gawd, how tacky."

"Look," she says, pointing. "That waitress is done up as Cybil."

"Don't *point*."

She points at my salad.

"You need to eat more," she says. "You're too thin."

"I know. It's the stress of the marriage break-up."

"Not eating won't help," she preaches. "That'll just make things   worse."

"It's not intentional. It's just loss of appetite."

"If things get too bad come and stay with me for a month or so. Not long term – a temporary measure."

"Do you think I should kick Will out? I caught him in bed with his 'friend' Johanna. 'We were just cuddling' he said. Cuddling my arse. But I controlled my temper – I didn't go ballistic. I just quietly asked Johanna to leave. I'm still deciding what to do about Will. Do you think I should forgive him?"

"Hell, no. You *should've* gone ballistic. You should've given him an earful. How dare he cheat on you? You two have been together for what...three years now?"

"Four."

"Four years. That must be a record for you."

"Yeah."

"So what the hell did he think he was doing? Honestly, if I caught Trevor with another woman I'd wring his neck. And his balls. He'd be lucky to live to see another day."

"I could just pretend the whole thing never happened. Pretend I didn't see. Blind, like Mike from the Milk Bar."

"That's just denial, burying your head in the sand. Face up to it."

"You think I should leave, then?"

"Of course. No hesitation."

I munch half-heartedly at a lettuce leaf.

"But where will I go?"

"Like I said you can always come and stay with me till you find another flat."

"I can't stay with you, Marge. You've got your own life. I'll look around for another flat, then I'll tell him I'm leaving."
"Okay. Your decision."

Count Homogenised swings by our table.

"Everything alright with the meal, ladies?"

"Great," says Marge.

She whips out a pen and paper from her handbag.

"Could I have your autograph please? My sister here and I used to love *A Haunting We Will Go*. And you were the best character in it. I used to do a great impersonation of you, didn't I, Leah?"

She kicks me under the table again, nudging me to respond.

"Oh yeah," I say. "And I used to do a halfway decent Mike."

Count Homogenised laughs.

"Not many people recognize me, you know," he says. "Hardly anybody remembers *A Haunting We Will Go*."

"Oh, we definitely do," says Marge. "We used to play our own version of it for hours, didn't we Leah?"

She kicks me again.

"Yeah," I say. "We did."

She's remembering how much fun it was to be the sinister cackling Count and the meticulous disciplined Mike. I'm remembering being smacked on the bum with a piece of wood. The Count autographs Marge's piece of paper.

"Don't you want him to sign something for you?" asks Marge. "You always liked being the Count."

Yeah, when you let me play him, I think. I fossick in my handbag for something to sign. All I find is an empty cigarette packet, but I can't give him that, because then Marge will know I've taken up smoking again.

"What about this serviette?" asks Marge, in a slightly exasperated tone.

She picks up her napkin and hands it over to the Count for him to sign. He obliges with a smile, then yells, *"Waldorf salad's off, we're fresh out of Waldorfs,"* and grins and marches off to check on another table.

"Fancy that," says Marge. "Fancy bumping into Count Homogenised at random."

She reaches out and grabs a bit of chicken from my plate.

"So, it's decided then. You're leaving that loser and moving on with your life."

"Yeah, but what if I wind up alone. Just me in a studio flat, drinking myself senseless every night."

"Move in with other people then."

"What, *strangers*? That's even more terrifying."

The Count returns to clear our plates.

"Drinks?" he asks.

"Cappuccino," says Marge.

"Glass of chardonnay, please," I say and Marge frowns.

"Alright, I'll dump him," I conclude. "I'll move in with you for a bit; then I'll find my own place."

Driving past a block of shops on the way home, I suddenly say, "Hey. Pull over."

"Why?"

"Just pull over."

For once, she does as she's told. I hop out of the car and nip into a costume shop; *Carrie's Costumes*. I purchase a black cloak, a bottle of fake blood and some fangs.

"Don't bother with a bag," I tell the shop attendant.

I swing the cape around my shoulders, spill the blood down my front, push the fangs into my mouth. Checking the mirror on the way out of the store, I leer at myself. I look pretty good. Marge is applying lipstick in the rear view mirror. I creep round the back of the car and tap on her window. She screams and jerks back in her seat, puts her hand to her heart.

"You scared the living daylights out of me."

"Ha!" I say. "Gotcha. Gotcha a good one."

"Little cow."

Snarling, I reach one hand in through the window and pick up her sunglasses, push them over my eyes.

"I vant to drinka your blood," I cackle.

"Stop it," she says. "Cut it out, get in the car. I need to get back to work."

But I'm having fun now, I can't stop clowning around.

"Is it a good likeness?" I ask. "Do I look like Count Homogenised?"

"God, no," she says. "You're way too short. But with your hair dyed like that, you look a bit like I used to. When I dressed up as the Count, that is."

I hop into the passenger seat. We drive on in silence.

Creationism

Last week I created my child. He expands, a dot of possibilities, something waiting to happen. A singularity. I have ensured that he will be a boy. He will not be like the others. He will be marked from the start, set apart. He will be different. He has everything he needs. Food, water, shelter, and me, of course, his loving creator. He shall be the best of the best, an übermensch, the kind of boy who could gain three PhDs by twenty-five and run a marathon in under two hours. A record breaker, a force of nature, a star. Walls shall not hold him in; he shall walk straight through them as if they were made of nothing but air. Shackles will not hold him; he shall slip Houdini style from any type of handcuff you might choose to place him in. Do you have a box? Do not put my son in it. He is made for soaring through skies and diving in deep seas, he is made for striding the earth and doing good work, he is not made for your jail cells.

I have prepared the nursery. Brightly coloured mobiles hang from the ceiling; they rotate in time to music. Lavender carpet, lavender walls. Soothing. This room will be a space apart; here he will have time out from the world. Nothing but the finest of classical music shall enter his ears (bar the cacophony from the mobile of course, but perhaps I could see to that, with a screwdriver and a pair of wire-cutters), nothing but masterpieces shall adorn my living room walls for him to feast his eyes upon, no television shall he watch in his infancy; no Barney and Friends, no Teletubbies, no bloody Wiggles shall contaminate his brain. My son shall watch films by Lech Majewski and Darren Aronofsky and of course, Martin Scorsese; and further, he will understand them. I shall explain them to him. He will not attend any typical educational institution; I shall home school him. Is it cruel of me, that I will not allow him to be "normal", your everyday, run of the mill kid? Is it cruel that I expect him to be exceptional? Perhaps I am putting too much pressure on the boy, and on myself. Maybe I should relax, take it easy, allow nature to take its course, although already he requires excessive nurturing if he is to make it. Do you call me over-protective? Very well then, I am over-protective. He is worth protecting. He is worth everything.

He is eight weeks old and approximately one inch long. He has a head and limbs. He can bend at the elbows and knees. I shall call him Henry. He is inside me. An ectopic pregnancy. They tell me it's dangerous, having him nestled there in my abdominal cavity. I will remove him early, at twenty-three weeks; they say it's too young, but he is mine, he will be fine. They say this, they say that. He will not only survive, he will thrive.

My wife left me six months ago. She said I spent all my time engaged in my genetics research. She didn't believe I would ever make any sort of scientific breakthrough. She didn't believe in me at all. I believed in myself though and here I am, about to become the first man in the history of the human race to give birth to a child. A universal first. I implanted him myself. And what a son! What a son is to burst from me. I have it all planned, right down to the colour of his eyes and the exact tone of his skin and the dark chocolate brown shade of his hair. I manufactured him in my laboratory, but he shall be no Frankenstein's monster, or if he is, a monster only by the monstrousness of his achievements which shall dwarf all others. He shall cast the longest shadow, a shadow that stretches from earth to the sun.

I take hormones every morning, to prevent my body from rejecting the foetus. They made me nauseous at first, but now they have no effect on me. Despite this parasite (for technically, let's face it, that's what he is) that is living in my body, I grow stronger by the day, enlarging as he enlarges, gorging myself on eggs and steak and protein shakes and vitamin supplements so that he has the best possible chance at life. Survival is everything.

He is twenty weeks old and six inches long. I believe I have felt the first kick. May it be the first of many.

Every day I walk for two hours, along the river and back, past the screeching gulls. Exercise is good for us. I am not attached to any corporation or university; I am a free agent – Doctor Higgins

64

– an expert in my field, if I do say so myself. A creator of new life. I wear a baggy jacket to hide the bulge that protrudes from my side.

I have not allowed my wife to come back to the house. I have changed the locks. She would only try to stop me if she knew.

Down there, in the darkness, something is kicking and kicking and wants to be let out.

Twenty-three weeks. I inject myself with a local anaesthetic. I am not squeamish, my stomach does not turn. I reach in and pluck the baby out, slice through its umbilical cord, lower it gently into the incubator that I have prepared. It is so tiny, so perfectly formed. It kicks its feet and tries to cry. My wunderkind, my creation, my child. It breathes and breathes and I stand watching it, marvelling. The swells of Beethoven fill the room.

They are coming for me. I hear them at the door. My wife must have alerted them. I must run but I cannot take him with me. My activities are illegal; I will be imprisoned if caught. He would die if taken from his incubator. I flip out over the window ledge and stride across the grass, leaving my precious son to his fate, to the hands of others. He, with his perfect genetics, what will become of him?

He is four years old now. I have finally found him. It is undeniably him. I was watching him at kindergarten, a boy who looked like him. He tripped and fell, cut himself in the playground, and I swiftly descended to scrape up some of the blood and ran DNA tests on him. He lives not so far from me, with a young couple, two teachers. They are not raising him correctly. They do not fill him with Brahms and Majewski, they are allowing him to be *diluted* by mixing with others who are not like him, who are ordinary. He will be polluted. I must find a way to rescue him, to take him back. He belongs to me.

I live in a luxurious waterside apartment. I am not short of a bob or two. I can give him everything. They can give him nothing.

I wait outside the boy's kindergarten. They have named him incorrectly Peter. He is not Peter. He is Henry. His mother comes to meet him, but there is a short wait, a space of time when he lingers by the monkey-puzzle tree. It is during this interval that I must swoop.

I snatch him and bundle him into my car. He kicks and tries to cry out but I put my hand over his mouth and smother him. I lock us in the car and drive home. One of the neighbours peers curiously out over her balcony as we approach. Nosey old woman, go inside and do not ask questions you do not want to hear the answers for. I take him to his room. Snot runs from his nostrils. I inject him and he falls asleep. In the morning he will like it here.

He does not like it here. He cries and will not stop crying. I have tried everything to comfort him.

"I want Mummy," he keeps saying, "I want Mummy."

"But I am your Mummy," I reply.

He screams and screams. He won't eat. I am beside myself. He is rejecting me, his host, the man who gave him life.

I consider putting him on a drip feed but that seems so clinical, so cruel.

I will return him to his surrogate parents. I will continue to watch.

Desert Life

Tiring of city life, I made my home on the edge of the Mojave desert. The daughter of an American father and a British mother, I had been born in the desert, but had moved to the UK as a teenager. I had spent years working in London as a lawyer and I wanted to shuck off my old skin and become somebody new. The rat-race had worn me out; working till midnight most nights. By the time I took the tube home and unwound enough to go to sleep it would be two in the morning. There was no *me* time, no time for friends or family, barely even time to eat. I was too thin and I knew it, clocking in at barely forty-five kilos. The truth was, I was too stressed out to eat much; my stomach was a small tight ball, a clenched fist. I didn't have a boyfriend; I scared them all away. I didn't understand the social rules. A lady must never ask a man out; a lady waits to be asked. A lady must not text a man too many times. A lady must not email a man too many times. A lady must make herself look presentable. The problem was, I wasn't really a lady, I was a *woman*. I didn't see why these rules should apply to me. If I liked a guy I just told him so and asked him if he wanted to go to the movies or out to dinner and this seemed to be too much for the male psyche to bear. I didn't know how to play hard to get; I didn't see why I should. It seemed like a stupid game that I didn't want to learn how to play. People said that I made myself look desperate, and that's one thing a woman should never appear to be, but I was just a woman who knew what she wanted and set about getting it. You don't ask, you don't get, that was how I had been raised. Don't get me wrong. I had my fair share of admirers. They admired me because I was high-flying, good at my job, an excellent, nay, dare I say it, exceptional lawyer. I didn't crumble under pressure, I held my own in what was still predominantly a man's world, at least at the firm where I worked, where all the partners and seventy-five percent of the staff were men. I had a first in law from Oxford, so I'd had my pick of city jobs and had stayed at the same firm all my life. I was loyal. I met men at the pub or at work or at the houses of friends. Nothing ever came of it, apart from the odd one- or two-night stand. Most nights I returned alone to my one-bedroom flat in East Dulwich, ate a small dinner, whatever I could force down, drank just the one glass of wine (I didn't want to turn into one of those sad lone female boozers) and knocked myself out with a Seconal.

*

It crept up on me slowly; "It" being the blues, burn-out, depression, a breakdown. My temper was frayed and I began to snap at colleagues, I cared less and less about the job and my clients, I had difficulty concentrating. The words I was meant to be taking in failed to signify – they were just black marks on a blank page, I couldn't get them to *mean* anything. I felt as if I was standing on an iceberg and a crack in the ice had appeared, with me on one side of it and the rest of the world on the other. I was drifting further and further away, out to sea, where nobody could reach me.

One morning I couldn't get out of bed. I tried to force myself to move but I just couldn't do it. The walls and ceiling seemed to close in around me. I couldn't face another day, another legal case. I rang in sick, spent the morning wallowing under the duvet and the afternoon plotting my escape. Like many rat-racers, I had often dreamed of an existence free from my shackles, my golden handcuffs. I fantasised about having a quiet life, having all day every day to myself, to do as I pleased, to diddle the time away, or perhaps pursue an artistic career. I had long dreamed of writing a sci-fi novel. Damn it, I would throw off this straitjacket the world had me in, rent a small house on the edge of the desert and write my novel. There was another factor drawing me back to Tepoca – my father was from there, my deceptive father, who hid his terrible secret from my mother and me for eighteen years until the day he was discovered.

I bought my airfare. Booked a hire car. I would take my work laptop – hell, they owed me something for sixteen years of loyal service. I typed up my month's notice and handed it in to the boss, but I was not planning to see out the month. No, before things got really bad, before I burned out, I would leave London, head for elsewhere.

I went to bed that evening feeling light and carefree. I had made the right decision, I was sure of it. A new life beckoned me. Perhaps my novel would become a best seller and I would never have to work a normal job again. At any rate, I had been good with my money, I had plenty of savings. The mortgage on my house was nearly paid off and once the place was sold I would have three hundred thousand pounds in the bank. A girl could live for ages in the desert on that.

The following day I rang a local real estate agent and asked them to sell my house for me and deposit the money in my account. I spent the week packing up my belongings, and saying goodbye to friends and family. They thought I was crazy. *What?? You're just ditching your job to head out to the middle of nowhere, where you know nobody??? You're insane.* I didn't care what they said. I was ready to fly.

We passed over the Grand Canyon. I looked down, into those deep orange crevasses and shuddered for a moment as I thought of what it would be like, not to fly, but to fall, down, down, through those fissures in the earth. The plane did not stall though, the engine did not fail, we puttered on, high up in the clouds, to touch down at Mojave Airport. I picked up my hire car and headed to the Death Valley Junction Hotel, where I had booked myself in for the night. Once I had unpacked my suitcase, I headed to the Tepoca Hot Springs to soak my tired bones.

I was lying in the hottest pool with my eyes closed, listening to the chirp of cicadas in the trees when I felt an arm brush against mine. I opened my eyes to see a large hirsute man standing next to me.

"Hi," he said. "I thought you looked lonely lying there by yourself. I'm Jake."

As a matter of fact, I hadn't been lonely, but I was too polite to say so. I just smiled up at him and said nothing. He sat down on the seat next to me.

"A lady needs company out here in the desert. It can be a pretty inhospitable place. Though you'll find the townspeople of Tecopa friendly enough. How long you been out here in Death Valley?"

"Just arrived. Hi, I'm Caroline."

"Well, if you need a tour guide to show you around, I'm your man."

I wasn't sure whether or not to take him up on his offer. Could I trust him, this stranger? What if he turned out to be a rapist or murderer? What if he had it in for me?

"It's gonna be a full moon tonight," he said. "So the coyotes will be howling. A welcome ceremony, welcoming you to town."

"Neat."

"If you like we could take in a show. We've got a performer here called Marta Becket who got a flat tire in Death Valley Junction in the sixties and decided to stay. She owns the opera house and has been performing here ever since. She doesn't dance anymore but she performs *The Sitting Down Show*, which involves her sitting in a high-backed chair, switching hats and describing a musical in which she used to dance and sing. Her voice cracks, and her movements are slow, but her wit is razor-sharp. Come on, you'll find it a hoot."

He was getting a bit keen. He was scaring me. Now I knew what it was like to be on the other side of the equation, the one who was on the receiving end of somebody else's come-on.

"Can I think about it?"

"Okay."

He went silent for a bit, and then started up the conversation again.

"Where you from then? You out here for good or just a holiday?"

"London. And I'm out here for good."

"Ah, the big smoke. We've got quite a few folks out here who've tired of their city lives and decided to head for somewhere more tranquil. You'll find desert life peaceful, but maybe a little dull for a girl who's used to inner city excitement."

"I'm sure I'll cope. I intend to write a novel."

His eyes lit up.

"Oh yeah? What about?"

"A sci fi set in post-apocalyptic London, called *After*. What do you do for a living yourself?"

"Paint houses. There's plenty round here that need doing. I'm never out of work."

"That sounds exciting."

"Hardly. But it keeps a roof over my head. Anyway, tell me more about this novel."

"Okay, well it's set in the year 2030. A nuclear bomb has gone off in central London and the only people left alive are those who were safe in bunkers when the bomb exploded. When the dust settles the survivors emerge from their bunkers. The bunkers are equipped with enough food to last the survivors for two years only. However, the bunkers each have their own supply of seeds and trowels, so the immediate task of the survivors is to till the soil and plant seeds so that they will have a sustainable food source. A hierarchy is established, with a man called Jeremy being the elected leader. Jeremy is selected as, pre-apocalypse, he was the CEO of an inner-city company, so the other survivors feel that he has leadership experience. Fights, both physical and verbal, are common amongst the survivors and it is Jeremy's job to keep the peace as best he can."

There was another space of silence as Jake digested all I had told him.

"Well, it sounds promising," he said eventually. "You ready for that tour yet? Had enough of soaking?"

"Just give me ten more minutes then I'll be done."

"Great."

He lay back in the pool and started humming to himself.

When the ten minutes was up we climbed out of the hot pools. I made my way to the Ladies' changing room, he to the Gents. I changed out of my wet swimming costume and into the tracksuit I had been wearing previously. I felt like a new woman; refreshed and ready to embark on my latest project – the building of a life out here in the middle of nowhere, out here in the desert.

He was waiting for me by the gate, hands in jean pockets, leaning against the gatepost. He linked his arm through mine in a manner that I found a little too overly familiar and led me towards his car. I hopped into the passenger seat and we began our tour of the town. There wasn't much to see; just a few dilapidated houses and dusty old shops – imaginary tumbleweed blew down the main street. He took me to the local bar. It was only three pm, too early in the day for me to drink. He had a beer, I an orange juice. The locals turned to stare as we walked in. Somebody wolf-whistled at me and hissed, "Wow, great legs. Great ass."

I felt violated, but I said nothing, just sat down at the booth with my orange juice.

"So whose house are you painting at the moment?" I asked.

"The house of an old couple who live three doors down from me. It's going well, I'm nearly finished."

I looked down at my hands as they lay upon the oak table; they looked gnarled, like witches' hands, claws. I finished my orange juice and told Jake I had better be getting back to my motel.

That night, as the coyotes started up with their howling, I began my novel. I wanted to hook in readers with a brilliant beginning. At midnight, the usual hour when I retired, I went to sleep. Out here in this quiet, peaceful place, I did not need a Seconal and drifted off to sleep naturally. I dreamed desert dreams, filled with coyotes and rattlesnakes and Joshua trees. I awoke with the dawn and, feeling perky, made myself a cup of instant coffee using the sachets that were provided. It was winter and freezing cold, so I wrapped up warmly, then walked out onto the small porch to stare out at the town. Lights were beginning to flick on in the houses. One by one, they sprang to life. I could enjoy life out here, I thought, away from the hustle, bustle and ruthlessness of London. A woman had space to breathe here, space to dream, to dream up a novel which would hopefully make my name in the literary world; if it ever made it out of the slush-pile, that is.

I sat down to write and was three paragraphs into my work when I was interrupted by a knock at the door. It was Jake. He just wanted to call around and see how I was. He asked me what I was going to do with myself today and I pointed to my laptop stating that I intended to spend the morning writing and the afternoon looking for a house to rent.

"Ah," he said. "Well, I can help out there. One of the houses I'm painting the outside of is vacant and I know that the landlord is hoping to get somebody in there."

"That would be brilliant."

"Leave it to me. I'll be back around noon."

Jake left and I settled down with my novel. He was starting to get a bit too keen, I felt, calling round to see me without telephoning first. I wrote on until midday, then broke for lunch, walking into town to the one and only sandwich bar, where I had tuna, cucumber and mayo on rye.

When I returned to the motel room, Jake was waiting at the door.
"Sorry to leave you hanging," I said. "Been here long?"
"No, just a couple of minutes."
I unlocked the motel door and we went inside.
"Good news," he said. "The landlord is happy to show you around the house at one pm today. He's keen to get somebody in there as soon as possible, so you're in luck."
"Great. Thanks very much for sorting that."
We sat out on the front porch for a spell, and then made our way to the house that was available.

The house was a run-down ramshackle affair, with the hot wind whistling through the gaps where planks had fallen out. The landlord was standing outside, a moustachioed man in a singlet top with tattoos all up and down his arms.
"Alright, love?" he asked, as we approached.
"Doing fine," I replied.
It was the truth. Looking back, I could see that I had been dangerously close to burn-out in London and I patted myself on the back for having made the decision to save myself from collapse, by coming out to this place, the desert. I still felt a little on edge, shaky, but the hot pools had done me a world of good and I knew that in a few days, once I had moved into my new home, I would come completely right.

We stepped inside the house. I don't know how long the house had been vacant but nobody had bothered to clean the inside up for my inspection. Cobwebs hung in the corners of the rooms, empty Coke bottles littered the floor, and there were unemptied ashtrays in the lounge and dining room. The windows were covered in grey film; dirt. It was no palace but, I thought, it would do. Any port in a storm, as they say. The rooms were enormous, compared to British rooms; I would have plenty of space here, space to unfurl and expand. The kitchen was filthy, crumbs and mice droppings on every surface. I opened up the oven – a foolish move; it was coated in black gunk. One good thing; – it was partly furnished; there was an old double bed with springs poking up through the mattress and a sofa in the lounge. A fridge in the kitchen, a washing machine.

"I'll take it," I said. "How much?"

"One hundred and fifty a week."

Cheap enough.

"Will you help me clean it?" I asked.

I couldn't quite face tackling the filth on my own.

"Sure. We could muck in this afternoon if you've got nothing else planned."

"Great. I wanted to get to the hot pools in the evening, but the afternoon's free. Do you have any cleaning-products or will we have to go buy some?"

"Don't have nothing," said the landlord with a shrug of his shoulders. "There's a broom and a mop in the laundry though, and a vacuum cleaner in the hall cupboard."

We walked into town, bought detergent, oven cleaner, glass cleaner and cloths. It took us three hours to get the place spick and span; I did most of it, down on my knees scrubbing the kitchen floor, spraying the oven, attacking the windows with all my might. The men just vacuumed and wiped down dirty surfaces. When finished, I stood back and admired our handiwork. The place had come up okay; it was habitable now. I would need to buy a writing desk and perhaps a chest of drawers for the bedroom, but there was no great hurry to do so.

I brought my suitcase round from the motel, went grocery shopping, settled in. At five o'clock I headed to the pools. Jake had said that he wanted to come too and was waiting for me at the gate, with his swimming shorts and his towel tucked under his arm.

"Hello there," he said, as I approached.

"Howdy."

I was warming to him; he had adopted me, taken me under his American wing. He wasn't standoffish, like British men, with their social rules that must be obeyed. He was friendly, even if a little overly so. We entered the pools, got changed and retired into the hottest pool for a soak. Jake chatted away and I listened. He had been born and bred in Tecopa; he rarely left. He'd been to Las Vegas once for a gamble, but the city had overwhelmed him with its flashing lights and card sharks and hookers. He was a big reader, he said, an armchair traveller, so it was interesting to him that I was going to try and be a writer. The library here was okay, he said. I should join. He'd read his way through most of the fiction section and was starting on the non-fiction. He asked me to join him for dinner at Pastel's restaurant and I agreed.

I went back to my new home and lay on the bed for an hour and a half, daydreaming about what life would be like when I was a successful novelist. Perhaps I would be invited to attend literary festivals, to meet with other authors, to appear on radio and television. How would I feel about doing all that? It could be an awful strain. Perhaps it would be better to be like Janet Frame or Thomas Pynchon, to all extents and purposes a recluse, shunning the limelight, hiding in the shadows. Jake arrived to pick me up. His car had been fixed. It was a red chevvy, a nice car and very American.

He'd booked a table by the window. We sat down and ordered – I a muccio panini sandwich (smoked chicken breast, roasted eggplant, portabello mushrooms, cheddar cheese, with a garlic aioli spread served with a side salad), he a Pastels Pizza with pepperoni. I never ate dessert in London, I never felt like it. I was always too stressed out to fit it in, but out here I was working up an appetite. I ordered the strawberry rhubarb shortcake and he the double dutch chocolate pound cake. The food was delicious; Pastels touted itself as "*the* place to eat in Tecopa" and it didn't let me down. I stuffed myself full, perhaps the first time I had really eaten to satiation in over a year. We had a fine red wine with dinner.

"Here," said Jake, pushing his leg up against mine under the table, "You don't fancy coming back to my place for a coffee do you?"

I thought for a bit. What harm could it do? I was a single woman, a free agent, and it was just a coffee after all, it's not as if he'd asked me to sleep with him, though I wasn't naive, I knew where coffee could lead.

"Alright then," I agreed. "As long as it's not instant. I'm sick to death of that horrible stuff that was in the motel room. I hate instant coffee but that's all there was."

"Would I make a lady *instant* coffee?"

We drove back to his place in his chevvy. His house was a damned sight better than mine; no missing planks, a well-cared for garden, a cactus collection and, once we stepped inside, I was pleased to note that the place was clean and tidy. Some bachelors can be terribly messy, but not this one.

"You got a boyfriend back in London?" he asked me.

"No. I scared them all off."

"Why?"

"Too forthright, I think. They don't like it. Britain is a place where the men are expected to make all the moves. The lady just sits there and waits for the man to take the lead."

"I like a forthright lady myself. Forthright and honest, that's the way. None of this messing about. Now, you take milk and sugar?"

"Yes," I said. "White with one, please."

"Take a seat," he said, gesturing towards the sofa.

I sat down. He prepared the coffee and brought it through, sat down on the sofa, up close next to me. He finished his coffee then put his arm around my shoulders.

"Wanna watch a DVD?"

"What have you got?"

"I'm a big Tarantino man myself. *Kill Bill, Jackie Brown, Inglorious Bastards.*"

"I've seen the others, so let's watch *Inglorious Bastards.*"

He put the DVD into the machine and hit "play", then snuggled up to me, his head on my shoulder. It struck me as a vaguely feminine thing to do for such a masculine man, but I didn't push him away. I was enjoying myself; this was the new me – liberated, free and obviously attractive, at least to somebody.

When the film was finished he leaned over to kiss me. I didn't resist, didn't push him away. Why not enjoy a little kiss. It was an auspicious start to my new life; why not let a little romance in? I didn't want to be lonely – and out here that was a real danger. One thing led to another and before I knew it we were in bed together, having sex. It had been three years since I'd slept with somebody, three years too long. He was a marvelous lover, surprisingly tender and sweet and in the morning he cooked me a big American breakfast; hash browns, eggs, bacon, with a side of blueberry pancake, washed down with good coffee. I felt that I had really landed on my feet, meeting this man. My old friends, who all had prestigious jobs, might have scoffed at me for hooking up with a painter of houses, but I didn't care what he did for a living. The main thing was that he was a good, kind man who knew how to treat a woman. Lady, I was a lady now.

I returned to my house and fired up my computer. The words flowed freely, line after line, paragraph after paragraph. I was on fire; it was the sex that had freed me, freed my mind, blasted the cobwebs out.

Out here in the desert, time was different. There was no routine, no structure. I was very strong-willed though and I disciplined myself to write two thousand words every day. The rest of the time, when Jake wasn't working, I hung out with him. He treated me well; bought me flowers and chocolates, encouraged my literary endeavours, egged me on when I was flagging. He was a gentleman. Then there was the sex, of course, which started out marvellous and remained so. We experimented with a variety of positions; Jake got sex books out from the library and we made our way through the pages together. The men I had met in London would sleep with me once or twice and then lose interest. Jake's interest in me grew with time. He liked to hear about my old life, the legal cases I had fought and won, my time at Oxford, my childhood in Dorset with my eccentric lepidopterist of a father and my mother, who had manic-depression and would be up in the air, flying from star to star one minute and down in the dumps, sitting round staring at blank walls the next.

We had been seeing each other for about a year when Henry suggested I move into his place.

"Why pay two rents when we can pay one?" he said.

I thought about it for a day or two. I didn't want to rush into a decision I might later regret, but in twelve months of dating, Henry hadn't put a foot wrong. He hadn't said anything to insult me, he'd never stood me up, he'd never put me down. He had done nothing but listen and encourage me. The man was a keeper.

We shacked up together. There were babies, first Celia and then a year later, David. They were good; they slept through the night almost straight away, they rarely cried. I sent my novel away to several agents in London. One of them signed me up and the novel was published. There were reviews online at Bookbag and Amazon, and in the Metro and, to my great surprise and delight, in the *Guardian*.

"A writer of real talent," said the *Metro*.

"A star is born," said the *Guardian*.

The money wasn't much, but it was an accomplishment nonetheless. I had done it. I had set up a new life for myself, created a successful, free existence. My old shackles were shattered. I was my own invention; my motto was *don't look back.*

Over the next four years I wrote the two sequels to *After.* Both were accepted and were moderately successful. The kids grew up and attended the local kindergarten. They were happy, as was I, happy with my desert life, my desert love.

Ghosts

For a long time I did not believe in ghosts. I thought they were like Santa Claus and the Easter Bunny and fairies; mythical creatures dreamt up to serve humanity's needs. My sister Petra believed though; she claimed that she could see them with her special eyes and hear them with her special ears; that they were all around us, ethereal spirits that she could tame to do her bidding. She thought of it, she claimed, as a circus master taming his animals.

"Some of them are very belligerent," she said. "You have to show 'em who's boss. Don't let them get the upper hand, keep them in line."

She said she had scars, not physical but psychological, from where they had maimed her, like Mabel Stark and her tigers.

"Some of them are peaceable," she continued. "They mean you no harm. But others, boy, look out! They haven't been satisfied in life, they died bitter and full of regrets and as spirits they are vengeful, they're like that girl in that cheesy Bob Geldof song *I Don't Like Mondays* – they wanna shoot the whole place down."

Everybody thought that Petra was funny in the head; what other logical conclusion could you reach regarding a girl who wandered around proclaiming she was in touch with ghosts? Petra was two years older than me and didn't have any friends and was picked on at school. I was determined not to end up like her, and put special effort into fostering relationships with girls my age, my little gang that I hung out with at lunchtime and jabbered on the phone to after school. One of these girls was Sally. Sally thought Petra was completely bonkers and told her so to her face.

"You're loopy, you are," she would say, circling one finger at the side of her head to indicate madness.

"Whatever," Petra would shrug. "You'll see, one day; one day when you *die* and journey to the spirit plane yourself, then you'll look back and understand that I was not lying, but telling the truth."

I had no idea where Petra had got her ideas about ghosts and spirits from. Maybe she had read too many Amy Tan books about girls with Yin eyes, maybe she'd been too affected by *Casper the Friendly Ghost*, which we'd seen together as kids, maybe she was just plain bonkers. She was a dyed-in-the-wool eccentric. She wore red skirts with green skivvys and yellow socks pulled up to her knees; she wore sandals in the summer and socks and sandals in the winter; she dyed her hair blue like Marge Simpson. She said the strangest things at the strangest times, like *How can our eyes recognise colours?* And *How does the brain comprehend language?* And *How does a baby know when it's time to walk?* It was as if her head had been fastened to her neck at a strange angle, as if she saw the world differently from everybody else. Being so odd can't have been comfortable for her. Most children want to conform, to be included, to be part of a group. They look with suspicion upon anybody who is different. Petra was perceptive enough to realise what other people thought of her, the way they shut her out, ostracised her, the way people gave each other *looks* when Petra opened her mouth to make one of her weird statements. Besides, Sally told her to her face on a regular basis what a fruit-loop she was. But she did not seem affected by other people's looks and comments. It was as if she was oblivious, blessed with a rhino's hide. Thick-skinned, she ploughed head-long through her life.

Petra was as clever as coffee pavlova and never struggled with her schoolwork, unlike me, who floundered about with physics and calculus and biology. She learned osmotically; she barely even had to take notes, just sat in lessons, absorbing knowledge through her pores. She was always alone at lunch-time, typically in the school library communing with the spirits whom she claimed lurked between the library shelves. She was my sister and I loved her dearly, but she was a right *weirdo*.

I was often embarrassed by Petra and would tease her by hiding in various spots around the garden when she was sunbathing and calling out her name in a ghostly voice.

"Petra. Oh *Petra.*"

She would sit bolt upright, put down her book and head in the direction of my voice. Usually she discovered me, lurking behind the rhododendron or the grapefruit tree, trying to sound spooky.

It wasn't until I was a little older and had left home and begun university that I began to wonder if there wasn't some truth in Petra's beliefs. Since leaving home, I had developed insomnia and often awoke in the wee hours of the morning, when long shadows flickered on the walls. I had gone to see the university doctor and he had prescribed Zopiclone, which did the trick, but which I disliked for the chemical aftertaste it left when I awoke. My life which, throughout high school, had been fairly uneventful, became riddled with catastrophes. It was as if the gods had it in for me. A flat I was living in burned down, when a flatmate left the light on in her room and it set fire to a rack of clothes drying on a makeshift hanging-rail, constructed from two chains screwed into the ceiling and a broom handle. I was away kayaking with a boyfriend at the time and returned to a blackened cicada shell of a house. Everything burned, everything gone. I moved in with my boyfriend, who dumped me over the following university holidays after I met his control freak of a father who didn't approve of me; of the way I spoke, the way I dressed, my hair. David hadn't even told his parents that we were going out, let alone that we were living together and when his brother let it slip, his parents asked to meet me, in their ever so posh six bedroom house up in the "heights".

"Hi, I'm Caitlin," I had introduced myself politely.

"Yeah," his father'd said. "So you're the one shagging my son. What kind of contraception are you using?"

"Umm," I said, flustered. "I'm kind of on the pill."

"Kind of? Are you or aren't you?"

"Yes, I am."

"Good. 'Cause the next thing you know I won't be supporting just you and David, I'll be supporting thirty-three kids as well."

Charming. The man had never given me a cent in his life and I certainly had no intention of having one child by his darling son, let alone thirty-three.

Not only was I suffering my own insomnia, but I also suffered the problems of other students. A friend dumped her boyfriend for her boyfriend's best friend in the middle of exams and the dumped one took to coming to the house at three am, threatening to kill himself as my friend shagged herself senseless in the next room with her new man.

"There, there," I would say. "She's not worth it. Let me make you a cup of herbal tea."

Another friend was beaten up by her boyfriend on more than one occasion; at four am I would get a phone call to go around and help try to sort things out. Drama was always taking place in the middle of the night. It was all those not-yet-adults and the vast amount of alcohol and pot we all consumed that created such a heady mix.

Petra was away at a different university and I was missing her; her quirky sense of humour, her eccentricity. Most of the other law students were awfully straight; they turned up the collars of their little chequered shirts and wore pearl necklaces and earrings and sunbathed on top of the university dorms with beer mats over their breasts and sung along to *Mustang Sally*. They were "rugby chicks" they hung about with thick-necked meatheads, hanging off their every word, worshipping them, hoping to snag a boyfriend who would turn into a husband so they could reproduce and bring forth yet more rugby freaks. What would they make of Petra? They would ridicule her, if she were here, mock her dress sense and her music taste, attempt to cut her down to size. But there was no cutting Petra down. She lived on Planet P, where the skies were shaded not blue, but probably a lurid purple, and multi-coloured animals roamed the landscape. She was studying Fine Arts and in the university holidays brought home portfolios full of her wild, surrealistic paintings and her wonderful curvy sculptures which had earned her A+ grades.

It was really the spontaneous window-smashing that made me wonder about Petra and her ghosts. I was doing a BA/LLB and one of my English papers was Modern Poetry. It was run by Trevor Peterson who was an overweight Californian who incessantly sipped Diet Coke and sweated a lot and was Wallace Stevens's biggest fan. I liked him anyway, he was funny and quietly brilliant in a savage sort of way and wrote poems himself which had been published in the States and in New Zealand. He seemed like he would share my hatred of rugby heads and burgeoning love of poetry. His lectures provided welcome relief from the endlessly dull, endlessly dry law lectures I sat through.

After the final no there comes a yes, he would quote and I would wonder to myself *but who is The Well-Dressed Man With a Beard* meant to *be? Why is he well-dressed?* Petra would have asked. *Why does he have a beard? Is he God? Charles Manson? Did Wallace Stevens have a beard?*

I was on my way to the library one Saturday when I saw Trevor coming down the English Department stairs carrying a heavy-looking box. As I approached his car, the front windscreen shattered into a thousand fragments. Nothing hit the window. The car was not moving. It was like something out of a poltergeist movie. I kept walking; I'd had houses burn down, boyfriends' fathers ranting at me, jilted boyfriends sobbing in the night, angry boyfriends with knives threatening their girlfriends and me. What did a little window-smashing matter? For Trevor, it was different. He froze and nearly dropped his box.

"My car window just smashed for no reason," he said.

He looked freaked, as if he'd seen a ghost.

"Maybe you need shatterproof glass," I said.

"Maybe I need a new car."

That night I thought about the smashed windscreen. It was inexplicable. Car windows didn't just *burst,* did they? I knew what Petra would say. She would say that angry ghosts had smashed the windscreen, hungry spirits who wanted to be listened to. *Mustang Sally* blared down from the house next door, where they were roasting a lamb on a spit. I wished for a power blackout.

I graduated from university and took a graduate position in a law firm. For a while, life settled down and became more predictable, dull even, with me grinding away, doing endless hours at the office, hoping to scale the ranks and make partner by the age of thirty. I lived with two men; the house was a pigsty, dirty dishes and clothes and games and DVDs and PlayStations and bits of computers everywhere. You couldn't move for tripping over some sort of debris. Petra came to visit; she'd graduated at the same time as me and was struggling to make ends meet as a painter, living and working in a small studio flat, on the dole, supplementing her income with the odd sale of a painting. She'd toned down her style a bit, matured. She spoke more quietly and thoughtfully, she listened to what others were saying, her dress sense wasn't quite so wild. She seemed more shy and withdrawn. She no longer spoke of ghosts or spooks or spirits. She was more like a normal person. I found this slightly sad, as if she had lopped off part of herself in order to fit into one of society's little boxes. I found out later that she was taking psychiatric medication that acted as a tranquiliser, but Petra didn't tell me that herself. I found out from my mother. One of my flatmates developed quite a crush on her and kept asking me if she was single. As far as I knew Petra was still a virgin; there had been no talk of boyfriends or one-night stands. When she left he asked me for her number and the two of them would chat on the phone for hours every night. Progression in the direction of adult behaviour.

Neither I nor my flatmates sleep-walked. It was odd then, that shortly after Petra had come to stay, electrical appliances began switching themselves on in the middle of the night. It started with the Expelair. It was firmly switched off in the evening after dinner; yet when I awoke in the morning and walked downstairs to get my coffee it was on full bore.

"Did you turn this on?" I asked the boys.

"No, not me."

"Not me."

The following night it was the heating and the TV. Off last thing at night, on first thing in the morning. I wondered if one of the boys wasn't playing a trick on me, having a laugh, but they'd never played tricks before, they weren't the type, they were too busy with their jobs and their PlayStations and trying to get girlfriends. Things hadn't been going too well for me at work; I had been passed over for promotion despite my seventy-hour weeks and had been given a series of rather gruelling cases to work on. Did the ghosts make themselves known during trying times? And what sort of entities were they if they could shatter glass and affect electrical flow – were they shrieking at frequencies inaudible to human ears?

I phoned Petra in one of those rare spaces of time when she wasn't on the phone to my flatmate.

"Hey, Sis," I said. "I think I've come round to your view that ghosts actually exist."

"Ghosts," she said. "What's this talk of ghosts? You losing your mind?" "But Petra! You always used to claim to see and hear them. What's happened to you?"

"Gee, I was a kid then, you know. Kids believe all kinds of crazy stuff. You used to believe in elves, didn't you?"

"I certainly did not."

"Oh, must've been somebody else. Listen, you've probably not been sleeping properly. You're stressed out, I can hear it in your voice. Take a bath with some lavender essence in it and get a good night's sleep. Call me back in the morning if you like, I'm always here, painting, painting, sold three last week; good week."

I did not sleep that night or the next. The dreaded insomnia was back, gripping me in its merciless, iron claw. I called in sick and staggered to the doctor for some sleeping-pills, which I hadn't done since leaving university. That night I slept the sleep of the dead, awakening to the familiar chemical taste in my mouth, which I washed out with toothpaste. The house was empty and all the appliances were on full bore; even the vacuum cleaner which had been left plugged in. It was time to move.

But they follow me, these ghosts; they like me. I move from house to house and always they make their presence felt, in insidious ways. These airy entities smash my mirrors and turn my laptop back on after I've switched it off and hurl eggs to the floor. What do they want from me? Trevor Peterson is famous now, after winning the Forward Prize for poetry. His name is frequently in the papers. Sometimes I wonder what he meant when he handed me Stevens's *The Snow Man* to study, but I don't think about it all that often.

Going First

We all assumed that my grandfather would go first. "We" included himself. At eighty-five, he'd had two heart attacks and, unlike my grandmother, who kept fit and active by playing golf and mahjong every week, he didn't do any activities. In June, I had a call from my mother, who was in Gisborne at the time, with my sister Nicola and her two young children.

"Nana's in the hospital," she said. "She's been diagnosed with acute myeloid leukaemia. Nicola and I are going up there with the kids tomorrow."

Leukaemia runs in the family; two of my grandmother's siblings contracted it, one dying at the age of fifty, the other still alive, receiving regular doses of chemotherapy. It was terrible news, but at first I assumed (despite the word "acute") that the leukaemia would be slow-acting and that my grandmother would be around for a few more years. Googling the illness, I found otherwise.

As an acute leukemia, pronounced Wikipedia. *AML progresses rapidly and is typically fatal within weeks or months if left untreated.*

My grandmother was being treated; perhaps she would be okay? I thought I should fly to see her anyway. She'd been *such* a good grandmother, baking *such* fine pavlova, teaching us how to play the piano and putt a golf ball, taking us to the beach and inventing stories with us when we got caught in the rain on the way home. She was kind; had a heart of gold. Then there was my grandfather, with his dry sense of humour. He and my grandmother had been together for sixty years – he would need all the support he could get at a time like this. I went online, booked a flight, packed my bags.

"Be prepared for a bit of a shock," said my sister, in the car on the way over to the North Shore and the Milford Hospital.

"Can she talk? Is she conscious?"

"Yes, but she's very weak. Fragile."

I couldn't imagine my grandmother weak; she'd always been such a pillar of strength, decisive, with a good group of friends. I felt an old familiar dread creep into my stomach. Life was about to deal one of its blows; one of those cuffs to the back of the head that always happened when you least expected it.

She lay in the hospital with oxygen tubes up her nose, wearing one of her floral nighties.

"Hello, Nana."

"Katy!" she said. "What are you doing here?"

"Oh, just come to see how you're getting on. You know I don't like to see my Nana sick."

"Oh," she said. "I'll get better. Be back on my feet in no time."

Her lunch was on a tray in front of her; she was struggling to eat it, taking tiny mouthfuls, and then putting the fork down on the tray, exhausted. She'd always been such a hearty eater, never one to leave food on the plate. Lifting a cup of tea to her mouth was a mammoth effort; my mother reached across to help her lift the cup. My grandfather shuffled in.

"It's an empty house without Nana in it," he said. "Strange sort of a place. Quiet, too quiet. Nothing happening."

"They're starting me on a new drug tomorrow," said my grandmother. "The white blood cell count keeps going up and up."

My grandfather slowly nodded his head.

"You'll come right," he said.

That evening he showed us a booklet he had on that particular strain of leukaemia. He'd highlighted a section that read – *With treatment, the majority of patients will recover.* I didn't know what to say when he showed it to me. I didn't want to take away his hope, but I also wanted him to be realistic. Nana was eighty-four and although she was in good health, this was a nasty disease. I wanted him to be prepared for the fact that she might *not* come right. In the end, I didn't say anything at all. I felt sorry for him, all alone in the house after so many years. The emptiness, I thought, must be crushing.

The following day we went to the hospital again. My grandmother looked even weaker, though she raised her hand to wave at us as we entered. My cousin Jean was there as well, with her three-month-old baby, Oliver, who was all big blue eyes and smiles. After five minutes with Nana, Jean went out into the corridor and I went after her to check that she was okay. She was crying, great lobs of tears running down her cheeks.

"It's just so terrible," she said. "She was in such good health, so fit and able. Why does something like this have to go and happen? Go and ruin everything."

"I know. It's very harsh."

I put my arms around her shoulders in an attempt to comfort her. She shrugged me off.

"It'll be alright," she said. "She'll pull through."

It was what we all wanted to believe. But later that day, the haematologist, a young woman called Rebecca, who oozed competence, took us all, excluding my grandmother, to one side.

"Acute myeloid leukaemia is very aggressive," she said. "A woman of twenty would be doing well to last forty-eight hours with what your grandmother's got."

We looked at one another in silence.

In the car on the way home, my sister said, "So, do you think they're trying to tell us that she's going to die?"

"Yes," said my mother.

I disagreed. "No," I said. "They're saying that she's doing well."

Every day we visited her. Every day she got worse, slipping away, till she was barely present. When I looked in her eyes I saw something trying to hang on, trying and failing. All she could manage at each mealtime was a mouthful or two. The nurses wanted to move her out of her current ward of four and into a private side room. I knew then that she was going to die; they didn't want her to disturb the other patients as she was going. There was to be a meeting at three pm, again without my grandmother. I didn't like the fact that she was excluded from these meetings; they did, after all, concern her future, or lack of it. I thought that she should be in the loop, informed as to what was really going on. Rebecca was joined by one of the more senior doctors, Dr Patel, who did most of the talking. I sat next to my grandfather, holding his hand.

"Thank you all for coming along," said Dr Patel. "We've tried three different drugs on your grandmother, and none of them seem to be working. Her white blood cell count is very high. It's highly unlikely that she's going to pull through."

I squeezed my grandfather's hand. Tears welled in his eyes.

"I don't want her to know," said my grandfather in the corridor, after the meeting. "I don't want anybody to tell her."

When we went back into the ward, my grandmother looked up at my grandfather and asked, "Do they say that I'm going to get better?"

"Yes," he lied. "Oh yes, on the mend."

She looked at me.

"Is he telling me the truth?"

I couldn't look her in the eye. Nor could I go against my grandfather's wishes. I just stared at the wall, nodding my head slowly, and then laid my head down on her chest.

"Oh," said my grandfather later, at home. "Oh, it's all a bit of a shock. I always thought that I would be the one to go first. It says in this booklet here. Look," (he tapped the page with his finger) *"with treatment, the majority of patients will recover."*

I was furious with whoever had written this; who were they and how dare they give my grandfather false faith, build his hopes up just to smash them? As for his desire that Nana not be told her disease was terminal, that put us all in an awkward position. We all felt that she should be told, should *know*. *If it was me*, we all said, *I'd definitely want to know.*

We, the family, went on twenty-four hour watch. There was somebody with my grandmother at all times, with first my parents and then my uncle and aunt taking the night shift. There were more meetings, meetings with the people from the hospice and with Dr Patel and Rebecca again. Nana was asked whether she wanted to be at home, or in the hospital, or in the hospice, so she must have figured out then that she wasn't going to get any better – no patient ever comes *out* of a hospice. She wanted to stay in the hospital she said. The doctor insisted that she be moved into a side room.

"It's just such a bugger, Katy," Nana said to me. "Such a *bugger*."

She didn't shed a tear, comforted her son when he cried.

"There, there Richard," she said. "I've had a good life."

What a trooper! She gave instructions for her funeral as she lay on her deathbed.

"I just want a small, private funeral. Just family and the following people."

She rattled off the names of her ten best friends. She kept her sense of humour right up to the end.

"I'll drive," she said, when my grandfather asked who amongst us was going to drop him home.

We got the call at five in the morning. My aunt and uncle were in the room with her.

"Nana's going to go soon," they said.

We jumped in the car, drove across to the Shore. She was lying in bed with her oxygen mask off, struggling to breathe, unconscious. I didn't want to see it.

"Bye, Nana," I said and kissed her on the cheek.

"She can probably hear you," said my uncle. "She just can't respond."

I waited in the lounge, flicking through the papers, not really taking anything in. An hour later, she was gone.

"She said *the train is coming*," reported my aunt. "*The train is coming.* Grandad's still in there with her. He doesn't want to leave."

"I'll go see if he's okay," I said.

He was sitting in the room with her body, holding her hand, which was growing colder by the minute. I took the chair next to him. He started crying, which was when I distinctly heard my grandmother's voice softly saying, "Aw, gee." I looked at her body. She was no longer there. Was it an auditory hallucination? Was it really my grandfather, not her, who had spoken? I looked at him. I didn't want to ask.

Consoling my grandfather, I said, "She's just gone to the next platform Grandad. She's waiting for you there."

But he misheard me. What he thought I said was, "she's just gone to another planet" – Nana was elsewhere, hanging out with aliens, laughing beneath reddened skies. He liked this idea and I didn't want to tell him that he'd heard me wrong. A simple train platform with its hard wooden seats and its litter was so much less exciting than a planetary elsewhere.

The funeral was simple; just close friends and family as my grandmother had suggested. My mother and I read a poem together, taking turns at the verses. Everybody cried except me, I felt dead, hardened, as if I had turned to stone. After the funeral, back at my grandfather's house, I felt distant, unreal, as if I was fading away. My father kept calling my name to jolt me back. I couldn't tell which direction his voice was coming from. A million miles away, I was thinking of my beloved Nana and her new home, up in the sky, and of the voice I had heard, a tiny, ghostly voice, barely there. *Aw gee.*

I reported the incident to a friend over the phone.

"It was just so *weird*," I said. "Am I losing my mind?"

"Was it the kind of thing she used to say?"

"Yeah."

"I dunno," he said. "Maybe there is an afterlife. Maybe you have special ears, sensitive ears, acute hearing. Maybe she was so upset by seeing her husband there, crying his heart out, that she spoke to you. Anyway, I'm sure she's gone to a happy place."

"It's so frustrating," I replied. "That we can't know what happens when we die. That we're not allowed to know. It's infuriating. Why can't we just be reassured by somebody? Yes, there is an afterlife. Or no, there's nothing, this is it, make the bloody most of it."

"One of life's great mysteries. We're born and we die, we know not why, as Bob Dylan would say."

I was quiet.

"Well," I said. "In her own words, she had a good life. She was *so* brave. If I knew I was dying I'd be an absolute mess, clinging on to somebody's hand, going *no, I don't wanna go.*"

"I guess you just accept it when your time rolls around. What else can one do?"

I hung up the phone. Sat by myself in the living room. It was so strange. Why couldn't she have told me something interesting, like, "It's terrific up here in heaven. Like a giant circus. All the candy floss you can eat"? Or, "It's great here on this planet. Strange flora and fauna, three-headed beasts, plants with teeth and eyes, animals with six tails."

Or, "I am just one stop along, at the next platform, the next stop down the line, peacefully waiting for you, staring at the clock on the station wall. Its hands have stopped."

But she had said nothing of the sort, nothing so exciting. Just *Aw gee.* And then silence.

Lady Bluebeard

Here he comes, my seventh honey. The others hang on hooks in one of my many spare rooms. The room is awash with blood. He looks so fine, with his Brad Pitt abs and his golden locks that hang to his shoulders. Neither he nor any of his five brothers wanted to marry me. He is the youngest of them all; it took money to persuade him, an offer of five thousand pounds. He was easily bought. He is a country boy, a farmer, destined to become a farmer himself, but for fate, in the form of me, intervening.

I am standing at the castle window, watching as he pulls up in the driveway in his silver Mercedes. He steps from the car, walks down the driveway, so innocent, knocks upon my front door. The butler lets him in. The cook has prepared a fine feast for our first dinner together; pheasant with boiled new potatoes and French beans. Crème brûlée for afterwards. I grin my wolfish grin. He looks so good I could eat him.

I descend the stairs and greet him in the hallway, which is hung with portraits of my dead ancestors.

"So glad you could make it," I say and show him to his room, our room, an ornately decorated boudoir with a circular bed featuring a control panel on the headset, the operation of which can cause the bed to sway gently from side to side or rise up or lower back down or revolve in a circular motion.

"Put your heavy suitcase down in the corner," I say. "I shall give you a tour of the castle and its gardens."

I show him through the castle's many rooms, avoiding, of course, *that* room, the locked one. The room he shall enter eventually, but not until he is a corpse himself. For now he is fresh blood, a living, breathing hunk of meat. He oohs and aahs over the castle's many architectural features, the large stained glass windows, one of which depicts a crucified Christ on the cross, the crown of thorns gouging into his forehead. He marvels at the gardens, the white garden, with its lilies and baby's breath, roses and orchids. So pure. And the red garden. Snow and blood. The sun is setting behind the hills, spilling its rosy glow across the evening sky. We make our way indoors; winter is coming on and there is a chill in the air, so I light the fire and we draw our chairs close in to it and I pour us a glass of port and we begin the process of becoming acquainted with one another. He is, after all, a stranger, picked from the village with the help of my butler. I have acquired, I am afraid, something of a sinister reputation among the locals; a distinct whiff of brimstone. My dark frizzy hair springs up from my head as if I have been freshly electrocuted, my eyes are so dark they may as well be black holes. And then there are my living arrangements, high on a hill that rises up behind the village, alone, a lone she-wolf, fond of prowling the night. Then there is my taste for murder, of course, and the rumours that circulate regarding this, though nothing has yet been proved. The police are too scared to come up here. The castle is, after all, surrounded by a moat which I have filled with snapping crocodiles and should any unwanted visitor threaten to come near, I can always raise the drawbridge. This one, my new husband, is either brave or stupid or both. Greedy, perhaps, for the money although, after all, five thousand pounds is not such a great sum, not to me anyway, although I suppose it is to him.

After the port, dinner is served. He tucks in with relish, forking in large mouthfuls, slurping back his wine. I am fattening him up, like the witch in Hansel and Gretel. I shall feel his little finger to determine when the time is right. I am most looking forward to the night, when we shall retire and make the beast with two backs. I shall dig my fingernails into his shoulders, wrap my legs around his back, howl like a tortured wolf as the full moon casts its glare through the window. I quietly eat my meal, careful not to drink too much wine, although the butler keeps my husband's glass fully topped up at all times, as instructed.

We were married last Saturday; a quiet ceremony. I myself have absolutely no friends and few living relatives, my parents having died in a car crash when I was two years old, leaving my now dead grandparents to raise me in this castle I now inhabit. I have various living cousins and uncles and aunts and so forth, but they all think of me as creepy and weird and although I sent out several wedding invitations, nobody replied or attended. By contrast, my husband had a plethora of friends and relatives who attended the ceremony, all full of good wishes and love, blessings for our marriage. Many of them cast me sideways glances, wary of my reputation, but happy all the same to bear witness to our union. There was a cake, three tiers high, with two dolls on top, a male and female. It was decorated with white icing and dark red cherries. We danced, my husband and I, turning in time to the music like ballerinas inside a music box when the lid is opened.

Dinner is finished. We retire to the dining room for a nightcap, a sherry. He has two. Mind yourself, love, or performance will be impaired. And then, to the boudoir, where he ravishes me five times as the bed rocks gently and then falls asleep exhausted as I trace patterns across his stomach. Such bliss I have never known.

The morning dawns. The butler brings us croissants and strawberries and champagne. We are still celebrating, after all, celebrating our new love, which surrounds us like a golden cloud, a sparkle of fairy dust or a protective spell nothing can penetrate. We live, we move, inside this bubble. The world cannot touch us. We are in fairyland, up high, up here on this hill, above the common horde of humanity, above the rabble. In the wardrobe hang a number of new shirts and trousers I have bought him. He came to me dressed as a farm boy. I shall transform him, make him over, in an image of my own choosing. When I am finished with him, he will not be ordinary, he shall be spectacular, a prince amongst men, a god. He is raw material, putty in my paws.

The two of us spend the morning roaming the hills, watching the hawks as they swoop and dive, creatures of prey, at home on the air currents.

"I rather fancy that I would like to be a hawk," I say.

"Lady Hawk," he murmurs, slipping his arm through mine. "My Lady Hawke. Milady."

I give a small curtsey, for I am a lady after all, despite my appetite for men's blood; I was raised to have the best of manners, the finest of clothing, the freshest foods. Raised like a princess in a tower; a tower that at times felt more like a prison. Yes, there is a stench of the penitential about me. I am something that deserves to be set free, yet who holds the key? This man, this boy, with his country air and his ungentrified ways? Will he be the one to unlock, just as he has already, defrocked me? Set me free to soar on the breeze, higher and higher, a kite whose string has been snipped? Perhaps, perhaps, we shall see.

And so the time passes, though differently up here than it does down at ground level, for the air is finer, more rarefied. My castle is its own time zone. If so desired, I can stop the grandfather clock that sits in the hallway, freeze time, so that we spin up here in eternity, immortals. We make love frequently, we stuff our bellies, we wander up hills and down dales. My beloved seems happy here, with me, and why should he not be? Have I not, after all, rescued him from a life of poverty and despair? Who else would he have married? Some little farm girl with her hair in plaits and her smocked frock, some Heidi or Sophie or Hannah who liked to dosey-doe at the fair of a Saturday? No, he is better off with me. His days are numbered. So are mine.

Today his relatives visit. They are in awe of my castle, my power, my wealth, but I, I do not lord it over them. They come to the door, I welcome them in, dish them up freshly baked treats, cookies and scones with fresh dollops of cream and jam and tea, of course, Earl Grey. An English tea. I chat congenially, hiding my sharpened fangs; I am expert in small talk. I can see that I am beginning to allay some of their fears, but then the little girl, the nosey one, Elisabeth, I believe she is called, runs away mid-English tea and goes snooping around the castle and discovers the locked room. She returns downstairs, saying, "What's in that locked room, what's in there? Can I have the key, please?"

Fortunately I have my wits about me.

"That's where I keep my sword collection," I say. "Most of the blades are made from the finest Sheffield steel. And then we have my pièce de résistance, a Hattori Hanso sword that glistens like a diamond. And nosey little girls will come to no good."

I mime a sword slashing through the air, Zorro-style. She cowers and hides behind her mother.

"I believe it's time for us to leave," says her father and they swiftly make their exit. There will be talk now, speculation about what *really* lies behind that locked door. They will whisper amongst themselves like the wind rustling in dry leaves. They will not leave it alone, they will come for me, they will bash down the door and discover the awful truth and that will be the end of me, my demise. I must act quickly or I will be doomed.

They will sneak in at night, catching me off-guard, before I have time to raise the drawbridge in order to keep them out.

His time draws near. I can feel it in my waters, the time for him to join the others, the dead ones with their staring glassy eyes and their cold fingers like thin sausages and their lank greasy hair, matted with blood.

But Oh, mercy grips me! I cannot bring myself to thrust the dagger into his chest, for he is mine and too fine to be murdered like the rest, to join that bloody horde who sojourn in that locked room. He will not join the dead tonight.

This one I shall keep forever or at least until they make their way back here, full of bloodthirsty vengeance, hoping to make me pay for my many crimes. Until that day, may God keep me safe from harm, up here, in this highest and loneliest of towers. Hear my voice as I sing my song, echoing out across the valley, a love song, a lonesome song, the wail of a banshee on a moonless night.

Ladies and Gentlemen

The day after my novel *Richard Returns* was short-listed for the Orange Prize, Aunty Ingrid came around to help me with the garden.

"Get out from behind that bloody computer," she said. "Get out and get some fresh air. You've got a garden full of weeds, you've got roses that need dead-heading and an out of control rhododendron that needs a good prune. Here take these."

She shoved a pair of clippers into my hand.

"Get snipping."

Dutifully, not daring to disobey, I began deadheading the Miss Flippins rosebush. Snip, snip, snip. Ingrid was going at the rhododendron like a woman on a mission from God. Great chunks of foliage flew out and onto the grass.

"Novels," she scoffed. "Too many novels, that's your problem. Always with your head in a book. You need more hobbies. Before I had my bees people never wanted to talk to me when I went out. Who wants to hear about a sixty-year-old who sews for a living? Now I've got the bees, I've got a real conversation starter. Everybody's interested in bees."

"I'm going to take up kayaking. Fresh air, ocean waves."

"Oh, there's no point doing that, that's like the cycling you do. Just round and round in circles."

"Maybe I should get some bees, then."

"They're a lot of work, love. I'm thinking about something like knitting. Why don't you take up knitting? Knit yourself a scarf or some bootees for your new niece. Or go down to Bunnings Hardware Store and see what home-decorating courses they're running."

I wonder to myself who wants to hear about knitting or home-decorating.

"If your whole life is reading and writing books you won't have anything to talk about."

Curious logic. I never talk to people about my own work, but I am always keen to discuss theirs. It seems to me that literature provides plenty of opportunities for general discussion. Don't people get Bachelor's and Master's degrees in Literature? Are not doctoral studies based on the stuff? Whoever heard of a degree in bees? But I don't say anything. Ingrid means well.

"A heart of gold," my father says, followed by, "She can be a bit overbearing sometimes."

In the space of a single day we prune everything in the garden that needs pruning, including chopping back two large trees that overhang the back steps. We sweep all the paths and also under and around the steps, we plant cactuses in tidy displays, mow the lawns and weed the veggie garden and plant lettuces and coriander. We go to Bunnings for a new clothes rack and an outdoor table for the patio, throw out my old duvet because the feathers are falling out of it, pull out my bed and discover three unreturned library books, chop all the dead fronds off the pungas, plant two new ferns, go to the Recycling Centre at the tip and purchase a roasting dish, a heart-shaped vase, three wine glasses, a new shelf for the fridge, a fruit bowl and six plates for only ten dollars. Everything is done at six times the speed of a normal person. When we drive, I sit in the passenger seat, giving directions. *Go right.* She turns left. *No, right, Ingrid, right!* We lose the car keys and then spend twenty minutes looking for them and calling the car-hire shop to see if they can drive out and give us a new set (never getting through, always getting the answer-phone). We find the keys dangling from the keyhole in the boot where Ingrid had left them. By the time I get to my parents' place, the only thing I can think to do is pour myself a stiff gin and sit on the sofa recovering. We go out for dinner to an Indian restaurant. I am in a state of shock and sit, unable to speak, staring into space. My mind won't go. Lights off, nobody home.

"Oh dear," says Ingrid, "I think I've broken Lucy."

Dad tries to speak to me about something.

"It's just a bit much," I say.

Then I say nothing for half an hour.

"Oh, she's snapped," says Ingrid. "Too many novels will rot the brain. It's not good for her, all that reading."

It's as if I am Charlotte Perkins Gilman and the year is 1888 not 2008. When I get home I check the wallpaper to see if any ladies are crawling around behind its pattern. There is nobody there.

Most members of my family are like this. Hard-working, honest, driven, well-meaning. Good morals. There's not much space in such a network for somebody who lives half her life with her head in the clouds, as my father says. What kind of person writes books for a living? Or worse, writes books and *fails* to make a living at it. There are no artists in my family. There are teachers and health care workers and electrical engineers and chemists and bankers and IT workers, but no "dreamers", as my aunty calls me – no painters, or poets, or actors. I am a black sheep, a throwback. I may as well be an orphan. When I told my father that I published thirteen pieces of work in 2008, he said sarcastically, *That's good*, followed by, *Your fridge needs a damned good clean-out. Throw out that mouldy cheese.* I am trying to become more practical. I eat three meals a day. I manage my finances. When I published my first book, I was greeted with, *Yes, but one book's not a lifetime is it?* And, *So how are you going to pay the rent?* And, *Today's news, tomorrow's fish and chips,* along with a hearty dose of public humiliation and social ostracism. Easy to stand your ground when it's one against one. Harder when it feels like three million against one. Perhaps I was complicit in my own demise, but only through being too *nice*. A *nice* girl. Odd. Asking for it.

Being Queen Bee means being stung to death by all the other bees, as Margaret Atwood would say.

But I wasn't being a Queen Bee, at least, not intentionally. I was a worker, an insomniac. I hated having nothing to do. Writing filled the time, filled the space. They punish young ladies in the Antipodes when they think they're getting too uppity. Perhaps they thought I was trying to show off, but that wasn't true either. I was merely trying to claw my way up from the seventh circle of hell. *A country where the people frown with disapproving Presbyterian mouths*, says Billy Connelly. They certainly frowned on me.

In my youth, part of the problem was that I was too naïve, too trusting. *You're going to make a film of my book? Neat. A dream come true. How much money? Thirty thousand bucks. Great.* Off I go, trotting around to somebody's house for lunch, Red Riding Hood marching into the mouth of the wolf. They could've been anyone. They could've raped me. It was all bullshit. They just wanted to spend an hour or two harassing me for their own entertainment, shoving two fingers into their mouths to imply that I had bulimia. What a hoot. Then there was the charming gent at Radio New Zealand who rose to his feet, pointed to the door and told me to 'fuck off out of his studio.' My former friends bullied me to within an inch of my life, found out I was having some kind of mental breakdown and did a comedy skit, mocking me, on National TV. What a gas. People would come up to me and harass me in the street. Somebody spat at my feet. Oh dear. Never mind. Welcome to your new role as humanity's whipping post. Starlings pecked at my father's garden. He shot one and strung it up by its foot as a deterrent to the other starlings. *Don't come round these parts looking for bugs.*

It didn't stop me though. I went quiet for a while, then fruit-picked my way to Britain, wrote *Richard Returns* whilst working as a secretary. I was ambitious, I had plans. I wanted to sell a novel, make my name and then release a perfume onto the market. The perfume would be called Vitriol, tagline, "A Scent For the Bitter", and would smell like lemons with overtones of vinegar. A sure hit – it would knock J-Lo's "Glow" and Sarah Jessica Parker's "Lovely" off the shelves. Who wanted to glow and be lovely anyway? Bugger that.

There were rejection slips galore.

We can't accept your book, but you sound like Nicola Barker.

This *sounds like* business always made me think of charades. An editor in a publishing house somewhere in London, tugging his earlobe, tapping two fingers to his wrist to indicate two syllables and then pointing to a marker pen. Sounds like...pen. No, *marker.* Sounds like marker. Harker. Farker. Karker. No, I got it, I got it, *Barker*, Nicola *Barker!* This was better than Sylvia Plath, whom New Zealanders said I sounded like. I had no intention of ending up with my head in an oven. I should've been flattered by the comparisons, but I didn't want comparisons. I wanted people to publish my work, whilst I remained unseen, hidden away, anonymous, like Thomas Pynchon, in a safe place where I couldn't be mauled. I wanted to be like Emily Dickinson, only I wanted my work to be published in my lifetime, rather than after I was dead. I want, I want, I want. To be out of sight. I didn't want to be in the public eye. *You can't always get what you want.* I liked dark shadows; I shrivelled when dragged out into the light. Twenty more rejection slips. *Lucy Solomon is completely out of control.* Was I? Doubts circled my head like vultures. Would I ever succeed? And what price would I pay if I *did* sell a book in the UK? They could shove you into the public eye, let the British media, who, like the New Zealand media, can be very cruel, loose on you. You could become like Amy Winehouse, a public spectacle, with everyone gathered around, feasting on the schadenfreude. They could give you the Heather Mills treatment. How dare she marry a rich, famous, powerful British icon, take a whack of his money and hog a chunk of the limelight? We can't let her get away with that. Might give other women ideas. Who gives a toss about her charity work? Pack hatred. Burn the witch. They could try and break you for blood sport. They could eat you, in one way or another. Male artists got treated like John Lennon. Female artists got treated like Yoko Ono. At least, that had been true in New Zealand, for me; I hadn't made up my mind about Britain, but I knew that the whole thing had the potential to turn nasty. They could munch you up and hoick you out, feast on your flesh, spit out the bones of you, bones that would lie skeletal on the sidewalk. Somebody somewhere might make some money off your work, but it probably wouldn't be you. A story was accepted by a New Zealand magazine but never printed. I politely enquired as to what had happened to my tale and was told by the arts editor, "I don't know where the fuck your story is." I slept with a copy of Germaine Greer's *The Obstacle Course* under my pillow. A Gideon Bible sat in the top drawer of my bedside table, bookmarked at Job. Beneath the bible was a copy of Christa Wolf's *Cassandra*, which is about a doomed prophetess fated never to be listened to. There was also a bowl of limes on the table, I would split one open and suck at its insides while reading. After a three-year struggle, I sold the book to an independent publisher for a small sum. A year later, it had sold a hefty fifty-three copies.

There were further literary exploits. I took a play to the Edinburgh Festival Fringe. By the end of Scene Two there was a woman asleep in the front row, having a bit of a snooze.

Wake up, love, still eleven scenes to go. Don't you know it cost me six months of work and a thousand quid to bring you this lovely show?

"That was *ridiculous*," an audience member snapped, in the foyer afterwards.

No, I silently replied. *Just a waste of time and energy.*

But I also know what it's like to be on the other side, the side that screens. Auditioning actors for the play, one young hopeful, slapping his copy of my script with the back of his hand, said, "I've seen black comedy before, but I mean *this*, this is ridiculous."

That word again.

"I need to be *choosy* about what parts I take," he continued. "I mean *I*, I'm an *actor*. I was an extra in *Cold Mountain*, you know."

"So why have you come here today?" asked the director.

"Oh, I just came to pick up my CV."

The director and I stared at him in disbelief. When he left the room we rolled round laughing on the floor.

"Well fuck off back to Hollywood then, Mr Bigshot," said the director. "Go have lunch with Milos Foreman. Maybe he'll give you a role in his next film."

"Why did he even bother to send his CV in the first place?" I wondered. "He knew it was for the Fringe. We weren't pretending to be something we're not."

I felt for him as well, though; I could put myself in his shoes. He was like me. He had dreams that hadn't come to fruition. Thwarted hopes. He felt "reduced" by auditioning for a play for the Festival Fringe, when he wanted to be the next Brad Pitt.

Richard Returns is a black comedy based on my failed marriage – in particular, an episode in that marriage where Richard, having left me for a lap dancer, returned for a brief and tumultuous spell as we tried to repair our flawed union. It was like trying to patch up a fishing net so that the water no longer runs through it. The marriage hadn't been too good to start with. I was always busy working and Richard was always busy snorting coke. I wanted us to save our money and buy a small flat in London together; he wanted to shove all his money up his nose. I took life fairly seriously – after all, you only get one shot. I wanted to make something of myself. I wanted to publish a book in Britain – not easy, especially when struggling to support yourself financially at the same time. Writing-time was stolen, snatched from the claws of the corporate beast. Richard just wanted to have a good time, to scratch London's seedy underbelly. He had plenty of friends, as you do when you buy everyone at the bar a drink and shout them a line of coke and a couple of "e"s. I had two friends, one male, one female; I didn't know how to make any more. Humans scared me. I buried myself in work. Richard would go out on a Friday night and arrive home late on Sunday, cook a roast and eat it, then pass out, snoring on the sofa. We were living in Hackney. The woman across the hall had a violent drunk for a boyfriend. He would come round at three in the morning and incessantly ring all the wrong doorbells, waking up everybody in the whole apartment block. His girlfriend would let him in, they would row loudly for an hour, she would kick him out and he would ring the doorbell for another hour. The lesbians who lived upstairs would push open the window and yell, "Oi, you! Piss off to your own home," and he would yell back, "Fuck up you Northern bitches!" Peace on earth, goodwill to fellow man. One time Richard caught him trying to break into our flat. He trapped Richard in the hallway and threatened him with his fists, saying, "Think you're so much better than me, you with all your fancy education." Richard had the American equivalent of O-levels. Then the mad Christian moved in upstairs, fresh from some mental institution or other. He would blare Christian hymns at four am, just after the violent drunk had quit ringing the doorbell. Disturbing thudding noises came from the room above – he was either body-slamming or throwing the furniture around. The blissful land of sleep was a precious territory that I was excluded from.

There were amusing episodes, such as the time Richard put a boil-in-the-can pudding on the stove and then fell asleep. The pot boiled dry and the pudding exploded with a hell of a bang, taking out the Expelair and splattering sticky pudding all over the ceiling. The explosion woke me from my sleep. Then there was the night Richard put the scissors through his wrist. That was less amusing than the pudding, though fun in its own way. He

103

was drunk and high, we had a fight, he picked up the scissors and shoved them into his arm, nicking an artery. The blood came out in spurts. I had never seen blood spurt before and was terrified, sat outside until three in the morning, shaking, and then called my best friend in New Zealand to tell her what had happened.

"Shoot," she said. "You can't stay in that situation. You need to get out. Just leave."

I went to stay in a hotel then found another flat. It seemed like an ending, but it was just a new beginning.

There were good times as well, going out to see musicians I had always wanted to see; Bob Dylan, Nick Cave, Beck, Basement Jaxx. In London, everything was right there on your doorstep. Literature, Science, Music – you name it, it was there. I went to lectures at the Royal Society, sat in the room where Faraday first demonstrated electromagnetism. There were trips to most of the European capitals, to Prague and Barcelona and Paris, and holidays in New York and Chicago, in Sardinia and the Greek Islands. I was happiest on holiday, especially if the trip involved an ocean. Living in London, the sea was the thing I missed the most. There is a photograph of me in the Costa Esmeralda, walking across a concrete strip that divides a swimming-pool in half. If you squint your eyes and tilt your head to the side slightly, it looks as if I'm walking on water.

We went to beach parties on the banks of the Thames, but it wasn't the same as a deserted New Zealand beach, such as those found in the Abel Tasman National Park – the golden sands, the crystal clear water, the lush greenery. The lagoons. Sometimes I loved London, sometimes I hated it. I loved the feeling of being at the centre of everything, the excitement of it all. So many great minds had lived in this city before you had. There were more opportunities in London than in New Zealand; the chance for international recognition, exposure to more ideas, different ideas. New Zealand was a paddling-pond; this was the big kids' pool. I was keeping afloat, but only just.

I often worked in the Reading Room at the British Museum, taking my own tea bags and getting free water from the

104

Starbucks across the road, too skint or perhaps too stingy to pay for the two or three caffeinated drinks that I would need to keep me going. My year of picking fruit had taught me the value of money. Sometimes strange shadows flickered; I fancied they were the ghosts of writers who had been here before me – I saw their names on the wall beside the door; Karl and Eleanor Marx, Virginia Woolf, George Eliot, Amy Levy. Such prestigious company. You couldn't sit in the room where a Marx had sat. back in New Zealand. The good times were very good, but the bad times were very bad. In winter, I bought myself brightly coloured clothes in order to cheer myself up – an orange cardy from Top Shop, a hot pink jersey from Primark, a canary-yellow jacket. There were days when I couldn't function, my brain froze, wouldn't go, couldn't jump through the hoops anymore, the basic hoops such as eating and sleeping and showing up for work each day and being able to type up the letters they were asking you to type and relate to the woman sitting next to you, with whom you had nothing in common. A woman who had no ambitions to be anything other than a secretary. When I first started typing up dictation from tape, I put the headset on upside down, didn't realise that the plastic that joined the two ear pieces together was supposed to hang down in the middle of your chest. I thought the thing should be worn like headphones, with the wire sprouting out from the top like an antennae.

"You look like an alien with that thing on your head," said my boss.

I felt like an alien too. The more I tried to force my mind to leap, the more it refused to budge, a stubborn horse that digs in its heels and won't take a hurdle. There were days, sometimes weeks, when I could hardly even move my mouth, went into a sort of psychological shutdown. I sat in a pub in Soho with my male friend, mute, nursing a glass of red wine for three hours, while he talked and I tried – but failed – to respond in what I thought was the socially correct manner. Tried and failed to hold a conversation.

"Well, Lucy," he said as he departed, "Good to see you. It's been a riot as always."

I sniggered. I was still capable of that.

Seeking money and a more interesting job, I slogged my way into Computer Science via a Master's degree in the subject, undertaken in the evenings while working full time. Two years of hard intellectual labour. At four pm each day, a great wave of exhaustion would hit me, and I would take myself off to the paraplegic toilets for a ten minute lie down, using a cardigan for a pillow. Twice I passed out on the tube on the way to work. Nonetheless, it was a smart move. Good money. They actually *pay* you to develop software. As a writer, I was working for free. In the world of IT, I met some brilliant people. In lectures I sat next to Jeremy Penzer, a statistician and lecturer at the London School of Economics. Jeremy would spend the lecture doodling cows and dragons, barely even seeming to pay attention to what the lecturer was saying, and then get an A plus in the end of year exam. I worked as hard as I could and got a B minus. Everything I did, I did *tired*. It wasn't the same as having a fresh brain – everything was harder. Most of the other students already knew something about IT. Before I started the course, I could open a Word document, write a sentence and save it. Everything was new to me. The learning curve wasn't so much steep, as vertical. My thesis supervisor was Trevor Fenner (aptly nicknamed Clever Trevor) whose mind seemed to work on a million different levels at once. He spoke to me about scary things like Fourier Transform.

It's n + k to the power of two, he would say, just assuming that I would know what n and k were. I didn't have a clue. Trevor was a lovely man, but his brilliance intimidated me, so I switched to another supervisor who ditched me via email for using (so he claimed) foul language. He was Greek – he spelt it "fowl". Perhaps he had overheard me clucking in the corridor. I didn't remember using language that was impolite or in any way bird-like, but perhaps a word or two had slipped from my tongue unbeknownst to me, speech without the will to speak, like somebody who walks in their sleep. I got an interview with a Blue Chip company. My nerves were fraying – I had bad nerves; when I sat exams my hands shook uncontrollably.

"You need a smart suit," the others girls on the course (all three of them) said.

"A suit, really?"

I was an idiot – I hadn't even thought of that. My mind was too full of Java and XML and genetic algorithms to think about clothing, appearances.

"Where do I get a suit?"

"Go to Next. Cheap. You also need a cocktail dress."

A cocktail dress? I didn't even know what that was. If this was the kind of company where cocktail dresses were required on a regular basis, I knew the whole thing was going to be an unmitigated disaster. I bought a good pin-striped suit and two smart shirts, an actor getting into costume. I was doing my best to invent a new persona, a corporate persona, to become somebody else, somebody new. They let me in. A hefty Golden Hello. Free subscription to the *Financial Times*. A hundred and fifty quid, the difference between what I had been quoted for having my book edited, and what I had been forced to pay, seemed like nothing now. How had it seemed like so much before?

Once employed, I worked under Harvey Jutel, who joined the firm as a consultant and within three years was Chief Technical Officer of a big publisher. We were building a shopping channel for a client in the States. *You've all been hand-picked*, said our manager, trying to boost our egos so we would work even harder. Harvey was a genius. The RAF had sponsored him through university, he had a PhD in Networks, he'd had an offer from NASA that he'd turned down to take this job. I could work on a problem for three days and then, stuck, turn to Harvey for help. Harvey would glance at it and then fix it in five minutes. Another nice guy, who often worked hundred-hour weeks. How did he do it? He was a big man, not fat but solid, six foot five and broad – he had more energy reserves than I did. This was brains on another level, a level that I hadn't been exposed to in New Zealand. This was *drive and ambition* on another level. You wouldn't catch a New Zealander working a hundred hour week back home. I was eclipsed by these people – they could walk upside down inside handcuffs. I kept still within my shackles, occasionally twitching a toe. They were experienced hands. I was the new girl.

"Lucy's got some good ideas," Harvey would say, and encourage me to share my ideas with the rest of the team.

I was always quite reluctant. I didn't want to show off. I knew where showing off could get me, especially as one of three women in a team of forty men. I worked as hard as I could for two years, always staying late, sometimes past midnight, never having time for writing, just managing to get my groceries and throw a load of washing in the machine at the weekend before collapsing on the sofa in front of a DVD. My manager was forever dangling the carrot just in front of my nose, *that's it, that's it, you're one of our stars, a bit more hard work and you'll get accelerated promotion.*

On four separate occasions, by four separate men, I was called a bitch, a psycho, a tart and a smart arse, but I didn't mind. What did I care? One male colleague, again Greek, said, *In Greece the man beats the woman like an octopus*, and slapped his hand down upon the table with quite some force. Whatever. The shopping channel was completed, and I was shifted to work under somebody else. One day I snapped from the pressure and said something grumpy to a colleague that I probably shouldn't have said, and this was used as an excuse not to promote me, after I had worked myself silly for two years and achieved excellent ratings.

"Lucy's not mature enough," they said. "What if she does that in front of a client?"

But I had seen Harvey rant and rave and yell and let off steam on several occasions and *he* still shot up through the ranks like a skyrocket. Nobody said *what if he does that in front of a client?* Nobody called *him* a bitch, a psycho, a tart or a smart-arse or spoke of imaginary far-off countries where women beat men like squids.

So, who do you think said you shouldn't be promoted?, my boss taunted me.

Umm, I said. *Adam?*

And?

And Tim.

And?

And Blair.

Ha! he said. *Yup, all of 'em.*

As if to say, that'll fix her, that'll put her in her place. A boot on the neck. A fist in the face. *They just use your mind and you never get the credit...* Somebody was always trying to put me in my place and not just men, females too. Former friends turned enemies. But what *was* my place? I didn't feel that I had one, I didn't *belong* anywhere; I felt like the Ancient Mariner, doomed to walk the earth for thousands of years, some kind of half-rotten albatross slung about my neck. Bewildered brain flounders again. Was I passing through a series of harsh tests in order to prepare me for something – a type of army training? And what if I didn't pass the tests, make the grade, leap the hurdles? Then what would become of me? My mind swam with questions that I had no answer for.

I lost heart. All that effort just to be chopped down by corporate types instead of literary types. Anything that seemed good could flip upside down to reveal its fanged and snarling underbelly. Why bother doing anything? Lily Allen was on the radio. *Mustn't grumble...just the way the cookie crumbles.* I tried to learn the rules. A lady must never lose her temper. A lady must always be polite and charming. A lady must never be shrill or shrieking. Nobody likes a harpy. *He who loses his temper loses the war.* Or was there another rule society was trying to teach me? Ladies must never succeed. Ladies must never shine. It seemed like that. Surely times had changed? Feminist wars had been fought and won by certain front-liners who had gone before me, so that I could have an easier time of it now. So why did it still feel like such a battle? Maybe I was just getting paranoid. I was getting close to the core, to the worlds of wealth and power. Here there be monsters, dragons. If you rubbed them up the wrong way, they could crush you like an apple seed beneath the wheel of a truck. Things began to disintegrate. People started doing the wolf laugh at me *oh ho hooo*, they said, if I made a social mistake, or an IT mistake, or a literary mistake. *Oh ho hooo.* I remembered the words of my old poetry lecturer John Dolan as I had left his final lecture of the year. *It's a rough world out there, kiddo.* At the time, I had thought, *It's not the external world I'm worried about. It's the internal world. Or worlds, plural.* Now I was finding out what he meant. The words of a lecturer at the Otago English Department also rang in my mind. *Look at what they did to Janet Frame.* The mental institutions, the ECT. The lobotomy that was narrowly avoided when one of the doctors noticed that her book of short stories had won a literary prize.

Other people were pushing me. I was pushing myself. It was a lot to expect of one person; that they could comprehend enough about IT and how the corporate world works, to scale the ranks whilst simultaneously trying to have some kind of literary breakthrough in Britain. It was *too* much to expect. I felt like somebody had sat me down at a chess board and told me to play against Viswanathan Anand, without even explaining any of the rules. I felt like an ant climbing Everest. Maybe I just lacked confidence. That had been beaten out of me as a young female in New Zealand. Emily Perkins seemed to have plenty of the stuff; but maybe she too had her moments of doubt and pain. Her last name suggested perkiness. My last name suggested wisdom. So why did I always feel like such a fool? Somebody somewhere was always trying to take me for a ride. Perkins always seemed to get away with the publication of her books without being berated. What had I done differently to attract so much flak? Perkins either had a magic key or knew how to pick locks. I bashed myself senseless against closed doors.

The British writers I met were all very nice to me, far nicer than New Zealanders had been. Most New Zealanders wanted to cut me down to size. The British kept trying to pull me up. They egged me on; they handled me with kid gloves. But they were all internationally famous and probably rich. They had houses in Kensington and husbands and wives and kids and pets and books in bookshops. These people seemed to have everything. I had almost nothing. They gave workshops and attended festivals. I hated leaving the house.

Sometimes they gave feedback on my work. *This line is a bit too much. This line isn't quite enough.* Like trying to teach the wayward kid in the ballet school to dance. *Pliè, pliè, turn, that's it now, <u>smile</u>! Don't forget to smile. Quit trying to do the can-can. We don't want no can-cans here.* But I *like* the can-can. Bleak exhaustion. I can-canned alone, in my room, after dark, cackling to myself, practising, but they wouldn't let me can-can onstage. My can-can was a can't-can't. *No* was a word I learnt early, but I didn't know how to say it. I appreciated the efforts of the Brits to egg me on, but it was like the CEO of some major corporation saying to somebody in the lowest echelons, *Come on, work harder, try harder, you too can be CEO, if you just put in a few more seventy-hour weeks.* I was doing my best, but not everyone can be CEO. Not everyone can be Brad Pitt. Not everyone can be Salman Rushdie or Fay Weldon. Underlings will also survive.

Now things are different, easier, cushier. Now, through my own hard labour, I own my own house, always a dream of mine. Not just a room of ones own, but a house of ones own. Lovingly, I stroke the walls. Now I have, through bad fortune turned good, an income that means I don't have to work. I am grateful, in a safe place. I know how lucky I am. But my psyche can't forget what it was to be locked out, struggling, a vampire, one of the Lost Boys, shoving my fanged face to the window, bashing at the pane with a leathery wing. Lacking the force to shatter the glass. Just a feeble tap. Tap, tap, tap. A Cessna, circling the airport, waiting to land. Cathy at the window howling at Heathcliff, *Let me in.* Bad dreams in the night. *So* cold. A person who has once been starving always remembers what it was like to be fed nothing, even though they may now be being fed something. A person who has been freezing, out in the snow and ice like the Matchstick Girl, may stay frozen inside forever, even after having been physically warmed. In older English dialects, "to starve" meant "to freeze." I know why.

Then there is Aunty Ingrid. Who are they, the Aunty Ingrids of this world and why do they want us to stop reading and writing? Is it because they don't read and write themselves? Do they fear what they don't understand? Is it out of envy? Is it because cutting people down at the knees is so ingrained in the New Zealand psyche that they chop away without even realising that they're doing it? What does it achieve, stomping on somebody else's ambition? The world is full of these women who would like me to shut my trap. Get a day job. Get some self-respect. Get out in the world. Live life. Quit hiding away. But she's such a good aunt in many ways, and the relative outside my immediate family that I am closest to. She sews a lot of my clothes – she can whip up anything. I can point to a dress in a

111

magazine and the next day it will appear in my wardrobe, like a seamstress fairy godmother has been at work. She sends me gifts; vintage brooches, dried flowers, Christmas decorations. The garden looks terrific since she attacked it with full force. And my father is such a good father, helping me fix broken cupboard doors and buy new appliances, reading my stories and helping me win insurance claims and just generally checking that everything is under control. He takes regular neuroses checks, looking for the tell-tale signs of mental frailty, as if I am a lemon tree infected with blight. Will I ever bear fruit? *Lemon tree fairly pretty and the lemon flower is sweet.* The neuroses checks include looking for outbreaks of eczema, gnawed fingernails, sleeplessness, loss of appetite and spacing out into what we call "the other place". Personally, I like the other place. I find some of my best ideas there, but I wouldn't like to live there permanently. Family-wise, I have won a type of lottery.

Today, Ingrid is here, for another visit. She arranges *Home and Garden* magazines on the hearth and puts fresh flowers in vases, telling me that this will make my house look more *homey*. This morning I got the call.

"*Richard Returns* has won the Orange Prize," I tell Ingrid.

"Orange Prize? What's that? Best citrus?"

"No," I say patiently. "It's an important prize in Britain."

"Oh, Britain. Well, what do they know? It's not New Zealand, is it? I've brought you a book on macramé."

"That's great," I say. "Thanks very much."

A green macramé owl perches on the cover looking solemn. Ingrid looks at her watch.

"It's time for me to go," she says.

"Alright. See you later."

"And no more novels," she calls as she backs out the driveway, nearly running over my recycling bin on her way out.

Braille

He went blind suddenly, overnight. He woke up sightless. His hearing seemed much more acute; he could hear the birds twittering outside the window, the distant drone of a lawn-mower, the hum of traffic on a nearby motorway. There was no Mrs Thomlinson to whom he could turn – she'd been dead for over a year now and he'd got used to the empty space in the bed next to him, the vacant chair at the kitchen table, the conversations he conducted with the air, with nothingness. Her death had excavated a hole in the centre of his chest, an abyss that he tightrope-walked across. He was a pensioner; his days followed a strict routine – he rose, ate a bowl of cornflakes, drank three cups of Earl Grey tea and got out in his garden for the duration of the morning. After a light lunch (typically a bun and a can of sardines or salmon, perhaps a kipper or two), he would walk to the local library and sit reading the papers for three hours before taking a short walk along the river, then heading home and reading a book until dinnertime. He'd once been proud of the fact that he didn't take out large-print books; his sight had been excellent, nearly 20/20, the vision of a much younger man. Now there was just this endless sea of black, like the outer darkness into which rebel angels were supposedly cast, the darkness with the weeping and wailing and the gnashing of the teeth. Mr Thomlinson neither wept nor wailed nor gnashed his teeth. He was a practical man. For every problem there was a solution. Life's hurdles were there to be leapt. Answers hovered, waiting to be found.

He swung his feet out over the edge of the bed and, clad in his red and black striped pyjamas, felt his way to the telephone and dialled the number of the local hospital. He spoke like a child.

"Hello, my name is Alan Thomlinson. I live at 7 Eckers Place and I appear to have gone blind."

"Is there somebody who can drive you to the hospital?"

Who could he ask? The neighbours, with whom he hardly spoke (he didn't even know their names) would already have left for work; he'd never seen anybody home during the day. His only child, his daughter, was in Melbourne. All his friends had died. He hadn't made new friends; he didn't belong to any groups or clubs. No, there was nobody to drive him. The receptionist said that she would send an ambulance.

He was collected. There was an MRI scan, a diagnosis.

"You've had a stroke," said the doctor. "Both occipital lobes, which reside at the posterior of the brain have been affected. Your vision will not return."

So, one of his vital five senses had deserted him. Well, he would just have to develop a sixth sense, or some sort of extra ability. Nothing is taken away without something being given. Something would compensate.

They arranged for him to have a seeing-eye dog, a white cane and a woman to come twice a week to help him with the housework and grocery shopping and preparation of meals. The dog was a golden Labrador called Candice. He hadn't realised how lonely he'd been until he had a canine companion. He ran his hands through her glossy coat, stroked her ears. The woman was called Janice. Candice and Janice. Janice told him all about herself, as she dusted his shelves and vacuumed his floors and held onto his arm as they walked down the grocery aisles. She was a recent divorcee. Before they'd married, her husband had seemed like a nice enough chap, a catch, even. He'd courted her the old-fashioned way, with theatre tickets to the latest shows and dinners in fancy restaurants and boxes of expensive chocolates with liqueur centres. After they'd tied the knot he bared his dark side, his anger; an explosive temper. He revealed himself to be a dormant volcano of a man – he could blow at any time. He became increasingly difficult; nothing she did pleased or soothed him – if a light bulb blew it was her fault, if the thermostat on the fridge gave out she was to blame, if there were specks of dust left on a surface after she'd done the housework he would collect the specks on his finger and hold them in front of her face accusingly. He was verbally and psychologically, but not physically, abusive. He would agree to meet her at various places and then not bother to show up, later claiming that he had forgotten or been too busy. He criticised her clothes, her choice of friends, her lipstick. She'd taken five years of it and then she'd left him. She'd only stayed that long because she'd hoped he would change. Like many sociopaths, he could be charming and in between the bouts of bad temper and abuse were weeks when he was like a man heaven-sent; kind, generous, witty, loving. Then a switch would flick, and he'd be in a different mode of operating, a dark state. A devil took up residence behind his eyes. She neither knew nor cared what had caused him to become that way. One night she gathered up all her belongings in their Toyota, drove to her sister's and never looked back.

"Men," she would say. "Better off without 'em."

The cane felt ordinary. He ran his hands along its smooth surface, had a small practice walk, tapping his way to the letter box and back. Mr Thomlinson had been blessed with an extraordinary memory. In his mind's eye he saw his town's streets spread out as clearly as if a map had been laid down in front of him. Two weeks after his sight had left him he set out without Candice, *tap, tap, tap* all the way to the corner store to buy a pint of milk and *tap, tap, tap* back. It felt good, free, independent. Another man might have let the sightlessness knock him for a six – not Mr Thomlinson. Mr Thomlinson was strong, he wouldn't let this cripple him, he would bounce back, better than ever.

With the arrival of Janice there had been added to Mr Thomlinson's life an extra dimension. Just the other day she had flicked his hand with her feather duster as she had been doing the mantelpiece and he'd felt a small spark, like electricity, travel across the surface of his skin. On another occasion, she held on a little too long to a mug of tea as she'd been passing it to him and their hands had brushed together. Finally, when he'd been out on his garden path tending to the dahlias that grew there, she'd waltzed past and her hips had lightly touched his buttocks that had been poking up in the air as he bent over his flowers.

On the days when Janice didn't visit he stroked Candice's fur and counted the hours until Janice's arrival. He felt like a lovesick teenager. He told himself to snap out of it, he couldn't be galloping through this gamut of emotions at his age. He was pushing seventy. Would he even be able to *perform*? Needing to push Janice from his mind, he set off down the road towards the river; *tap, tap, tap.* Halfway along the street he stumbled and tripped over an old shoe that some damned fool had left lying there and the tip of his cane smacked down forcefully upon the pavement. The overwhelming perfume of roses filled the air, an otherworldly, heavenly scent.

"Hey," he heard somebody yell. "Hey that old guy just made roses appear in the middle of the pavement!"

Had he? Could he really have done that? He groped the air in front of him, felt his hands touch petals, thorns, leaves. He turned around and rapped the tip of the cane down hard. He felt ahead. More blooms sprouted. He stepped sideways, out and around the roses. Continued on his way.

It was a Tuesday and he was out in his garden when she brushed against him next. This time it was unmistakeably intentional, frottage, her chest against his chest, her pelvis against his groin as she edged past him along the garden path. If his eyes could see they would have seen hers looking into his. Not knowing how to react, he froze. Janice smiled knowingly to herself and edged away, along the path to where a patch of Remember Me roses bloomed a deep copper orange. She took a pair of secateurs from her pocket and began snipping away the deadheads. They fell to the ground and lay on the path reminding Janice of the ex-husband she'd chopped out of her life. A deadhead, that's what he'd been. A worthless dried up old thing. She looked back at Mr Thomlinson. Here he was, this sweet sprightly, elderly man, a man who wouldn't harm a fly.

"Men, better off without 'em," that's what she used to say, but she'd never really believed it.

The words had been a crust, a carapace around her heart, protective words designed to keep her from harm. What she really thought was that there was somebody out there for everyone, that nobody should have to make the brutal journey from cradle to grave alone, that everybody needed a hand holder, somebody by their side to ease the pain of daily existence, somebody to share experiences and emotions with, somebody to lie down next to at night and wake up beside in the morning.

Janice enrolled Mr Thomlinson (Alan, she had to start thinking of him as Alan) in Braille classes. She attended with him, closing her eyes, hands moving across the raised letters, the single dot of the 'a', the vertical two dots of the 'b', the horizontal two dots of the 'c'. A, B, C. Every now and then, she would reach out her hand and rest her fingers upon his; two hands like two spiders crawling across the page.

Alan had yet to reciprocate Janice's advances. He didn't flinch, he didn't pull away, but neither did he respond in kind. Typically, he simply sat there, like a man cast in stone, immobile, a monolith. Certainly, he was grateful for Janice's company. But then, he was grateful for the dog's company, too. A love affair didn't necessarily follow on from companionship. His wife wasn't that long dead – a year passes at the speed of light when one is in one's later decades. Her memory was still fresh in his mind, images of the two of them at the beach, building sandcastles, or together in the garden or simply sitting at home watching television. It was too soon to get involved with somebody else.

Then there was this business with the cane. The blooming had not been an isolated incident. Whenever he rapped the tip of his cane down upon the concrete something flowered. It wasn't just roses that bloomed; there were chrysanthemums, crocuses, tulips, irises, hyacinths, birds of paradise. A veritable jungle blossomed all along Eckers Place. Janice remarked on it on those mornings when she turned up at his door. She didn't know that it was him that was causing the concrete to burst into flower. Her joke was that elves were at work, digging little holes in the pavement late at night or first thing in the morning and pushing in plants.

Vast improvement, Mr Thomlinson, she would say. *Elves hard at work. Yours must be the prettiest street in the entire neighbourhood.*

The irony of it, the grand irony of it, was that Mr Thomlinson couldn't see any of his handiwork. Oh, but he could feel it though; hands outstretched, he touched gorgeous silken blossoms, delicate shooting leaves, spiky thorns. Each morning he tap-tapped down the street and then tap-tapped back, stopping along the way to reach out and feel the foliage, the fauna that he had created – this something that he had conjured from nothingness. He did not search for an explanation – he simply accepted the cane's powers. The cane was magical; somebody must have cast a spell on it.

They were sitting in the lounge, she watching and he listening to *Wheel of Fortune* when she put her hand upon his thigh. A warm glow spread along his leg in both directions, he felt as if his flesh was melting, turning from solid into liquid, becoming molten. He didn't respond, he simply sat there, wondering what would happen next. Nothing happened. Janice left her hand where it was for the duration of the programme. Mr Thomlinson remained frozen, and at the end of the episode he rose to his feet, offered her a cup of tea and then felt his way through to the kitchen where he prepared them both a cup of Earl Grey tea.

The next morning when she came to the door he could hear the note of upset in her voice.

"Oh Alan," she said (it was the first time she had called him by his first name). "Oh Alan, everything's *withered*. Something must have happened; somebody must have been out there spreading poison."

He walked down the quiet street, felt crispy leaves, wilted stems, atrophy. She had followed him, trotting along just behind – could he hear her quietly weeping? He stopped, turned around, reached out tentatively, put his trembling arm around her shoulders and considered his future possibilities.

Memory

I am underneath a bridge. The river runs by at my feet; my face is turned towards the sky. My mind is a perfect blank – I cannot remember my own name. I feel my vitals to check my gender; I am a man. Everything aches; my skin, my bones, the roots of my hair. Slowly, painfully, I rise to my feet and head down to the river to wash my face. The water is icy cold and stings. Blood comes away on my hands; there are grazes. Cars zoom by overhead. I walk up the bank of the river to the road and stick out my thumb. I don't know who I am, nor do I know where I am going. After five minutes, a white Honda pulls over with a blonde woman wearing dark sunglasses behind the wheel.

"Where are you headed?"

I shrug.

"The next town," I say.

"Jump in," she says, and I do.

We say nothing for the duration of the drive. I search for my wallet to pay her some petrol money but my pockets are empty.

I am in a small town. A doctor is what I need, a hospital. I find the information centre and ask my way to the nearest hospital. It is within easy walking distance, so I make my way there by foot.

"I am having difficulty," I say to the woman behind reception, "remembering anything. It's all gone, wiped."

"Name?"

"I don't know."

"Occupation?"

"I don't know."

"Do you have any documents on you? A passport, a driver's licence, papers?"

I search my pockets again but there is nothing there. I shrug and hold out my empty hands.

"Well," she says. "If you take a seat I can get a doctor to come and speak with you. Do you have a place to stay for the night?"

"No. I don't have anything."

"I see. Quite a conundrum. Is there a friend or relative you could ring to help you out?"

"I don't remember any names. Is there some sort of emergency fund?"

"You can speak to the doctor about that. Please, take a seat. Somebody will be with you shortly."

'Shortly' turns out to be about two hours. When the doctor finally does arrive he looks like a boy, fresh out of medical school.

"Follow me," he says, and leads me down a white, sterile corridor to a small curtained room.

"Please," he says, gesturing, "Take a seat."

I sit.

"Can you tell me your name?"

"I can't tell you anything," I say. "I woke up under a bridge and hitch-hiked here. Where am I, by the way?"

"You are in Ipton," he says. "There is a possibility of concussion. We'll have to check you out."

A nurse appears. She takes blood and urine samples. They test balance, vision and orientation.

"We'll book you in for a CT scan," says the doctor. "I'd like to keep you in overnight."

"Good; because I haven't got anywhere else to stay. Nor have I got any money."

"Well, perhaps we can help you arrange a visit to social services when we discharge you. They might be able to provide you with some sort of emergency fund."

I nod.

"That'd be good."

"You are in safe hands," reassures the doctor, but his words do not remove the panicking bird in my head that bashes its wings against my cranium.

"I'll bring you some magazines," says the nurse. "Would you like anything to eat and drink?"

"A sandwich?"

Suddenly, I am ravenous.

"Sandwiches," I say. "Two please, if possible. And a cup of chamomile tea?"

"We only have gumboot, I'm afraid."

"Gumboot, it is. Milk and two sugars."

"We'll notify the police and see if they can match you up with any missing persons records."

"Okay. That sounds good."

"I'll see you tomorrow morning," says the doctor and exits.

The nurse brings me two sandwiches, one beef, one egg, a cup of tea and a stack of magazines; *Heat, Now, Woman's Day*. I can read about Tom and Katie, Gwyneth and Chris, Brad and Angelina and Poor Old Jen. Who are these people? I devour the sandwiches, swallow the tea and flick despondently through the magazines. Curious and bored, I pull back the curtain that separates this cubicle from the next and see a thin young man, sitting upright in bed, staring into space and muttering to himself. Quickly, I close the curtain. Heavy thuds come from the centre of the ward, as if somebody is jumping up and down.

"Can't stop it," a man rants. "Can't stop *it*."

I peer out and see a hirsute man slapping his face with his right hand and (I was correct) jumping on the spot. Two nurses swiftly appear, take one arm each and bundle him back to wherever he is housed. It strikes me; I am in the psych ward. They think I'm a lunatic, they think there's something wrong with me and perhaps there is. Most people, after all, have no trouble in recalling their name, their date of birth, their occupation. Part of my brain, my memory, has been wiped out. I am a cripple now, crippled by my own mind, a prisoner.

I lie on the bed and pull the pillow over my face. What kind of future has a man whose memory has been wiped? Will my memory function correctly from here on in, or will I wake up each morning, unable to recall the events of the day before, as if it has snowed in my mind overnight? I ring for the nurse, ask for a pen and paper, so I can start a diary, a record of my new life. Then I can check that I am remembering events from day to day. As long as I remember about the diary that is. I could be anybody; a serial killer, an electrician, an out-of-work actor. I could be nobody at all. There is no clock in my cubicle but there is a clock on the far wall. Five-fifteen pm. I write down everything that has happened to me today, so that I can check it tomorrow and make sure that I recall the events correctly (and in the correct order). At six, the nurse brings dinner. The food sits unappetisingly on its plastic tray, but I am still starving, so I eat it all, washing it down with the orange juice provided.

"Can I please have a sleeping-pill?" I ask.

I need oblivion. She brings me what I ask for and I black out into a deep and dreamless sleep.

In the night, the man in the bed next door to me starts screaming. He screams and he screams until the nurse comes running and gives him a shot of something and then he konks out. I make a mental note to self never to start screaming. If I start I might not stop.

The doctor arrives in the morning after I have had breakfast with one Citalopram, which is supposed to help me with any depression I may experience as a result of my 'condition'.

"Let's get you in for this cat scan," he says. "Just in case."

Battling claustrophobia, I lie down on the bench provided and they slide me inside the machine. I am scanned.

"We'll have the results of those for you later today," says the doctor. "If it's all clear we can let you go."

The panic bird beats its wings.

"But where will I go?"

"We have an outpatient facility. We can arrange to have nurses visit you twice a day. We think you should be on some sort of medication to help you cope with what's happened. Amnesia on this scale can be very...challenging."

"And accommodation?"

"Social services will be able to help you."

"But what work can I do? I have to work."

"Social services should be able to help you find something appropriate. Of course, we don't know your skill level in any given discipline."

"But I could have been a doctor, a lawyer, an IT consultant, anything and now I'm just going to have to start from...from scratch."

The doctor gives a sigh.

"In these first weeks, what you need to worry about is your basic survival. Once you are back on your feet you can retrain, or you may begin to remember who you were before. Your name, your area of expertise."

"Do I have to go alone? What if I can't find my way back?"

"We'll arrange taxis for you there and back. I'm afraid our nurses are too busy to be able to come with you."

Too busy. I'll go it alone then, go and plead my case to some bureaucrat with the power to help or hinder me. I have a good case. I am in dire straights. No money, no memory, no name, no friends, no relatives. If Social Services are not there to help people like me, who are they there to help?

"When would you like your taxi?"

"In about half an hour? Then I have time to collect my thoughts before I go."

"Fine. One of the nurses will be back to check up on you tonight and I will be in to bring you your results. We'll give you a letter to take to Social Security."

"Can you bring me any information on amnesia?"

"I'll see what we can do."

I check my diary. I can remember the events as they have been noted down there. I make a few notes, points that I wish to discuss with Social Security. I want to live alone; I don't feel I can face other people on a daily basis. I want a job in an office, even if it's just admin work, typing and filing and answering the phone, making appointments. I want to be able to support myself; I don't want to rely on welfare though I am well aware that in the immediate term I have no choice. A nurse escorts me to the front of the building, where my taxi is waiting.

At Social Security I am given a ticket and told to take a seat. This is what institutions are; waiting in line, waiting your turn. The red electronic numbers flick up and up until finally my number appears and I make my way to booth three, where a small Indian lady sits behind a pane of glass.

"Hello," she says. "How can I help you?"

"My situation is very unusual," I say and I hand her the letter from the hospital.

She reads it, nodding.

"I see. Well, I think you would fit our emergency criteria. We need a new name for you though. I'm not sure how this works, but I think you should re-register yourself with Births, Deaths and Marriages, so that you're in the system. Everybody has to be in the system."

Ah yes, the system.

"I would like to be Clarence," I say boldly. "Clarence Whitehall."

"Alright, then please fill out this form in that name and I'll do my best to get you a number and to process your application. You'll be entitled to one hundred and fifty dollars a week plus an accommodation supplement of forty dollars. But first you'll have to get a bank account that we can pay the money into."

"And work? Can you help me find a job?"

"We have a list of available positions on our database. You can search at one of the terminals over there."

"What about somewhere to live?"

"Sorry but we don't usually help people to find accommodation unless they are disabled and unable to do so themselves. You could try the paper or one of the accommodation websites."

"Alright," I say. "Thanks for your help."

I fill in the form as Clarence Whitehall, inventing my date of birth as 28 June 1974. *Clarence*, I think, it has a ring to it. Clarence will make something of himself, invent himself, survive.

On the journey back to the hospital it begins to rain heavily, the water pelting down upon the windows of the taxi and spraying up around the vehicle as we drive.

There is information in my cubicle; a pamphlet *Amnesia: What You Need to Know* and some information on Henry Gustav Molaison, as if reading about somebody worse off than me is supposed to make me feel better about my own situation. It is possible that somebody has performed an operation on me, chopped out parts of my hippocampus, my parahippocampal gyrus, my amygdala. Have my memories been surgically removed? Surely nothing so barbaric has taken place. It's more likely, I think, that I owed somebody some money, that they beat me up and dumped me over the edge of a bridge, not expecting me to survive. If that's the case there could be somebody out there who, were they to learn that I am still alive, has it in for me, would kill me if they could. Maybe I attempted suicide, threw myself off the edge of the bridge. Did I jump or was I pushed? There are too many questions for which I do not have answers. I turn to the magazines; Kate is growing tired of Tom's controlling ways, Sam Mendes is working on yet another film, Madonna's trying to adopt another African. Guy says that sleeping with Madonna was like sleeping with a piece of gristle.

Petty swipes, from one hurt party to another. And me, Mr Nobody, stuck inside these four walls until I am discharged to fend for myself in this vicious world. Again, I make notes in my diary of all that has happened to me today so that I can check that I remember it tomorrow. The doctor arrives with the results of my cat scan. All clear, no tumor, no missing parts of brain. All in good working order, at least on paper.

"A member of the police is coming to visit you at three," he says. "They'll photograph you, ask you some questions."

"Okay."

I feel like a sheep, being herded from pen to pen.

The police officer is a woman, very nice, with a soft manner. She handles me with kid gloves. She takes my photo and my fingerprint. There is talk of sampling my DNA but she doesn't do it today.

"Typically in a case like this," she says. "We will be able to match your photo to that of a missing person. You must have had a job or friends or relatives. Somebody will have noticed that you are gone and reported it. It's only a question of time. I'm sure we will find out who you really are."

I eat dinner, am brought another sleeping-pill and sleep the sleep of the dead.

The following day. I read my diary first thing and am pleased to realise that all the events noted there also exist in my memory; the cat scan, the trips to and from social welfare, the small Indian woman who did her best to help me. The doctor tells me that I will have to leave today, they are pressed for space, there are other, more urgent cases. He gives me a month's supply of Citalopram.

"But I haven't arranged accommodation yet."

"There's a night shelter you can go to. For homeless people."

He hands me a scrap of paper with a phone number and address on it. Homeless; the word sends a shudder through me. It's up to me now; I will have to find myself a home.

"Alright," I say. "This is it. My new life. Reconstructed from scratch, from nothingness."

He smiles a tight grin, more like a grimace really.

"I'm afraid so. But let us know when you move on from the shelter and we will send nurses to visit you to make sure you are adjusting to your new life. I suggest you find yourself a local GP who can refer you to a psychiatrist. Somebody will visit you in the night shelter."

Clarence, I decide, will become a lawyer. He will work in admin by day and study law at night. In my diary I write *charity shop – new clothes, Births, Deaths and Marriages – register Clarence, bank – open account, internet – find flat, social security – search for job, GP – register.* It's a daunting list. Not everything will be able to be completed in a single day. I will have to pace myself, find my feet slowly, raise myself, inch by inch, from a horizontal position to a vertical one. Stand upright. I will fly, I will not fall. The name is first.

"Do you have a phone-book I can borrow?" I ask. "I need to find a few addresses."

The Department of Births, Deaths and Marriages is located near to the centre of town in an old, crumbling brick building. I still have the letter from the hospital, explaining my case, my special case. I am allowed the name of Clarence; I become him. I am handed a certificate declaring my new name. I will need a bank account before I can do anything else. I walk to the nearest branch of the National Savings Bank and open an account, giving the homeless shelter as an address. I am given a debit card. They will have to post the pin out to me, they say. Everything is going smoothly, far more smoothly than I had anticipated. I return to social security and tell them my bank account number; my first payment is to go in tomorrow. I am doing it; I am reconstructing a life, an identity. I decide to grow a moustache; it will be part of my new look. My spirits are buoyant; I feel light and free, as if nothing ties me down. Wouldn't many people like to be in my situation; their old life, their old problems wiped out, tabula rasa, everything gone, free to start again? I am a new man. I book into the homeless shelter and spend the rest of the afternoon sitting in the park, watching the birds, the ravens, bouncing across the pasture, the gulls squawking and shrieking across grey skies.

The homeless shelter is not a pleasant place. A nurse arrives in the evening to check that I am settled in. I reassure her that I will be fine and she goes away. The bunks in this place are pushed up close together, twenty people to a room, so I spend the night with a variety of noises, the snores and farts and groans of strangers. The smell is terrible; most of these people stink like skunks.

In the morning I check my bank account first thing and find that the funds have gone in as promised. I walk from the bank to the charity shop. It's another grey day, with drizzle falling from the sky. From a man with six piercings in his face I purchase two pairs of pin-striped trousers and three work shirts, a pair of jeans and a woollen jumper, scarf and hat. Winter is coming on; I will need to be warm. In an internet café I search for a small, cheap flat; a studio is all I will need. There are three in the area, all within my price range. I have decided not to be fussy, any of them will do. Only one is furnished and this is the one I take, giving the address to the hospital so they can send their nurses. Maybe I do need looking after, after all.

The job is the final hurdle and easily leapt. I take a position in a small law firm, where hopefully I can work my way up from admin boy to lawyer. I will take my degree via correspondence. I will work all day and study all night. There will be no time for wine, women and song. It will be head down and bum up. I am to start next week; there is time, then, to acquaint myself with this town.

A river runs through it; is it the same river I woke up next to? I don't know. There are two small art galleries that I visit. They display local art; watercolours, sculptures, oils, installations of cardboard cows. The Museum of Natural History is tiny, but it exists, displaying fossils that have been found in the area and a selection of gemstones and rocks. I walk the length of the town, along the river and bank. Ducks float on the slimy black swell. I register with a local GP, but aside from that, I do not talk to anybody during the course of this week. What could I possibly have to say?

Work. My colleagues are pleasant, the job dull but easily manageable. The correspondence course I wish to take doesn't start for three months so I have plenty of time to settle in and save some money. It's not bad, being nobody, starting on a blank slate. I like the look of one of my work colleagues, a secretarial temp called Judy who has lovely red lips and a full figure, but I dare not act on my desires. I don't want complications; I want purity, simplicity, no strings attached to this puppet. At night I watch the television that I picked up for only ten dollars from the charity shop, I watch shows called *Eastenders* and *Coronation Street* and *The Catherine Tate Show*; I don't remember any of these people, these actors, from what I have come to think of as "the time before".

It is during the second week of my new job that I receive a visit from my friendly police lady. She sits opposite me, in one of the cheap chairs with the springs poking through the seat.

"We have discovered who you are," she says. "Your wife filed a missing persons report a week ago. She says she waited because she thought you might come back of your own accord."

"I have a wife?"

"Yes. Susan Robinson. You are a scientist called Howard Robinson, a geneticist. Apparently you were in the throes of a major depression before you left her. We think you attempted suicide by throwing yourself off the bridge and received a blow to the skull which has resulted in your amnesia. The doctor at the hospital also thinks your condition may be psychological. You don't *want* to remember who you are. You want to forget."

On the television, a man called Gordon Ramsey is shouting and swearing at a hapless wannabe chef who bursts into tears. It comes back to me now. Small flashes. My workplace at the university, Susan and our child, an olive skinned boy whose name does not come to mind.

"But I'm Clarence now," I say.

"No, you're not Clarence," she says firmly. "That is an assumed identity. You are Howard Robinson, a married geneticist with one child, a boy."

"Shall I pack my things?"

"Your wife will be here in the morning. It's up to you how you wish to proceed. What we advise is that you return to your home and that your memory may come back in time. You should also see your old GP to receive treatment for your problems."

My wife arrives. I recognise her. She is beautiful and crying and I give her a hug.

"Oh Howard," she says. "Oh God."

She has brought the boy, Sam, with her. He clings to my leg as if afraid I will disappear into thin air. Nobody talks on the long drive home.

My wife makes roast pork with apple sauce and crackling. Apparently this is my favourite meal. My son sits on my knee receiving a horsey ride. Mozart plays on the stereo. My son burps. But I don't fit here, I don't fit anywhere. I am a non-person, blank space. I no longer exist.

Mike

I met Mike at the local swimming-pool. He said I wasn't swimming right, that my stroke needed improvement. He showed me how to lift my arm a bit higher, how to reach out a bit further, how to glide through the water like a silver arrow. He seemed nice enough. Mike claimed to be a swimming instructor, he said that if I met him at the pool at six every evening he could give me free lessons. And so began our romance.

It was more than just swimming with us. We took long walks along the beach, listening to the cries of the gulls that soared overhead, we shared expensive dinners in restaurants that had rose petals scattered upon the tables and elegant, tapering candles in glistening silver candlestick holders. We went on holiday to Rome together and drank in the city's arts and culture. Mike opened my eyes to a whole new world, a world apart from the mundanity of my everyday existence.

By day I slogged it out in Blockbusters. The work was hell. The customers didn't listen when I told them that all our Tarantino movies were out. *Have you got Kill Bill 3*, they'd ask, *Have you got Jackie Brown? Have you got Pulp Fiction?* It was enough to drive a strong mind insane. I was trapped. I'd never been to university, I didn't have a degree, I couldn't afford to study part-time, there was nothing else I was trained to do, apart from work in a supermarket, and I'd already spent two years doing *that*. Mike said he could help me to create a better life. A new life. A free life. A life without shackles. How I trusted him, how I fell. Hook, line and sinker I was taken in. It was ages before I cottoned onto the fact that there was something funny going on.

Two weeks after we'd met, I read about the chooks. *Police alert local farmers and chicken owners to the high number of chicken slayings that have been taking place recently in the town. Bloodied chickens have been found, both inside and outside their coops. Urban foxes have been thought to blame. Properties are to be made more secure.* That night, Mike and I went out to dinner. He ordered butter chicken, but I thought nothing of it.

When we'd finished our mains and were sharing a chocolate fondue, he popped the question, asked whether he could move into my place. I ummed and aahed. Said I thought that it was a bit early, that we hadn't known each other long enough – it had only been a couple of months. He ground me down over the next few weeks till I gave in. After he'd moved into my place, I was rearranging some of his stuff when I found his box of tapes. Some people listen to dolphin noises. Mike had been listening to canine noises; six tapes worth of them, a horrid insane *howling* that echoed in my mind long after I had hit stop on the tape player.

That same night I caught a glimpse of his fangs. I was walking past the bathroom when he was in there and I stopped and peered in, curious. He was too engrossed to know that I was watching. He was leaning in close to the mirror, examining his teeth, shaking his head in dismay at what he saw. Then he reached into his pocket, took out a pair of plastic fangs, inserted them into his gob, snarled at himself in the mirror and smiled, satisfied. Well, what would *you* think? I was in shock. I'd dated some quirky guys in my time, like Darren who'd been heavily into leather, and Gregory who collected monarch butterflies by the thousands, displaying them on all his walls, but never had I seen nor heard of a grown man wearing *fangs*. Terrible, terrible. That's not the kind of thing you can just ignore either, not taken on top of the howling tapes. I was forced to confront him.

In the bathroom doorway I stood, hands on hips.

"Mike?" I said his name forcefully, as if trying to jolt him from a daydream into reality.

"Wha – what's going on?"

"Mike, are those *fangs* in your mouth?"

"No."

"They are too. Here, spit them out. Let me have a look at them."

"Keep back, keep away, they're my fangs."

"Now Mike, stop acting like a child."

He stomped his foot.

"I'm *not* acting like a child."

"Give me the fangs, Mike."

He pouted, sulking, then pulled the fangs from his mouth and handed them, slobber-covered, to me, muttering, "Here, take them then."

I ran one finger along the edge of a tooth. A thin trail of blood sparkled on the tip of my finger. The teeth were sharp – they weren't plastic at all, they were dentures. Sharpened dentures. Somebody had been at them with a file.

"There's something else Mike. I found the tapes, the howling tapes. I don't like it, Mike, it's weird. Funny business. This is meant to be a normal set-up, a man, a woman, sharing their lives together, helping each other through. Not a *freakshow*."

"Tapes, what tapes? I don't know anything about tapes."

"That big box of tapes I found amongst your stuff. Tapes with noises of dogs or wolves or something recorded on them."

"*Wolves?*"

"Something inhuman anyway. Deny it all you like. I don't want you getting all crazy on me, Mike, I've had enough weirdness from guys in the past."

"Fine, just gimme my fangs back."

The more I thought about it, the more uneasy I felt. Something wasn't right, something was out of whack. I had a queasy feeling in my guts and a nagging headache that Panadol wouldn't take away. It's not as if I suspected him of being outright mad, but the fangs and the tapes most certainly had a whiff of lunacy about them. And lunacy was the last thing I wanted. I wanted stability, security. Two weeks later I found the suit. I was reaching into our wardrobe, putting mothballs in the pockets of some of my old woollen coats when I felt something strange brush against my fingers. It felt like those tufts on Mike's back. I reached in with *both* hands this time, and pulled something heavy off its hanger. It was, unmistakeably, a fur suit. Not a gorilla suit, or a monkey suit, but a *wolf* suit, undeniably a wolf suit. Well, how could he be so stupid? Knowing that my suspicions were already aroused, he went and left *incriminating evidence* practically lying about the house! Relationships should be based on openness and honesty, not furtiveness and deceit. I cornered him in the bathroom again that evening. The bathroom was the perfect place to ensnare him; it was a small, tight space, you could corner him there, like a rat in a trap. I could block off his exit simply by outstretching my arms.

"Err, Mike?"

I held up the suit in front of me.

"Yeah, what?"

"I found this in the wardrobe. Would you care to explain?"

"Oh that old thing," he said too casually.

"What do you mean *that old thing?* What the hell is it?"

"A wolf suit, of course."

"You told me you weren't into that stuff, that crazy stuff. And then I go and find direct evidence to the contrary."

"Alright, alright, keep ya knickers on. It's from a fancy dress party I went to a year ago. I couldn't throw it away, damned thing was expensive."

"Why didn't you just hire something?"

"What is this, the Spanish inquisition?"

"Mike, I'm trying to live a life that is as sane and devoid of bizarreness as possible."

"Come on, love! Don't be awkward about it. It was just for a fancy dress party. There's nothing odd about it."

"Fine. I'm throwing the suit out then."

"Oh, don't do that!"

"Yes, it's going out in the trash."

That was when he snapped, lost control, lunged at me yelling, "Don't throw out my wolfsuit!" before bursting into tears and running out the door. Well, Mike had never displayed violence before. I'd been out with a physically abusive guy before and I'd be damned if I was going down *that* road again. Sure, I'd been smitten with Mike at the beginning, but you know what it's like. Anybody can put on their best face during that initial "honeymoon" phase – and then you get really to know a person. Warts and all. And Mike was revealing some pretty big warts. He re-entered the room, dressed in his wolf suit, fangs firmly in place, yelling at me.

"I should've known! You're just like all the rest, trying to put me in a box, keep me in my place. People like you, all you value is conformity. A nice nine to five job, 2.3 children, TV every evening and sex twice a week. Difference is a celebration. It's not something to be ashamed of. You've heard of gay pride well this is wolfman pride! Yes, you have discovered my dark, dirty secret. I like dressing up as a wolf. So what? Plenty of guys like women's clothing; the French knickers, the camisoles, the lacy frocks. Transvestites, they're everywhere. For all you know there could be three in this very street. If I'd known you were going to be such a closed minded person I never would've helped you correct your lousy over-arm. Not to mention your breast stroke, which is *abysmal.*"

I must admit, I found his hysteria rather catching.

"Leave my swimming out of this, Mike. The swimming's got nothing to do with anything. What we're *trying* to deal with is you and your bizarre *habits.*"

"Oh a *habit* is it, is that what it is? It's not a *habit*, it's a way of life. There's a group of us you know, we *support* each other. Not that you'd know anything about being *supportive.* All you know about is cutting a person down at the knees, putting somebody in their place. Just because you've got a job that a *robot* could do."

"Stop turning everything round back to me."

"Yes, we're known as the wolfmen of London and we meet once a month by the light of the glaring full moon. Bella luna! We gather on Tooting Common, we howl, we paw at the dirt, we, we, we… dance about. Yes, that's it, we do the wolf dance. How do you like that, eh, the wolf dance."

He danced about the room, intermittently pointing his 'muzzle' at the ceiling and giving a small howl.

Something in me broke then, and I screamed at him, "AT LEAST I'VE GOT A JOB!!"

He froze.

"That's it. I've had enough. I thought you were a *kind* woman, an *understanding* woman, a woman with a heart of gold. But you're cold, cold and hard on the inside. "

I felt my old fear come creeping back, fear of being alone, without a partner to lean on.

"But Mike…"

"But Mike nothing. You had your chance, your chance to love me for what I am. And you blew it."

He eyeballed me before adding, slightly pitifully, "I'm going back home to my parents."

"Fine. I'm better off without a weirdo like you anyway."

"Fine."

"Fine, fine, fine, fine, fine. Five fines, just to show you how very *fine* it's going to be."

"I was fine before I met you and I'll be just fine without you."

"Say it one more time, Mike, maybe you'll convince yourself that it's true."

After he'd gone I drank two bottles of white wine and passed out on the sofa. When I came to my senses at three in the morning, the house seemed awfully cold and empty. But I pulled myself together, I soldiered on. There were videos to rent out, there were walks in the park to take, there were lengths to swim at the pool….and *that*, predictably enough, was where I bumped into him again. He was standing by another woman who looked a bit like me. He had his arm across hers and was giving her exactly the same sleazy spiel he'd given me. I overheard him telling her that if she met him at the pool at six the following evening he'd give her a lesson. The same lingering touches. The same unblinking eye contact. Fake, all of it fake. I was livid. I didn't know whether I was angry about the wolf suit or him using the same lines, the same tricks, on another woman as he'd used on me. I vowed revenge. That night, I drove round to his parents' house and peered in through the lit window. I could tell that his parents were out – their Ford Mondeo wasn't in the driveway. There they were, the two of them, as cosy as can be, all curled up on his sofa. He reached out and put his hand on her leg. I turned away; I averted my eyes.

It must have been that same evening that I got to thinking that maybe he wasn't a fake, but a *real* wolf. Maybe his human skin was just a disguise. He'd bought various *adornments* to try and throw me off the scent. That got me thinking about how I might have to, well…I hate to say it… kill him. If he really was a werewolf, then I couldn't just leave him roaming the streets, claiming chickens and probably women as victims. Oh sure, I could've gone to the police – they would've dismissed *me* as the lunatic, laughed me out of the place, considered me crazy. I did, at this stage, have a bit of a psychiatric history; I'd twice been hospitalised for depression and once, at Blockbusters, I'd gone on a sort of manic high, threatening people with scissors. I'd very nearly lost my job over it, but in the end I got a note from the doctor saying that I was mentally unwell, so they let me stay on as long as I took medication. However, my own history aside,

I couldn't just leave Mike roaming free, wreaking havoc. A silver bullet was out of the question. I would have to use a stake.

I dug out a fencepost from the backyard and sharpened the tip of it into the form of a spear. I threw the stake into a backpack, pulled on my black jeans and my black jumper and cycled round to Mike's place. Peering in through the bedroom window, I could see him sleeping peacefully, his arm around his new beloved. I raised my spear high over my right shoulder and sent it crashing through the windowpane. Foolish that, I should've picked the locks, crept in quietly through the front door and gone sneaking down the hallway to where they lay sleeping. Typical me, to be cacophonous when I should've been silent. Instantly, they were awake and on me – Mike ran outside and down the path at the side of the house, pinned me to the ground, yelling at his new girlfriend to call the cops.

Well there was a court case. They claimed I was mentally unstable, imagining my ex-boyfriend to be a werewolf when of course he was just an *ordinary,* even, they said, a *decent* guy. Who cared if he liked playing dress-ups? It could've got nasty – they could've had me up for attempted murder; instead they sent me to a shrink. But they don't know what I know, they haven't heard what I've heard; the distant howling on foggy nights when the moon is at its most full, the gnashing of fangs outside the window.

Dummies

The first mannequin was called Theresa. She was something of a looker, if you liked the Barbie doll thing, with long blonde hair that stretched to her tiny waist and enormous breasts that jutted out from her front like the prows of twin ships.

"She's a typical size 12," said Mike.

I eyed him sceptically. *I* was a size 12 and my vital statistics were nothing like Theresa's. He'd picked her up cheap from the recycling centre at the dump. Nobody else had wanted her – according to the bloke behind the counter, she'd been sitting there for the last five years. Maybe people had thought she was for display purposes only; they hadn't realised that she was up for sale. For Mike, it was love at first sight. Those were his own words, "I saw her standing there, so lonely, and it was love at first sight. Head over heels. Just like when I met you, love." He'd nudged me and I'd backed away, not much liking the comparison to a plastic thing, a doll, a *dummy*.

I tried to dispose of her. I put her out with the garbage on a Wednesday morning, after I was sure Mike had headed off to work, but blow me down if that wasn't the morning he forgot his sandwiches and came home at morning tea time to find her standing out there by the gate. Mike didn't have much of a temper on him, but he blew his fuse *that* morning. He stood in the lounge, Theresa gripped firmly under his right arm, his left arm gesticulating wildly as he vented his spleen.

"I didn't pay ten quid for Theresa just so you could get rid of her whenever it took your fancy to do so," he ranted. "What harm is she doing to you, anyway? She doesn't *encroach*. All she does is stand in the corner looking pretty. If only *you* were so easy to please."

With that, he plonked the doll back in the living room corner, adjusted her hair so that it hung down over her breasts, straightened her skirt and pulled the wrinkles from her top, gave her a peck on the cheek and returned to work. I couldn't stand

Theresa. The way her glassy eyes stared out at me from her plastic face, the way her gaze seemed, Mona Lisa style, to follow me around the room, the way she took up so much of Mike's time and attention. He even started having his dinner in there with her, rather than sitting with me at the kitchen table as he'd always done in the past. He was wrong when he said that she wasn't encroaching. Theresa was an intruder. She was taking over. Mike had always been a bit of a hoarder, a collector, but this, I felt, was taking it too far. I'd allowed him pets (three goldfish, a couple of canaries, a black Labrador), his carnivorous plant collection (the Venus Fly traps, the pitcher plants, the butterworts), his accumulation of old radios that spat and crackled. You could never find the channel you were searching for. I didn't see why I should allow him this.

Risking a return of Mike's fury, I attempted to take her back to where she'd come from; to the dump. I threw her in the boot of the car, tying the boot closed with a bit of old frayed rope and roared off to the tip before I could be apprehended. They wouldn't take her back.

"What, that old thing," they said. "We don't want her round here, she hung around for years, never brought anybody any luck, people said she was cursed, like an Egyptian mummy. During her reign, Jim Brady who used to work on the front desk here, contracted lung cancer even though he'd never touched a fag in his life, Kyle Langford, a young buck who used to help us out lugging the heavier furniture around came down with double pneumonia after getting caught in the lightest of rain showers and Bill Sampson who'd worked here all his life and exercised regularly and ate healthily had a heart attack and had to go in for a bypass."

The phrase "during her reign" bothered me; it gave Theresa a queenly aspect. *She'd better not try any funny business when she's living with us*, I thought. I didn't want her getting ideas above her station; I wanted her to know her place.

Back home we went. I sat her down on the living room sofa and did my best to turn my back on her, to ignore her. She was forever catching my eye. When vacuuming or dusting I would catch a glimpse of her out of the corner of my vision and feel compelled to turn and look. I could swear to God that she was shifting when my back was turned, readjusting herself this way and that, striking poses. When I had put her down she'd had her legs bent and her knees together, with both hands resting on her thighs, but when I waltzed past, hoover in hand, she had both her legs stretched out in front of her and her arms folded. I blinked hard, twice; surely my mind was playing tricks. Perhaps I had shifted her myself and then forgotten about it. Maybe this was the pose I had initially put her down in. There had to be a logical explanation.

*

Jasmine, the second mannequin was called. She was brunette, her dark hair curled in a neat shoulder-length bob.

"Here y'are tiger," Mike addressed Theresa. "Here's a companion for ya. Don't say I don't treat ya right."

He put Jasmine down on the sofa, and then swiftly vacated the room. When he re-entered he was clutching one of my newest dresses – I'd bought it just a week or two previously and it had cost a pretty penny.

"Mike," I squeaked, "You can't dress her up in *that*. That was expensive. What if she spills something or tears a hole in it?"

"She's a *dummy*. She doesn't eat or drink, she doesn't move of her own accord. Your dress will be fine, stop being so selfish."

He pulled the dress on over Jasmine's head, and shoved her arms through the sleeves. I thought, for an instant, that I saw a small smile of victory flicker at the corners of her mouth, but that, surely, could only have been a figment of my stupid, overactive, imagination.

I didn't plan it.

On the evening of Jasmine's arrival I went out with "the girls", the little gang I'd known since high school; Bridget and Andrea and Karlene. We dined at the local Thai, and then retired to our usual haunt, the Mucky Duck. I gave the girls a quick summary of the situation.

"It's creepy," I said. "It's like I'm being *invaded*. I mean, where is it going to end? Is he going to bring home a whole clan, an *army* of them? Are they going to take over? Am I being usurped from my own home?"

"I think you're worrying too much," said Bridget. "It's just two dolls. I'll admit it is a little *odd*, a grown man, a married man, showing an interest in mannequins like that, but they're hardly a *threat*. It's not like he's having an aff..., an aff.., an *affair*."

She gave a small sob. Her own husband had been caught in the broom closet with his secretary the previous spring. One of his colleagues had told Bridget about it and she'd been devastated. She kicked him out of the house and got a divorce, but everybody knew that she wasn't really over the break-up. She would burst into tears at random moments; not quiet, weeping tears, but great big howling, choking sobs.

"Sorry," she would say, "I know that I'm being embarrassing, it's just, it's just..."

"It's alright," one of us would reply, patting her back. "We understand."

No, it wasn't as if Mike was having an affair.

"Maybe he's having a mid-life crisis," said Andrea. "A nervous breakdown, a second childhood. Maybe you could get him off dollies and onto train-sets or something a little more masculine. Maybe he needs a hobby, or to take up a new sport.

"He *has* hobbies," I said, thinking of the Venus fly traps and the clapped out radios. "And he hates sport, Mike's a bit of a slob. Still, a train-set is a good idea. Less shameful if somebody comes to visit. After all, there are plenty of grown men who are into model trains. Aren't there?"

"Sure there are," replied Andrea. "That kind of thing is perfectly normal, everybody needs their little outlet, their tinkering time, their time out from the world. See, what *I* think the problem is, is that we live in a world where it's push, push, push. From the moment we're born, there are demands on us; to succeed at school or university or work, to buy a house, to find a partner, to settle down, to breed. The world *impinges* on us, it doesn't let us alone, won't leave us to our own devices. Everybody needs their quiet time, their time sitting doing nothing at all, or completing crosswords, or listening to music. Now, for some people, these pressures just build up, and they break, you know, they crack, they can't hack it. They're often the ones who haven't learnt how to take it easy, who don't know how to relax. So, maybe these dolls are a healthy thing, a small *blow-out* in order to prevent a larger explosion."

"You know what I think," said Karlene. "I think he's secretly satisfying his wish for children. Didn't you tell him that you didn't want any kids? Maybe the dolls are his substitute for a family."

"The whole thing's got completely out of hand," I said. "One thing's for sure, I don't want any more of those damned dollies cluttering up my living room."

Famous last words. Over the coming weeks Mike bought home a doll every other day; he didn't get them from the dump, he'd taken to going round the local shops and paying them a fairly hefty sum for the mannequins that sat in their front windows. By the end of the month we had over twenty of the damned things, all striking various poses, all dressed up in *my* dresses, all mocking me, silently mocking me.

*

It felt like living in a morgue. Dozens of dead eyes followed my every move. I was being spied on. It wouldn't have surprised me if the damned things were bugged, electronic devices embedded in plastic chests in order to record what was going on in the house when Mike was absent. Surveillance. I had suspected his suspicion for several months now; the accusatory looks, the probing questions. Since he'd brought the dummy home I'd been a lot more careful. We didn't do it in my marriage bed any more, or in the front room, during the day. Instead we booked hotels and motels, cheap sleazy joints with sagging mattresses with the springs poking through and clogged swimming-pools upon which floated a charming variety of dead leaves and rubbish, old crisps and fag packets, empty soft drink bottles and general scunge. We stayed in rooms that were coated with more than a sprinkle of mildew, rooms whose ceilings dropped soft, steady drips upon our consummating heads. He couldn't afford anything more and I could only justify so many of my expenses as "household appliances" (the Kitchen Whiz broke down, we needed a new one, of *course* it cost three hundred quid, that's cheap, new hoover, the old one died, always having to actually *buy* the damned things, of course, making a mark-up to help cover the expenses of my dalliances.) Mike gave me an allowance, but it wasn't much – he kept a pretty tight hold on the purse-strings. I often wished I had a career of my own, some way to make a buck, to pay my way in this wicked world, but I had left home at fifteen, not the sharpest tool in the box and my choices had been secretarial school or some sort of menial work, such as filleting salmon at the local fish factory or cleaning. I gave the cleaning a go, lasted about a week, developed dreadful eczema from all the products, the Jif and the Ajax and the Mr Muscle, my arms were red and raw and itching. No, it was better to put my efforts, my attentions into finding and netting a rich husband. I met Mike down at the Mucky on a Friday night; I was doing karaoke – Tina Turner *Simply The Best*, dressed up in my new tight, stone-washed jeans and high-heeled white boots with the gold tassels and a skimpy red top that showed off my assets. When I came offstage, he approached and offered to buy me a drink. Sure, I said, glass of chardonnay, make it two. It took just three sentences. He said he liked the high kicks I had done while I was singing, said I had flair. He said he thought I had a good singing voice and could probably find work part-time as a backing singer if I wanted. He said he was studying to be a lawyer and I was hooked.

It was so swift, so easy, just in and out, in and out....

We had a good marriage for the first three years, but as time went on I became increasingly dissatisfied. Dissatisfied with my gilded cage of a life, dissatisfied with the general lack of excitement, dissatisfied with the sex which was plodding and predictable, in, out, in out, finish (always *his* finish, never mine). Finish, roll over and snore. Dare I admit it, I began to turn to a tipple during the day and sometimes a Valium or two – Mother's little helper. I suppose that children may have helped to fill the void, but I didn't want any screaming brats circling my ankles with their snotty noses and their yelps and their incessant demands. My days were spent doing the housework and shopping and lunching with friends. A decade of housewifery. Who can blame me for seeking something more, for straying?

He found me through Facebook. I'd been going online more and more in an attempt to beat the *ennui* that threatened to engulf me. I'd made myself a Facebook page, put on a few holiday snaps of myself in various exotic destinations (that was one good thing about Mike – the vacations) and I'd had a few posts from other people who'd been to my high school or known me in my youth, but his was the one that really stood out.

"You were gorgeous then, and I'll bet you're gorgeous now. Swimming-pools have never been the same for me since. Get in touch if you fancy it. Trevor."

I should never have answered. I should've closed the open window, shut down my PC, walked away. The swimming-pool incident had been shoved into the wardrobe in the far corner of the room of the mind, and there it should have stayed; it never should've been rehashed, trotted out to prance and preen in the full light of day.

"Hey Trev," I replied. "Long time, no hear. Life is good, still living in Upton, have you moved away? Let me know if you fancy meeting up for a beer one day this week."

He answered within twenty minutes, which should have made me suspicious about his motivations. Mind you, shouldn't I have been suspicious about my *own* motivations – what was I playing at, inviting an old boyfriend out when I was a happily married woman? Well, married anyway.

We didn't go to the Mucky, too risky, that was where Mike and the girls drank. Instead we went to a Wetherspoons where he shouted me from the two for the price of one menu. I had scampi and chips and a glass of white wine. As I reached for my wine, he extended one hand and furled his fingers around mine.

"It's been so long," he said.

I thought I might drown in two pools of murky blue.

"I still get excited every time I smell chlorine," he added.

My heart increased its beat. Gosh, he was handsome, I'd forgotten all about the strong jawline and the masculine forehead. I know that sounds odd – "masculine forehead", but, boy, you should see *his*. Not to mention the eyes, which were like slivers of sky. He clammed up after the chlorine comment, said nothing for the rest of the meal, just chowed his way steadily through his burger and wedges, glancing in my direction from time to time, as if to check that I was still there. I did my best to pry information out of him – where he'd been, what he'd been doing with himself for the past decade or two, but he would just shrug and avoid my questions, he'd always been a shy guy, maybe it was all a calculated ploy, maybe he thought an air of mystery helped to make him more attractive. Or perhaps he was ashamed, maybe he'd been doing something illegal, like dealing cannabis or heroin, or working as a pimp, or in money-laundering. Wherever he'd been, whatever he'd been up to, I was none the wiser after asking him a few questions. Well, I didn't want to *interrogate* the guy; everybody's entitled to their privacy.

When I was done with my scampi and he with his burger he spoke again.

"Listen, I know a great little place near here, they do two for one cocktails at this hour of the night. You wanna give it a try? Don't know about you, but I can sink an awful lot of Tequila and still stand up straight."

Tequila made my head spin and my guts heave.

"Sure," I said. "Just gotta make a quick call."

I'd told Mike that I was going to my sister's place.

"Mike," I said. "I'm going to stay over at Susie's. One of the kids is sick and she hasn't had a good night's sleep in three days, so I'm going in the kids' room so that if they wake in the night, I can tend to them and Susie can sleep right through."

Susie was a solo parent.

"Fine," he said.

All bases covered. If I was home that night, I could just tell him that the kids seemed fine and Susie said it was best for me to go home.

He was asking for it, really...

Home was not where I wound up. Several sambucas, three tequilas and a worm later, I was in the first of many sleazy joints. Did I feel guilt? Oh, there was something tweaking vaguely at the corner of my conscience, but I was having too much fun to pay it any real attention. Mike had never been up to much in the sack, nor had he ever bothered to learn any real *skills*, so what had he expected? At any rate, he'd never find out and what he didn't know wouldn't hurt him. Millions of women, all over the world, at this very moment, were doing exactly what I was doing now. Some of them got away with it, some of them didn't. It was human nature, it was biology, it was inevitable. Such excuses I made for myself, such justifications. Trevor and I had been at it for about six months when Mike brought home Theresa. I wondered if he wasn't getting back at me, wondered if he knew, if he was really saying, *ha ha, two can play at that game.* Upping the stakes.

Three months after I'd first met Theresa, I caught Mike in bed with Jasmine and one of the others. There was a hierarchy, you know, amongst the dolls, as there is in a harem. In this case it was first in, highest status; Jasmine and Theresa would tend to lord it over the other girls, boss them about and so on. They thought I didn't know about it, but I had extra-sensory ears when it came to that sort of thing. I knew they moved and gossiped and whispered when my back was turned, as in those stories about toys in a nursery who have their own lives, their own existences, quite independent of their owners. It was a Saturday. I'd gone out to do the grocery shopping, but came back early having forgotten my purse. There he was, in the sack, buffing Theresa's breasts with a shammy. I stood in the doorway, mouth agape.

"Just giving her a buff," he shouted, overly defensive. "She was getting grubby. Her and Kylie here."

He gestured to the other doll who shared our marital bed with him, a ginger-nut with fake freckles spattered on her cheeks and a pouting mouth. If it had been just the single incident maybe I could have forgiven him. I'm not trying to make excuses for myself, but I caught him a total of *ten* more times in bed with the girls, *ten* and always an excuse – *just cleaning, just buffing, just doing her hair. We were just watching Hymns of Praise together.*

All day long I thought of those dummies, they infiltrated my consciousness, they took over. At night, when I closed my eyes, I saw their plastic faces floating before my mind's eye, I heard their admonishing, criminatory voices calling in a chorus, *we know what you're up to, we know what you're up to.* They would tell on me, they would blow the whistle. Their own crimes were endless. They had stolen my husband, ruined my marriage, driven me half out of my mind. Driven me further towards the bottle.

They say that I murdered my husband, you know, knifed him in the full light of day. It wasn't me, it was one of the girls, nobody's quite sure who; I suspect somebody lower down in the hierarchy who was envious because she wasn't getting enough love and affection from my husband. It's me who's paying, of course, locked up in this place, avoiding the dykes – the only things I look forward to are the day's hour of exercise and the TV watching we are allowed in the afternoon. But I'll be out, soon enough; a life sentence is never really life these days and then I'll find my beloved Trevor and tell everybody the truth.

The Faker

I faked my death, just as I faked so much in my life; passports, degrees, orgasms. I was a fraud. My English Literature degree from Oxford I had bought online at www.fakedegrees.com five years ago. My New Zealand passport, which would allow me to stay in that country indefinitely, had been purchased from a dodgy friend who had "connections". Even the software on my PC (Microsoft Office, Dreamweaver, Photoshop) had not been bought legally, but acquired for free from other people who had burnt my CDs. I lived with the constant fear of being "discovered", "rumbled", found wanting, needy, substandard and inadequate. An impostor.

I left a note; *Dear Jake, I have had enough of this world and have decided to leave it all behind. Thanks for the time we had together.* I signed it with a lipstick kiss. I packed everything I would need into a hot pink suitcase I had bought from Argos the week before. Dressed casually in jeans, trainers, dark sunglasses, a blonde wig and a grey hoodie, I caught a cab from our flat in Peckham to Heathrow, checked in and sat waiting for my flight. I felt tense, furtive, as if somebody might have followed me and at any moment might put one hand on my shoulder, *Hey you, you're coming with us.* Nobody arrived to drag me back.

On the flight, after two gin and tonics, I relaxed slightly. There was a lightning storm as I was leaving; it lit up the early morning sky with its spidery electric fingers and made me feel that the heavens were complicit with me, cheering me on, putting on a sort of farewell-to-your-old-life and good-luck-to-your-new show in order to signal their approval of my decision, which had not been a snap decision at all, but rather had been meticulously thought out and planned and pondered over for many months prior to this morning's departure. I ate my meal of rice and stir-fried chicken when it arrived on its plastic tray and drank a glass of red wine and buried myself in the Jackie Collins novel I had brought with me.

147

We refuelled at Hong Kong airport; I couldn't sit still, but wandered the airport restlessly, admiring the orchids. In my wallet was a picture of the shack (New Zealanders would say "bach") in Te Anau that my Uncle Quentin had left me upon his death. Planks were missing; space for the wind to whistle through. The paint was chipped and falling off the wood. It would be my space apart; I needed time out. I treated myself to some noodles which I ate quickly and then wandered around the airport in that stupefied limbo you enter on long-haul flights. It seemed that there was nobody else around, just me, and yet, at the same time, the airport was packed with people, busy. Perhaps it was more that there seemed such a great distance between them and me, as if they stood on one side of an ice floe and I on the other with an ever-widening crack opening up between us. I felt as if I were a different species. Purposefully, I had left my mobile, my Blackberry and my laptop at home, so there was nothing to tether me to my normal channels of communication. This was the moment I had dreamed of for months, and how many others, ordinary Londoners like me, also dreamt of slipping free of their chains; their jobs, their mortgages, their established relationships and setting out into nothingness? I was doing this for everybody, I thought, rather too grandly, to see if it could be done. Was it really possible, to set up a life and then vacate it, leaving the empty rooms of your old existence behind to gather cobwebs and dust?

In the ladies' room, I took off my itchy wig and had a good scratch, feeling a little like one of Roald Dahl's witches. Was that a wart sprouting at the bottom of my nose? No, and no newts in my hand luggage either. I remained, beneath my costume, good old Harriet May, a less-than-notable journalist who had, during her four year career, written for a number of not-so-prestigious UK papers and who now wanted nothing more than to live in a shack and eat, what did they call them? Oh, yes, huhu grubs. Huhu grubs and supplejack. My uncle had sent me a brochure on the Wild Foods Festival a few years earlier and I had cast my eyes over the fine specimens that were available there. New Zealand – a green land, lush. There were mountains, proper ones, with snow on them and fjords and deep lakes and beaches both tame and wild. They had a summer there, not just two weeks of the year when the sun made a pitiful effort to shine. They had swimming-pools in their backyards and quarter-acre sections and you could still buy a halfway-decent house for a hundred thousand pounds. Jake would be frantic by now. He would've called the cops. They would be looking for me.

*

Back on the plane, I felt lighter, freer as if I was shucking off the baggage of the years. There was ten thousand pounds in my bank account; my life-savings. I had no commitments, not any more. I had, to put it bluntly "buggered off". I did not intend to be easily traceable. I wanted to pull off a vanishing act, a disappearance, *whoosh,* up in a puff of smoke, into thin air like some third-rate magician performing a cheap trick. *Now you see her, now you don't.* Vamoose. An escape artist.

I spent two days taking in downtown Auckland (I bought a second blonde wig to match my first) and exploring the beaches of the North Shore. Wanting to see the city, I had allowed myself this time before flying down to Queenstown, from there to take the bus to Te Anau. I was missing my laptop a little; my fingers were in the habit of rapid typing and with no keyboard to drum upon I found myself tapping away at the top of the little wooden dresser in the Sky Hotel. I had checked the top drawer upon arrival; no Bible, Gideon or otherwise, though the liquor cabinet, I had gratefully noted, was stacked high with miniature bottles of spirits of which I made short work, reprimanding myself as I did so.

Easy on the liquor, I told myself. *You don't want to make a habit of drinking. You will need will-power and discipline to make this new life work.*

Queenstown was hideous; it was the ski season, so the place was packed with tourists – Japanese, German, American, they were there in droves, swarming over the city like ants. The whole place was geared up to cater to them, with its expensive boutique shops and over-priced restaurants. I hid in the YHA and cooked a simple dinner of steak, beans and spuds washed down with a couple of Steinlagers.

I didn't want to think of myself as a tourist; I wanted to be local, a Kiwi girl, at home. I didn't want to be camera to the eye, click, click, clicking. I wanted to blend in to the landscape.

The one electrical appliance I *had* bought was my iPod. Sigur Ros, which Jake had given me last Christmas, provided good company on that winding bus trip, through the spectacular scenery that greeted my eye as we wove our way towards Te Anau. Closer and closer, closer to the dream. Further and further away from the life I had come to despise and in which I had felt so trapped. I was shedding neuroses like a tree sheds dead leaves, springing back to life like a Jack released from its box. I applied a fresh coat of lipstick and wriggled my toes. The lipstick was called Fuschia Shimmer – it was a shade of pink that Jake always liked me to wear. Jake worked at Reading University, in the Cybernetics Department there. He was part of a team that was developing a robot that had, or at least could, simulate, emotions. It was a long commute for him; he worked from home two days a week and occasionally stayed over in Reading. According to him, his research was of global importance.

"Imagine it," he used to say. "A robot that can feel. They'd make great companions for old people, or else they could be used to help raise kids. A sentient machine. Something that would fly through the Turing test."

He was very engrossed in his work; it wasn't work so much as a grand passion and he found it difficult to disconnect, to switch off. I would be talking to him about something, what to have for dinner, or what I had accomplished during the day and I would get no response and realise that he wasn't with me at all, but off, somewhere else, lost far in his mind, "on another planet" as they say, not the planet of our marriage but "planet AI" where he was a sort of God who had the power to create life. The robot he was developing was his real wife and he gave more time and attention to it than he did to me. Lovelace was the team's name for the robot they were creating, named after Ada, rather than Linda. I had only met Lovelace once. We had a most pleasant conversation; she was very congenial. I liked her. She seemed to have a personality all of her own and I was most disappointed when Jake switched her off. I found myself wondering if he

150

didn't sometimes wish that *I* had a switch so that he could shut *me* down when I became tiresome. All that was behind me now. My tiny world was about to expand. I walked the three miles from the bus stop to the shack.

*

The shack was unlocked. Three large bugs with enormous feelers, which I recognised as wetas from the Wild Foods brochure I had been given, consolidated in one corner. I swept them out with a broom that Quentin, or whoever had been here last, had thoughtfully left behind. The place was musty and stank, so I threw open the creaking windows and let in the cold winter air. It was freezing, below zero, but I was rugged up, prepared, with my hot pink beanie with its matching scarf and my polar fleece and my thick wool trousers and socks. The shack was simple but it would do. There were four rooms; a bedroom which contained two bunks, with the plastic casings around the mattress worn and split, a kitchen which contained a jug (thank God!) and a small electric hob with a grill beneath it. The cupboards were completely bare but for an ancient tin containing five teabags, a few chipped plates and cups and half a packet of rice. I would have to walk back to the supermarket tomorrow. Stupid old me, I should've thought about food before coming all the way out here. There was a bathroom, which contained only a bath and a sink, no shower. A mouldy-looking sofa sat in the living area, a number of springs poking up through its cushioned surface. A fireplace was in the living area; there were ashes in the grate and I wondered how recently there had been a fire. There were no mirrors anywhere so I could not check my reflection. The bookshelf in the living area held a few musty old volumes of Encyclopaedia Britannica, the Gideon Bible I had looked for earlier in the Sky City Hotel and an old map of the area, which began to fall apart at the creases when I opened it. The toilet was outside, an outhouse; I would have to buy a torch then. There was no garden to speak of, though you could see that there had been one once, for stones had been used to divide the yard up into sections. Behind the house was a large patch of native bush and to the front was the pebbly shore of the lake and the jetty which I had seen in the photograph. Best of all, parked up outside the shack (I knew I had to start calling it a bach) was

151

a rickety old push-bike that would serve me well. I didn't want a car. A bike was just the ticket. I wouldn't have to walk to Te Anau tomorrow, after all.

I spread out my sleeping-bag and placed my belongings on one of the lower bunks in the bedroom and was boiling the jug in order to enjoy a mug of tea when I heard heavy steps, a man's steps, crossing the front porch. A brief knock.

"Hello, anyone home?"

I quickly applied some face powder then moved towards the door to answer him.

"Hello there!" I said. "You must be a neighbour of some sort."

"Indeed I am. Name's Dave. Pleased ta meetcha."

He was enormous, well over six feet tall; if I had to estimate I would say six foot four or five and built like the proverbial. His hands were what I really noticed; great callouses bloomed on them and the knuckles were red and swollen up to half again the normal size.

"Come in," I said. "I've just boiled the jug."

"Oh na na, I can't stay. I was just on my way to mend a fence that borders your land. I've got the land behind yours but I live in town. You might see me out here from time to time, so I just thought I'd introduce meself to the new girl so as you didn't get a fright if you see me around and about."

"But they would have the rabbit out of hiding," I quoted, but it was lost on him of course, he simply said 'Eh?' and squinted down at me from his gigantic height as if he was hard of hearing.

"Do you need me to contribute anything? For the fence, I mean. If it borders both of our properties, is it my responsibility or yours?"

"Well, nobody's been out here for years, see, so I've always taken care of it but I suppose that technically it's half your responsibility."

"Oh, I'm happy to pay."

"Oh the money's nothing. It's more the effort, if you see what I mean. Checking that the fence posts haven't rotted and that the wire hasn't been damaged where some animal's tried to get through."

"I see."

"Don't worry, I won't throw you in at the deep end. But if you'd be happy to help out from time to time…"

"Yes, of course."

"What do you do for a living then?"

"I write romance novels."

It was only half a lie. I hadn't yet written one, but that was what I intended to do out here, in the middle of nowhere; lose myself in a doctor/nurse fantasy, or the tale of a ski instructor seducing a pupil or a man gradually helping an amnesiac woman to regain her memory, or a story of love across the class divide – the son of an earl falling for a shop assistant.

Dave looked amused.

"Righto then. I'll be seeing ya round, I guess. Nice to meetcha. What did you say your name was again?"

"Oh, I didn't say. Lola. Lola Sullivan."

"Lola! Gosh that's unusual. Met her in a bar down in old Soho eh? You're not a tranny are ya?"

"No, no, I can assure you that I am one hundred percent female. Last time I checked anyway."

"Yeah, good on ya. I'll see ya later."

Stomp, stomp, stomp and he was gone. What was he doing out fencing at dusk? I made my cup of tea; sat out on the porch sipping it slowly, smelling the fresh native forest which smelt like heaven.

Dinner was a plate of congealed rice, with nothing to decorate it.

I will have to be more sharp, I thought. *I really should've remembered to bring groceries with me.*

*

Early morning frost coated the grass at the side of the road. The bike creaked and groaned and felt like it hadn't been ridden in many years, which undoubtedly, it hadn't. I pumped up the tyres, but the chain needed oiling. I pushed my way back into town and parked my new vehicle outside the local store. My requirements were simple; meat, vegetables, bread, perhaps some pasta, matches for the fire, that torch of course and light bulbs in case the ones in the bach blew. And seeds.

"Do you have any seeds?" I asked the gentleman behind the counter and he pointed me towards a small rack, a scanty collection; my choices were spinach, radishes or carrots. I

153

bought two packets of each and because he didn't sell potting mix and informed me that nowhere else in the town did either (*You'd have to go to Queenstown for that, love*). I prayed that the soil on my patch of land would be rich enough in nutrients for the seeds to sprout and thrive.

I creaked and groaned homewards, with my bounty on my back, then changed into my swimming costume, intending a dip in the lake. That would wake me up, bring me to my senses, keep me "with it". Then I could tackle cleaning the bach and getting everything organised. Organisation and structure would be key, or else I would just drift through my days without getting anything done and I *did* want to get things done, I had plenty to do. I wanted to get on with those romance novels.

There was a speedboat on the lake. It bounced across the surface of the water, its roaring engine cutting the silence. I dipped one toe into the water. A mistake; the lake was freezing. Better to simply leap straight in. I took a breath and dived; the shock of the cold left me gasping. I did four brief lengths of the jetty before hauling myself out of the water and drying myself with a towel. The trick had worked; I felt awake, alive, my senses shocked. A fish leapt, breaking the surface of the water with a splash before diving back under. The boat was out of sight now, but you could still hear the distant drone of its motor.

When I returned to the bach, Dave was sitting on the front steps.

"I was just in the area," he said. "So, I thought I'd come see how you were settling in."

"Oh, fine, fine."

It was vaguely creepy having him there; he was after all, still a stranger, an unknown quantity.

"Won't you come in?" I said politely, opening the door.

He rose to his feet, stomped into the bach.

"Oh, you've done wonders with the place," he said jokingly, looking around.

"Yes, it's not much to write home about, is it? Still, it's mine. Home for now."

"What part of the UK you from?"

"London."

"Ah, the big smoke. I've been to Blighty meself a couple of times. Didn't think much of the place. Better over here."

"Yes, I dare say."

"It's a bit odd though."

"I'm sorry?"

"It's odd you being out here. A woman alone and all that. Come all the way from London just to live in a tumbling-down old bach."

I didn't say anything.

"How's about that cuppa then?"

He plonked himself down on the old sofa, his legs, with their muddy brown boots on the ends of them, stretched out in front of him. He was enormous, like somebody had stuck a straw in a normal man and inflated him. Enormous and nosey.

"You got a husband then? Kids."

"A husband. No kids."

"He gonna be coming out here too then?"

I murmured something that sounded like, "no".

"You're a brave one."

"Brave or stupid. Milk? Sugar?"

"Milk and two thanks. I like it sweet."

I took him the cup of tea.

"Any biscuits? I love a good piece of shortbread, me."

"No, sorry."

"Ah."

He blew on his tea, then slurped at it noisily, while I merely sipped at mine.

"I used to have a wife," he said suddenly.

"Used to? I'm sorry."

"Don't be, she isn't dead. She ran off with a chef from Queenstown who was down here having a holiday. Bitch. She had everything a woman could want down here and what does she do but run off with the first ponce who comes her way spouting talk of 'fine dining'. Fickle, like all women, no offence intended."

I sipped my tea.

"She'd never have the guts to do what you're doing, just rough it in a shack on your own. That's admirable in a woman. Independent-minded."

I checked my watch.

"Well, I can see you're keen to be getting rid of me. Listen, I'll need some help on that fence early next week. I'll come by and get you. You got sturdy shoes?"

"Running shoes."

"Oh na, you'll need some decent boots. I'll bring you a pair of Trisha's old ones. She left a lot of stuff behind. You can have some of her old clothes too if you like."

"Oh no, that's quite alright."

"Yeah, I'll bring them anyway. Somebody might as well get some bloody use out of them."

Stomp, stomp, stomp and he was gone.

I had bought five exercise books with me from Britain, hopeful of filling them up. I should've brought the laptop after all, I'd probably have to buy one now, that'd be a trip to Queenstown. I wrote three romantic beginnings, but none of them held much promise so I tidied up the shack a little and then went outside to chop firewood, using an axe that I had found by the back door.

In the night, I awoke to the sound of heavy breathing outside my window. Terrified, faking bravery, I grabbed the torch that was on the floor beside me and headed outside, shining the light directly into a face which contained two small gleaming eyes. A black shape scurried off into the bush. Heart thudding, I returned inside. Sleep did not return until I took a Seconal.

*

"Possums," pronounced Dave, having been told of the incident when he arrived the following morning, with a truck full of fencing posts and wire.

The chemical taste of the Seconal was still in my mouth though I had cleaned my teeth twice to be rid of it. He handed me a rubbish bag full of old clothes.

"Get changed into something old," he said. "Those poncey clothes you wear aren't good for working on the farm."

I did as I was told.

"Jump in the ute," Dave said, when I emerged from the bedroom.   "You are good for it, aren't ya?"

"Oh yes," I said. "Yes I'm 'good for it' as you say."

In the ute, Dave pushed a pair of boots much like his own towards me and said, "Here, put these on. You need decent shoes out there, not those little city things you ponce around in. You need what real women wear."

His world, I suppose, was divided into "ponces" and "real people"; a dichotomy, black and white with not much room for shades of grey.

The ute jerked and shook along the gravel road. Window down, with the breeze in my face, it felt good. Wasn't this what I had dreamed of, back in Britain – wide open roads? Dave stank; old sweat and unwashed clothes – his odour assaulted my nostrils.

"My land stretches for miles," he said, when we arrived at the fence that needed repairing. "As far as the eye can see."

He gestured to the open fields where cattle and sheep grazed.

"I think I'll get you pulling out staples," he added and handed me a pair of fencing pliers.

It was tedious work, but not difficult. Dave was busy digging out old fence posts that had rotted. I wanted to keep up a conversation, but had no idea what I could talk to him about. What did we have in common, this rugged man and I? What could we talk about? Sheep and rugby? Dave said nothing, just gave the odd grunt and the occasional nod in my direction to indicate that he was happy with my work. At eleven, he boiled the billy and handed me a cup of tea and one of his beloved shortbreads.

"Gotta keep the tucker-box stacked," he said, patting his stomach.

When we returned to the bach, Jake was at the door. I froze. God, how had he tracked me down to this remote corner of the earth? He stared at me, scowling, as Dave and I approached.

"Found your itinerary on your laptop," he said. "I guessed your password. Your sister's name. You're lucky I haven't called the cops. *Yet.*"

I nodded slowly, feeling like an animal caught in a trap. He stood to one side of the doorway.

"Aren't you going to invite me in?"

"Do come in," I said icily and pushed open the door.

Both he and Dave followed me inside. Jake turned to Dave.

"And *who*, may I ask, are you?"

"I'm Dave. Lola's mate."

"*Lola?* Who the hell is Lola?"

Dave pointed at me. Jake sneered.

"Had a name change have we? Listen, *Harriet*, this whole escapade is completely juvenile. I don't know what you think you're trying to prove."

"I'm not trying to prove anything."

Jake held out his wedding finger.

"We're *married*, Harriet. Doesn't that even mean anything to you?"

"Who's Harriet?" interjected Dave.

"My wife!" snapped Jake.

I sighed heavily and lowered myself down onto the sofa.

"Listen, Jake. It's over between us. I'm a new person now. I won't say all of it was bad, but I grew to hate my old life, the life I had in London. I need a fresh start. It happens. People get tired of their old shackles and they want to start again somewhere new. Just let me go. Set me free."

He looked like I'd slapped him in the face.

"But what about *us*? What about the seven years we spent together? Don't they mean anything?"

"You heard the lady," said Dave. "It's over."

"You keep out of it buddy. This has nothing whatsoever to do with you."

"Forget me, Jake! Just go back to London and find a new woman. Work hard on Ada. Get famous. Dazzle the world."

"But I've flown all this way. I'm not returning without you."

"You're not returning with me."

His shoulders slumped, defeated.

"Fine."

He yanked off his wedding ring and threw it into my lap.

"You can have that hunk of metal back. I assume you don't want any of the possessions you left behind, either?"

"No, you can sell it all on eBay."

"Good. I'll do that. See ya later. Good fucking riddance."

He strode out of the shack, slamming the door behind him.

"Moody bugger, ain't he?" commented Dave. "You okay? Fancy a cuppa?"

I nodded.

*

David and I sit out on the front porch, drinking cups of tea. I am no longer Harriet May. I am the beginnings of Lola.

The Latest Lighthouse Keeper

The lighthouse went up for sale in November. Serena and her friend Joy had been taking their usual Sunday drive along the coast when Joy, seeing the "For Sale" sign, had pointed it out. Serena had been sceptical.

"But the isolation…" she had muttered, before Joy cut her off.

"It's perfect for you. You're always complaining that the real world encroaches on you and your so-called 'artistic vision'. You complain of Jehovah's witnesses coming to call, of friends popping round to visit, of ex-lovers showing up, pestering you, wondering if things could be taken up where they left off. This place could be your island, your sanctuary, your space apart. Granny would be proud that her money had been put to such good use."

Serena's grandmother had died that spring, kindly leaving her three hundred thousand dollars. The money had sat in a savings account for two months, gathering interest, while Serena decided what she wanted to do with it.

"It's probably outside my price range," said Serena.

"Don't ask and you won't know," replied Joy, jotting down the number on the For Sale sign.

They drove on, to Devon and their favourite café, Café Alf Resco, where they both had eggs benedict (Serena with a side of spinach) and a cappuccino, as was their Sunday tradition.

Back at Serena's, Joy dialled the number she had taken down and had a short conversation with the person on the other end of the line. When she hung up, she had a smile on her face.

"That was the owner," she said. "There's no agent involved – it's a private sale. A hundred and eighty grand. A bargain. With the leftover money you could put in a shower and a kitchen unit. You'll be set for life. I can see you growing old up there, maybe with a couple of cats for company, or a cocker spaniel…"

"I can see me growing crazy up there," retorted Serena.

"I can see you producing masterpieces up there; your vision finely honed, your hearing attuned to the cries of the gulls, who sound at times almost like angels shrieking; your mind a television set, receiving and transmitting the finest paintings..."

"I'd be insane within five minutes. Painting murals on the walls with my own blood and feces. Turning into a haggard old witch with matted hair and long twisting fingernails that haven't been trimmed in over a decade, cackling to myself and cursing like Caliban. A curmudgeonly misanthrope, mind warped."

"Well, give it a try. If it gets too much for you, you can always sell up and come back down to live amongst the earthlings."

"I'll think about it."

"Great. See you later. Gotta go meet Jake at Zilli's."

Joy gave Serena a peck on the cheek and dashed out the door, pulling on her red wool overcoat.

That night Serena dreamt of the lighthouse. It was all lit up, not just with the one bulb, but with a number of lights, roughly twenty. They created a circle of light that beamed out across the ocean. Serena stood in the centre of the circle, wearing a long white dress, like a wedding gown, with a vast lacy train that trailed out behind her. In her hands she clutched a bouquet of dark red roses that were the colour of Joy's overcoat. There were two gulls inside the circle of light with her; they swooped and dived and tried to attack her face, like something out of Hitchcock's *The Birds.* Reaching out with both hands, she caught first one bird and then the other, like Miyagi Sensei catching flies with chopsticks in *The Karate Kid.* She put a thumb beneath each bird's neck and four fingers on the opposite side and with two swift movements, snapped. Two heads hung crooked, at an angle. She threw one bird to the floor. From the other she plucked all the feathers, and poked them into her hair, which was tightly curled at the back of her head in a chignon. Then the Great Broadcaster of Dreams changed the channel and she was in a grand hotel with many rooms, struggling to find the exit.

Serena, who believed in the power of dreams, took it as a sign that she was meant to purchase the lighthouse. She had lived most of her life this way, trusting in fate or God or the gods or the muses to send her signals about which road to take. She knew it sounded bonkers, but she wasn't that crazy; it's not like she thought God was talking to her through the TV set or through secret messages etched out in the marmite on her toast or anything like that. She didn't believe in horoscopes. It's just that, when it came to major decisions, she always looked for some signal from the heavens regarding what she should do. Joy was over the moon.

"I know you won't regret it," she said. "It'll be brilliant. I'm sure you'll sell loads at The Space."

The Space was the gallery where Serena exhibited the majority of her paintings, though she also had a number of clients who collected her work, seeing her potential, banking on the value of her work to increase. Joy called the current lighthouse owner on Serena's behalf and made an offer of one hundred and sixty grand. The owner said she'd think about it, and rung back half an hour later saying what about one hundred and seventy. Joy asked Serena and Serena said okay. "Woo-hoo," screeched Joy, when she hung up the phone. "You are now the proud owner of one lighthouse. Or you will be when everything's signed and sealed. I'll go out and get a bottle of champers to celebrate."

The deal went down. Serena had a kitchen unit and a shower fitted. The kitchen was tiny, just a sink and a microwave. She had everything she needed.

Serena moved into the lighthouse. Joy helped her shift, borrowing Jake's white van for the occasion. Serena didn't own much in the way of large objects; a pullout sofa that doubled as a bed, a fridge, an armchair, a TV set, although these four heavy items seemed difficult enough when they reached the winding staircase that spiralled up the centre of the lighthouse.

"It's lucky you don't have a real bed," joked Joy. "You'd never get a double bed up these stairs."

They positioned the furniture, the fridge, the TV and then stood staring out of the windows for a while, gazing across the flat, glassy surface of the ocean.

"Well," said Joy eventually. "I'll leave you to get on with your work. Give me a call next week and let me know how you're getting on."

When Joy had left, Serena stood for a while in the centre of the lighthouse, imagining herself surrounded by the circle of light she had seen in her dream. Then she squeezed some colours onto a palette, dipped her brush into the paint and made a small mess on a formerly blank canvas. Over the course of that afternoon, it became a face, a man's face, probably the ugly mug of Gerald, whom she had dated six months ago, or if not him then Richard who had pre-dated Gerald and if not Richard then Gary who had pre-dated Richard. There was a string of them, a long line. It was any man's face. You could project yourself onto it. When the face, the any-face, was finished, Serena poured herself a glass of red wine and sat in her single armchair and looked out of the window at the far horizon. A crow was perched on the sill, looking in at her with its sad beady eyes. Such an anomaly, a crow at the seaside. This was a place for white-feathered gulls, screeching and fighting amongst themselves, not crows who belonged inland, bouncing across pasture, emitting the odd squawk. She went to the window to shoo it away, but it didn't budge when she waved her arms at it and bashed on the glass, it just sat there stubbornly, as if its claws had been stuck to the sill with glue. She poured herself another wine and ignored the crow, switching on the television, watching the news.

After the news she thought about calling her sister, Rachel, who had been committed to the Maudsley the previous year. Rachel had also been left three hundred thousand dollars by their wealthy grandmother – it was being held in an account for her until such time as she was deemed fit to control her own finances. It wasn't Rachel's first bout of mental illness – it was her third; major depression in her late teens, which had included a bout of self-harming; depression again in her mid-twenties, and then this, a complete nervous breakdown when she was in her early thirties. The doctors were saying she had bipolar disorder and that she had been manic when they found her, wandering deluded around Victoria Station, unable to find her way home to her flat in Peckham, her fragmenting mind confused by the signs and the crowds and the announcements, stopping at random

163

intervals to ask strangers if they could take her home. Frightening people. Eventually she had collapsed outside Starbucks and been taken in an ambulance to St Thomas's Hospital, where they had discharged her into the care of the Maudsley, where they had decided she was too ill to be an outpatient and kept her inside. She didn't seem to mind it there. She said the nurses were very nice, that they handled her with kid gloves. She said they walked on egg shells around her.

Serena knew she didn't call Rachel as often as she should. She found the conversations awkward; she didn't like to think of her sister as sick; she preferred to think of her as she had been when she was a kid, full of beans, bursting with life, starring as lightning in the school play, racing around amongst the clouds, the cumulus and cirrus and cumulonimbus, emitting zapping noises, making sandcastles at the beach and decorating them prettily with shells and seaweed, weaving daisy chains, playing with Mutt, the family dog. It pained her to think of Rachel sitting in some day room somewhere, with the other loonies. (Serena knew she shouldn't think of them that way, but she couldn't help it.) But what could she do to help? She felt powerless, as if her hands, the hands that she wanted to extend, had been cut off, severed. She supposed she could have moved to London, to be nearer her sister, but she liked Devon. It was her home, it was where they had grown up and she didn't want to leave. Rents were cheaper than in London, a gigantic sprawl of a city that could chew up artists and spit them out. Sure, those who scaled the giddy heights became world-famous millionaires like Tracey Emin and Damien Hirst, but what about the other poor buggers that were left starving in the gutter, never given a look-in? Or those who had to work at office jobs they despised just to support themselves and so had no time for their art, their dreams left lying scattered by the wayside. Devon was kinder, softer. It had fewer fangs and claws. Its eyes did not move shiftily from side to side, wondering how best to take advantage of you. London was always trying to get the upper hand. Dog devoured dog. Big fish ate the smaller. All the clichés. No, the phone calls to Rachel were all she could manage.

Rachel picked up after the first ring. She always did. She probably had little else to do, poor thing, other than sit around waiting for the telephone.

"Hello?"

"Hi, it's Serena."

"Oh hey, how's it going?"

"Yeah, not bad. How are you getting along in there?"

"Oh alright. They say I can go home in two weeks time. I am officially *fixed*. I'll still be an outpatient though; they'll send round nurses once a day to check up on me. Not allowed to go back to work yet and when I do go back it will have to be on a part-time basis at first – just ten hours a week. If that goes well then I can ramp it up, slowly, over time."

Rachel worked in administration at Playboy. They gave her free bunny ears and T-shirts and bags with the Playboy logo printed on them and also a free subscription to Sky – perfect for Rachel who was addicted to watching nature programmes on telly, who liked nothing better than witnessing a great white shark or lion or eagle devour its prey.

"Hey, that's great news Rachel. How are you feeling about going back to the flat?"

Leading up to the manic/fragmented episode, Rachel had been under the illusion that there were demons in her flat, springing up from behind the sofa, leaping out at her from the mirror when she checked out her own reflection, lurking in the veggie drawer of the fridge.

"Actually," said Rachel. "Not that great, I have a lot of doubts about it. What if those demons are still there? What if it was them that drove me crazy?"

"Well…"

"I considered going to Mum and Dad's but the thought of going back home at the age of thirty-three makes me depressed. I don't want to be a cripple, sponging off my parents forever, unable to stand on my own two feet."

Serena knew she should offer to have Rachel in the lighthouse – it was the thing to do, the kind thing, the good thing, the sisterly thing; it was what she would want Rachel to do for her, if the boot should ever be on the other foot. But could she, Serena, hack it? Rachel, off on paid sick leave, would be hanging around all day, they might fight, get on each other's nerves. She had a vision of Rachel, falling like a boulder from the sky and landing splat in the middle of the lighthouse floor. She would make a sizeable dent. Serena's better nature won out over her doubts.

"Well," she said. "You can come and stay with me for a bit. I just bought a lighthouse with the money Nana left me. You'd have to sleep on the pullout sofa with me; I don't think I could get another bed up here. Space is pretty tight."

Serena had expected Rachel to jump at the chance, but there was a pause, a silence.

"Mmmm," said Rachel. "What if we fight? What if we get on each other's nerves?"

"We'll be alright. We managed it when we were kids didn't we – I don't remember us scrapping too much."

"Alright then. If it doesn't work out I can go back to my flat and attempt to wrestle those demons! I'll just have to make sure there's an outpatient team at Devon that can come and visit me."

"Do you want me to come pick you up, or do you think you can find your way here?"

"No, I can find my way. Where is it?"

Serena gave Rachel instructions as to how to find the lighthouse.

"Alright then," said Rachel, eventually. "See you in two weeks time."

"Yes, see you then."

Over the following two weeks, Serena didn't speak to another living soul. She had her routine, every day the same, rising at seven am for an hour of yoga; breakfast – coffee and muesli at eight; then settling into paint through to midday when she would break and have two eggs on toast, go out for a walk along the shore, come back and do another hour of yoga, then back to work through till five pm, when she would knock off and have a glass of wine. She had taken up yoga five years ago when experiencing a mild depression of her own; it kept her supple, stopped her from seizing up. The two weeks was a very productive period, the period of faces, men's faces, faces with moustaches, faces with big sad puppy-dog eyes, faces with large, bulbous noses with the red veins sticking out thereupon. They sat stacked up against the wall like over-sized playing cards. They kept her company at night, kept her own demons out.

The raven never seemed to leave, whenever she looked up it was perched in the same old spot, and yet it must fly away sometimes, to eat. It peered in at her knowingly. It had secrets hidden amongst its glossy black feathers.

Rachel arrived when she was doing her afternoon yoga. She had been holding a downward dog for over a minute and her shoulders were beginning to ache when she heard the footsteps coming up the stairs, then a friendly 'yoo-hoo'. She rose and turned. There was Rachel, looking a little pudgier than when she had last seen her, over a year ago, but other than that, the same old Rach, blonde hair cut short like Jean Seberg in *Breathless*, green eyes, cat's eyes. The two of them looked nothing alike; Serena had long, wavy brown hair, down to her shoulders and dark chocolate-coloured eyes. People said she looked a bit like a skinny Nigella Lawson. Serena was flattered by this comparison to the domestic goddess but would laugh and toss her hair and shrug it off.

"Oh don't be silly," she would say. "Nigella's *gorgeous*. I look like something the cat dragged in."

"Don't let me interrupt your yoga," said Rachel. "I'll just plonk my things then go out for a bit of an explore."

She deposited her bright pink suitcase on the floor beside the pull-out sofa. Serena listened to her heavy tread going back down the stairs, then watched through the lighthouse window as Rachel walked along the seashore, stopping occasionally to pick up a shell or a piece of driftwood and examine it thoroughly as if the secret cure to her illness lay etched thereupon.

When Rachel was out of sight, Serena zipped open Rachel's suitcase and went through it, looking for razorblades or knives in case her sister had lapsed back into self-harming. Nothing. Serena removed the two sharp knives she herself owned from the kitchen drawer and stashed them underneath her mattress. She wasn't taking any chances. She set to work on her latest face, which looked a little like her father; bushy beard and eyebrows and deep set bright blue eyes. A pair of psychiatric nurses showed up, and – annoyed that Rachel wasn't there – left medication with Serena for Rachel to take.

Rachel was gone for hours. When she returned she was flushed and breathless.

"God, it's gorgeous out here! What have I been doing in stinky old London all these years? Took it for granted when I was growing up, but now I'm seeing it with new eyes. Isn't it weird how your perspective on things changes?"

Since leaving home at sixteen, Rachel had not been back to Devon. At Easter and Christmas, which Serena always spent with her parents, there was an empty chair at the dining room table where Rachel should have been. At first, Serena had felt slighted by her sister's absence, but as time went by she had gotten used to it. Rachel was just Rachel; eccentric, slightly crazy, keen to prove her independence, not wanting to lean on anybody else. Until she became so sick that she was forced to.

"You ready for dinner?" asked Serena. "I could make us some pasta or else we could go out to some place cheap."

"Pasta's fine. Happy to eat here. Great views, by the way."

"Cool, let's do that then."

Serena was sleeping deeply and not dreaming when a smashing sound rocked her awake. She sat bolt upright in bed to see, in the dim moonlight, her sister kicking and tearing at one of her canvases. Two destroyed works had been pushed off to the side.

"Rachel!"

Serena jumped out of bed and tried to restrain Rachel, who then turned the force of her fury from the painting to her sister, hammering blows down upon her head.

"CUT IT OUT!"

Serena grabbed Rachel's right arm and twisted it up behind her back. Rachel squirmed and tried to break free but could not.

"Okay, okay. I give in."

Rachel went suddenly floppy like a rag doll that has had all the stuffing taken out of it.

"What the hell do you think you're playing at? Those paintings could have sold for a grand each. My career's starting to take off, Rachel; the work that I produce is actually worth something these days. I know you've been unwell, but really."

168

"Sorry, I'm sorry. I was sleep-walking. Sleep-smashing. I only woke up when you grabbed me."

Serene eyed her sister sceptically, but let go of her arm. Rachel had always been a very proficient liar.

"I can't have you here if you're going to be destructive," she said. "I've got a life to live too. I can't have you stampeding through like a, like a...raging bull."

"Sorry. Hell, how many times do I have to apologise. I was out of my head. I didn't know what I was doing."

Rachel walked to the armchair and slouched down into it, long limbs sprawled every which way, like a drunk spider.

"If it happens again, you're out of here."

"Okay."

Serena went back to bed, but sleep eluded her. She lay awake in the darkness, listening to the deep breathing of her sister, who had fallen asleep in the armchair – in, out, in, out, steady like a heartbeat.

The lighthouse had no curtains. When dawn broke, Serena, the light hurting her tired eyes, rose and prepared a plunger full of coffee. Rachel slept on. The crow was still there; its claws and beak looked a brighter shade of orange than usual, as if they had been painted. It was probably just an illusion; the effects of having got too little sleep. Serena picked up the pieces of her destroyed paintings; surveying the damage. Terrible, all that effort laid to waste. Each painting had taken at least a week; she had laboured over each eyelash, each freckle, each skin tone. Impossible to reproduce exactly. She would just have to throw them out and start again. At least Rachel hadn't destroyed them all; there were still a number of works left intact. She would call up Joy and get her to come in her car and take them down to The Space where they would be safe from her destructive sister.

Joy came by at eleven, when Rachel had gone out for another of her seaside walks. Serena did not mention her sister or the damage that had been done. It felt too raw; a fresh wound. To speak of it would be to tear the wound open further, to poke a skewer inside and twist it around. Joy jabbered away about Jake, whom she had been dating for six months now. They'd had a bit of a tiff apparently, something about Jake accusing Joy of flirting with other men when she thought he wasn't looking.

"You know me," said Joy. "I'm just friendly, the chatty type. I'm like that with everyone; men, women, animals, it's all the same. It's just the way I am. I told Jake that if he had such a problem with it then he could just push off. So he did. Roared off in his beamer. Probably went home and watched porn on Sky."

Isaac at The Space accepted her work with welcoming arms.

"Brilliant," he said. "We've sold out of all your other pieces. Sales have really escalated since last year, when…you know."

He broke off, shuffled his feet.

"So, anyway," he continued brightly. "I'll give you a buzz if any of them sell. That reminds me, I've got a cheque for you too."

He wandered off to a spare room out the back and came back with a cheque for three thousand pounds.

"That should keep you going for a bit. Well done, Serena. And thanks for dropping these new works in. You girls just off for a coffee or something are you? Wouldn't mind joining you if you are."

Serena winced. He always did that, called her a girl. His subtle way of letting her know her place. Or maybe he didn't mean anything by it. People were always accusing her of being over-sensitive.

"Actually, we'd better get back. Got my sister staying; she hasn't been too well. You heard I bought a lighthouse, Isaac?"

Isaac just stared at her, nodding slowly, as if attempting to digest some indigestible piece of information. He probably thought she was bonkers living in a lighthouse on her own, secluded, tucked away. Joy linked her arm through Serena's and led her away, waving her fingers at Isaac. The bangles on her arm tinkled and jangled.

"I'm so proud of you," said Joy, when they were in the car and heading back down the coast. "You've come such a long way since last year and the Maudsley. Everybody always says how well you're doing. But what was that stuff about your sister?"

Serena froze.

"I'd better get home," was all she said. "Can you take me home to the lighthouse?"

"Serena, you don't have a sister. You haven't stopped taking your medication, have you?"

"Can you take me home?" asked Serena. "I'm trying to get back home."

Joy drove Serena back to the lighthouse in silence. Serena ascended the stairs. The crow, that she had thought such a permanent fixture, had gone, flown away. The sill seemed bare without it; too white, too bright. The faces that she had painted stared back at her, none of them smiling, all of them fierce. The smashed canvases lay in a heap in the corner. Tomorrow, she would take the pieces outside and light a fire, laugh as the smoke spiralled heavenwards, the flames leaping upwards, the tongues of hell.

The Levitator

On his seventeenth birthday, my brother Victor demonstrated his newfound ability to levitate. He waited until after the birthday dinner, the roast pork with its crisp crackling and apple sauce, the spuds and the fresh green peas that my mother had shelled herself, had been consumed. He waited until after the pavlova, neatly decorated with whipped cream and strawberries, had been sliced and devoured. He waited. When the family, satiated, pushed back their chairs and sat together in silence, he cleared his throat and made his announcement.

"I've taught myself how to levitate," he said. "I can't get up all that high yet, but I'm doing my best, I get a little higher every time. Last night I rose two feet off the floor. It was brilliant. My only concern was that there was nobody there to witness my feats. So, tonight, for the benefit of you all, I would like to demonstrate this new art I have mastered."

My cynical father scoffed.

"What do you think you are?" he asked. "Some kind of flying saint?"

"No, no," said Victor. "I'm just your average guy. The same old Victor I've always been. Just a Victor with a newly discovered talent. If you can call it that."

"Go on, then," said Dad. "Prove you can do it, prove that you can fly."

"I never said I could *fly*," protested Victor. "I just said I could levitate."

"Go on then, levitate."

"Alright, I shall."

Victor rose up from his chair and sat cross-legged in the middle of the living room floor. He closed his eyes and rested one hand on each knee. A strange buzzing sound, like that of a honey-bee swarming round the hive, came forth from his lips. Dad sniggered and Mum made a shushing sound. Slowly, inch by inch, Victor began to rise up off the floor. Dad's sniggers were silenced. The buzzing sound continued. When Victor reached a height of two feet, he outstretched his arms and hovered in space for two or three minutes before bringing his arms back in and slowly, steadily, descending to the floor in a calm, controlled manner. He seemed to lose his touch a little at the last instant, losing control and hitting the ground with a thud. He opened up his eyes.

"Well?" he asked. "What do you think?"

I couldn't speak for the rest of the family, but I was flabbergasted. How had he done it? Were there hidden wires, strings? Had he made some kind of Faustian pact with the devil in exchange for supernatural powers? Had he mastered the force of gravity? I had a contradictory relationship to his secret – I both wanted and didn't want to know.

Dad didn't hold back.

"How did you do it?" he asked.

"Force of will," replied Victor. "Mind over matter. Believe you can and you will. It's only our disbelief that holds us earth-bound."

Dad sneered.

"Check *him* out," he said. "*It's only our disbelief that holds us earth-bound*. What crummy books have you been reading?"

Victor looked upset. "I knew I should have made sure you were out. You're always so mean, Dad. You always have to piss on my parade."

"It's just that I've got my feet on the ground, Victor. Which is more than I can say for you."

A major point of contention between Victor and my father was Victor's decision to attend Fine Arts School when the university year started. Dad was a maths teacher, a man of logic. He thought that Victor's decision to attend arts school, majoring in sculpture, was frivolous, light, frothy. He thought that no good would come of it.

"You'd better practise saying 'Would you like fries with that?'" Dad had said, when Victor announced his decision to become a sculptor, "Because that's what you're going to spend your days repeating."

Mum was a teacher too, Chemistry, but she was a little more encouraging of Victor and his chosen pursuits.

"You just do whatever you think will make you happy," she'd said, and patted him, somewhat patronisingly, on the head.

Victor had turned our garden shed into a studio, in which he chipped and carved and sanded and buffed. His favourite stone was serpentine, with its lovely green, red, yellow and white lines running though it. He made lamp-holders, paper-weights, ash-trays. He sculpted faces, women's faces, mostly. Often, when I went out into the shed to visit him, I would find him lovingly running his hands over female eyes, lips, noses. Victor had never had a girlfriend – these stone women, severed at the neck, were his substitute.

*

In two years time I would have to make the decision that Victor was now facing; what to study at university. I had settled upon IT – I liked computers and had taught myself how to program at an early age. IT would provide a steady income and career opportunities. IT could take you places. I also liked to paint, but I wasn't as stubborn, or determined, or perhaps downright foolish as Victor, to believe that I could make a career out of it. For me, painting was just a hobby, a way to pass the time. Like Victor, I didn't have too many friends; ours was an odd family. We lacked social skills. We said the wrong things at the wrong times. We all had the habit of putting our foot in it. I was the worst of the lot; whenever I opened my mouth, somebody somewhere took offence. It was as if I had been raised by wolves. My speech came out as a howl.

Victor fared a little better. At least you could hold a conversation with him. I wasn't sure what the other kids would make of his ability to levitate, but I hoped he wouldn't be foolish enough to demonstrate his powers in front of them. Kids didn't like anybody who was Different (most definitely with a capital "D"). Kids liked conformity. But Victor liked attention; his ego needed it. He didn't walk the same or talk the same as anybody else. If he had a new skill, he was likely to flaunt it.

It was no great surprise then, to see him, the following day, on the bottom field, impressing a small crowd of onlookers with his abilities. He hovered in the air, while the other kids stood in a semi-circle around him. He was higher than he had been before, maybe three or four feet. Mouths gaped. A large boy called Lance tried to grab at Victor's legs and yank him down, but Victor rose up higher, out of reach. I was watching from a distance, standing outside the gymnasium, half-hidden behind an old, gnarled, oak tree. I knew that what Victor was doing was dangerous; kids like Lance, who was nearly twice my brother's size, could get jealous and turn nasty. I wished that Victor had kept it in the family, rather than taking it outside. The world was vicious and cruel. It could eat my levitating brother alive.

Victor made it through that day in one piece. There was mockery, a kid sitting on a bench outside the assembly hall, cross-legged, humming, saying *Look at me, look at me, I'm Victor the Great*. There were a couple of kids standing outside the school gate at 3.15, smoking and saying, "That Victor, he's such a show-off". General anti-Victor sentiment. That evening, I entered the room that Victor and I shared. He was hovering above his bed, eyes closed, buzzing. He had no idea that I was in the room with him. As I silently watched, he moved first to the left and then to the right. Sideways movement was a new addition to his repertoire. Learning to fly. Left, right, left. I cleared my throat and he opened his eyes and dropped back down to the bed, stretched himself out, hands behind his head, pleased with himself, self-satisfied.

"What's up, Champ?"

I hated it when he called me "champ", but I didn't say anything. I sat down on the end of the bed.

"It's the levitating, Vic. I don't think you should do it in front of the other kids."

"They love it. Best show they've seen in ages."

"They'll make you pay. In some way or other."

"Don't be silly. They can't hurt me. I can just rise up high, where they can't get me."

"They have their ways and means, Vic."

"Listen to you! You sound like a paranoid freak! You've always been such a scaredy-cat."

It was true; I was nervous, anxious, the type to thrash about and drown in a puddle of water. Victor was calm, smooth. Nothing ruffled his feathers. He was blasé – about everything. I thought his nonchalance would be his undoing.

That Wednesday, he didn't come home from school. At dinnertime, Mum expressed her concern.

"Where's your brother?"

"Dunno. Haven't seen him. At a friend's house?"

"Victor has friends?"

"Well, actually, no…"

Victor was too arrogant, too grand, to build true friendships with other people. His superior ways put the other kids off.

"If he's not home in an hour or so, you and your father will have to go out looking. Have you tried his mobile?"

"No, I'll do it now."

I rang his number.

"Switched off," I reported and helped myself to another spoonful of shepherd's pie.

*

After dinner, Dad and I jumped in the SUV to which he'd treated himself last Christmas and headed out. It was summer and still light. The streetlamps cast elongated shadows upon the pavement. The school was the first place we checked; he was nowhere to be found. For two hours we cruised the neighbourhood, stopping intermittently, jumping out of the SUV and calling Vic's name. No reply.

"What a bloody idiot," said Dad. "Your mother's worried out of her mind. Worried sick."

Arriving home, we found that Mum had hit the gin. She was sitting at the kitchen table with a bottle and a glass beside her, half cut. A couple of squeezed lemons sat on the table, next to the bottle.

"Didsha findim?" she slurred.

"Oh, Abigail!" said Dad. "You didn't have to take to the drink. It's not *that* bad. He'll come home. When he gets hungry enough."

But he wasn't home at eight o'clock and he wasn't home at nine o'clock either. He wasn't home by midnight, when the old grandfather clock that sat in the hallway chimed the melancholy hour, its hands together as if in prayer.

That night I slept uneasily, fitfully, tossing and turning, waking every hour and looking across at the empty bed on the other side of the room, pulling back the curtain and gazing out through the window at the lamp-lit street. Victor was out there somewhere. God only knew what had happened to him; like Piggy in *Lord of*

176

the Flies, he could've been taken out to the beach, and killed by a falling boulder, dropped down from the cliff above, he could be being held hostage in somebody's basement, tied up with a gag shoved in his mouth, he could be roped to some railroad tracks somewhere, waiting, with a knot of fear in his stomach, for the oncoming train. Once, in the night, I thought I heard him come in through the door, but it was only the wind, which had sprung up and was rattling a window which had not been put back properly on its latch.

At school, I checked the faces of the other kids to see if any of them looked guilty, responsible for my brother's disappearance. Nobody gave anything away; they all looked just as they always had – bored, restless, inattentive. No clues. I asked around at lunchtime – *anybody seen Victor since after school yesterday?* Nothing. He was as good as dead. I desperately hoped that he wasn't. He was somebody to talk and laugh and bicker with. He was *there*. Or he had been until now. Now he was elsewhere. Vamoosed. I had a strange feeling in my gut, a feeling like he wasn't coming back in a hurry.

No Victor, all that week, no Victor. I heard Mum crying through the wall at night and Dad comforting her, *shush, love, shush, he'll come home in his own good time.* I heard rumours, reports, circulating round the school like the wind rustling in dry leaves. Victor had been spotted in central London, levitating in Trafalgar Square, level with the head of one of the lions. He'd been seen in Canterbury, hovering inside the Cathedral, up high, near the ceiling. There had been a sighting at Cambridge, in one of the dining halls, Victor, suspended before one of the paintings that hung on the walls. Victor was a busy guy. He got around. Somebody showed me photographic proof of Victor levitating in Brewer Street, outside the Glasshouse Stores, but it looked to me like something that had been doctored in Photoshop. Dad filed a missing persons report. The cops were alerted to his absence. And at night, the empty bed opposite mine. Nothing where there should've been something.

It was a month before he returned, a month that seemed to drag by, shuffling its feet and sniffling pitifully, each day stretching out into an eternity. We were seated in the living room, watching *Wheel of Fortune* on the telly, when he waltzed in, as if he had been gone for only an hour or two. His hair was matted and he had grown a beard. He wore the same clothes as on the day of his disappearance; he reeked. His fingernails were long, with dirt encrusted under them. He said nothing, just plonked himself down in one of the armchairs and fixed his blank gaze on the TV. It was my mother who broke the silence.

"Well, Victor," she said. "Where have you been?"

He shrugged.

"Out and about," he said. "Taking care of business."

He crossed his legs upon the footstool in front of his chair, leant back with his hands beside his head. The same old Victor. Giving nothing away.

"Victor," scolded Mum. "That's not good enough. You've been gone for a month. We've been worried sick. Now, we need to know where you've been."

"What is this? The Spanish Inquisition?"

"We're your family. I think you're failing to comprehend the trouble that other people have gone to on your behalf."

"I've been in the desert, fasting, tempted by the devil."

"Stop being a smart-arse."

"You don't need to know where I've been. What you don't know won't hurt you."

He was infuriatingly smug. Showing off, he rose, two feet up off his arm-chair and hung suspended in mid-air. Annoyed with Victor, I took myself off to our room, and continued work on a labyrinth I had been programming for the last six months. Victor came in half an hour later and lay supine on the bed.

"How've you been, Champ?" he asked.

I ignored him. I was furious with him for causing all of us, but especially my mother, so much grief.

"Fine," he said, "Be that way then."

He picked up a copy of *War and Peace* from where it lay beside his bed and started reading.

After returning from his time in the wilderness, my brother was different, changed. He seemed distant, far away, not all there in some fundamental way, as if part of him had broken off and drifted out to sea. His grades started slipping; I found a paper beside his bed that had been marked "F". The Victor of old had never got anything less than an "A". Sometimes, during dinner, he would pause with his fork halfway to his mouth and stare into space like somebody who had been freshly lobotomised. Before he'd gone away we used to have conversations long into the night, him in his bed, me in mine, yakking about life, the universe and everything. Now there was nothing but silence between us. Silence and space.

Vic's spaciness began to attract attention; he wandered around in a kind of trance, waving his right hand in a circle as if commanding a host of invisible spirits, occasionally rising a foot or so up off the ground and put-putting along, like a thing motorised. The teachers began to complain about him levitating in class; they said it distracted the other students. They said that he buzzed too loud. There were phone-calls home to Mum. I overheard her saying that Victor had become unmanageable, beyond her control.

"He's not the boy he used to be," she said. "I don't even know my own son anymore."

She was drinking every night now, three or four gins before Dad got home from work, cooking the dinner half sozzled, often burning our evening meal.

I wasn't there when the first stone was thrown. I heard about it from one of the other kids, Kylie, as I was walking home along the Railway Reserve that ran the length of our town. The long golden grass reached almost to my waist.

"Hey," she said, puffing on a cigarette. "I heard they got your brother down on the bottom field and they're pelting him with stones. You'd better go check it out and make sure he's okay."

A fist clenched in my stomach. I was being cast in the role of Vic's rescuer; I wasn't sure I was up to it. How could I, a puny fifteen-year-old, possibly ward off a whole army of attackers? Still, I was his sister, I had to do something. I couldn't just leave him to his fate. I put my shoulders back, held my head up high and walked back the way I had come, to the school and down towards the field.

They had him surrounded. Fifteen or twenty kids his own age. They were chanting, *Victor the leper, we are gonna getcha*, over and over, as if on loop tape. They had bucketfuls of rocks that they'd collected from somewhere, probably from the stream that ran along the edge of the school. Stones whizzed through the air, hitting home, striking their target. One hit Vic on the head and cut his forehead open. Blood pissed down into his eyes.

"Come on Victor the Great," yelled somebody. "Let's see you levitate now."

"Not so bloody great now, are you?" shouted somebody else. "Now you're just like the rest of us!"

I could see Vic trying to levitate, there was a certain look he got in his eye, a glazed look, but determined at the same time. He rose a couple of inches up off the ground then fell back down again, weakly. They were sucking his energy, his special powers. It wasn't just the rocks that were doing it, it was the taunts as well. What could I do? How could I save him without becoming a target myself? I hung back, trying to think up a course of action. Another rock flew and hit Vic in the head, right in the place where the first stone had struck. He staggered backwards, his arms up to protect himself. Rocks flew into his stomach and legs.

"Come on, fly boy, *fly!*"

That was Lance, who had probably master-minded the whole sordid thing. Vic fell to the ground and curled up in the foetal position. I took out my mobile, dialled 999 and asked for the cops.

Lance grabbed Victor by the legs.

"Come on," he said. "Let's take him down to the river."

A couple of kids took hold of Vic's arms and hoisted him up into the air. Vic was too far gone to protest.

"Hey," I said. "Hey, that's my brother, let him go."

But nobody took any notice of me. I was just some dumb fifth-form girl, waving her arms about and squealing. I followed them down to the river, which seemed to me to be flowing more swiftly than it ever had before. I kicked at Lance, trying to trip him up, but he ignored me, as if I wasn't even there. Lance was a big bloke, burly, half my size again. It was like trying to attack a monolith. Lance didn't give the other boys instructions; they all seemed to know what to do. They took my squirming brother to the river and held him under until he stopped breathing. I saw the bubbles rise, then fail to rise. I was as helpless as if both my hands had been severed, cut off at the wrist. I vomited into the grass at my feet.

The cops arrived too late. Victor wasn't breathing and the murderers had split. An ambulance was called and I went home with the cops. Mum was beside herself; she reached for the gin, but Dad put the bottle out of her reach, helped her into a hot bath and then into bed. A hole gaped in the centre of my chest, a hole where Victor used to be. I went out to the garden shed, ran my hands over the faces, Victor's faces, then gathered up his sculptures and shifted them all into one corner, making room for my own blank canvasses.

The Rewind Button

There were days when all Roger Burton's bad decisions came back to haunt him, buzzing round his head like tortured flies and on these days he left work early, mumbling some excuse to his boss, and went home to have a lie-down. He would lie in the darkness of his bedroom, a wet flannel over his eyes, and recall all the things he had done wrong in his life. There was that beat-up Holden he wasted good money on back in 1987, the damned thing clapped out after only two weeks; there was the decision to follow his parents' advice and study law, rather than following his dreams, his heart, and becoming a painter. The result had been years of monotony, with layers of resentment building up like sediment in his chest. Then there was his marriage; turbulent at best, at worse, downright abusive, with his wife coming home from work and venting her frustrations at him on a daily basis. He should've married Celia, his childhood sweetheart, the girl next door, the girl who'd woven daisy chains for him in his childhood. He'd met Cynthia when she'd been performing a karaoke version of "Simply the Best" at a local bar. Cynthia was neuroses-addled, with a two millimetre long fuse – she could snap at any moment. As an adolescent she'd been a mental in-patient, plied with psychiatric medication and given electric shock treatment; they said it was major depression, but it could have been anything. Roger should've known better than to marry her – a woman with problems, a woman with issues, a woman, marriage to whom was bound to be problematic.

Roger discovered the rewind button quite by accident; well, of course, he had always known that it existed. It was its *functionality* he discovered by accident. The tape-recorder was a tatty old thing, battered and worn, salvaged from amongst his aunt's belongings after she'd died. He'd never used it; it had sat in the corner of the garage, gathering dust for over a decade. His work had been, of late, very stressful and – his CD player broken – he'd bought a relaxation tape to listen to. He took the tape downstairs to the garage, inserted it into the machine, rewound for two minutes, then hit "play". The years slipped away and he was back in Cynthia's apartment, perched on her sofa, clutching the tape-recorder, listening to the rattle of ice cubes as Cynthia prepared their drinks. In his pocket was a small velvet box that contained a diamond engagement ring – this was the night that he proposed. Cynthia came through into the living room with two drinks on a plastic tray.

"Here you are then," she said. "One G&T with a twist of lemon."

She sat down next to him on the sofa, knees together, a lady – her brow furrowed, as usual, as if she was watching a slightly disturbing movie on the television screen of her mind.

"So," she began. "You said you had something you wanted to ask me."

"Oh," said Roger. "Did I?"

"Yes, you certainly did."

"Well," Roger fumbled. "It was just about your job. Is everything going okay?"

Cynthia was a junior librarian at the local library.

"The boss is still being a bit of a bitch, lording it over me, but apart from that, everything's going okay. Why do you ask?"

"Oh, just wondering."

Roger leaned over and gave her a kiss. He took a few sips of his drink, then hit fast-rewind on the tape-recorder, rewinding a couple of minutes, back to where he'd come from. His life was now a CFZ – a Cynthia Free Zone. He stretched his arms out, expanding in the empty space, spinning on the spot, loving the sense of freedom, of aloneness. If only he could go back now to the moment when he'd decided to be the good obedient son and study law, he could choose a different path, could choose to follow his dreams, rather than being dictated to by somebody else's idea of a future.

Noting down the number on the tape-recorder's dial, he rewound for four minutes and hit "play". He wasn't in the right place, he was abseiling down a mountain, his university friend Jake a few feet above him. He remembered this moment; a few minutes later, one of Jake's crampons was to come loose and Jake was to fall five metres, hit his head on the rockface and be knocked unconscious. Finger on the button again – back a little further now, to an earlier time, a time that Roger recognised as the last week of high school, with everybody discussing what university they intended to attend and passing around garments for everybody else to sign, and girls wondering whether or not their relationships with their boyfriends could be sustained over long distance. Perfect. This was the week he'd sent away his Law School application – all he had to do was grow a bit of a backbone, stand up to his folks, and insist on going to Arts college. It felt so awkward to be in an adolescent body once again – the gangly limbs, the zits. After school, he went home to find his mother, a house-wife, pruning the dahlias.

"Ma," he said. "I've made a decision. I'm not going to law school. I'm going to become a painter – you know I've come top of my art class for the last five years running – I really think I could make a career of it."

"Oh Roger," said his mother. "Do you really want to live a life of poverty, destitution? Don't you want a steady income, share plans, a pension?"

Roger shrugged.

"No Mum. I know what that's like. It's not the life for me – mine is the life of freedom, of art. If I never make money, then I never make money. So be it. At least I'll live as I believe."

"Well, wait until your father gets home and discuss it with him."

"My mind has been made up. I won't change it for the world."

Roger's mother pursed her lips and frowned.

"I think you're making a big mistake," she said. "But then, it's your life and you can do as you please."

When the news was broken to Roger's father, he flipped his lid.

"An *artist*," he scoffed. "Don't be so ridiculous. Ponsing about in bars and cafes, having epiphanies. Pah! I didn't raise my son to be like that. I raised a man of the world, not some airy-fairy…"

Roger held up his hand for silence.

"It's my decision, Dad. There's nothing you can do or say that would make me change my mind."

Roger ascended the stairs to his room. Two sets of application forms sat on his desk – one for law school, one for arts college. He tore the law school papers into shreds, filled out the arts school application, pushed it into an envelope, stuck a stamp to the envelope, cycled to the nearest Post Office and pushed the envelope inside. Sealed his fate. Hit fast-forward on the tape-recorder and scooted forwards to the number he had recorded.

Clearly, as an artist, he'd been a roaring success. He found himself in a converted Soho loft, white walls hung with his own paintings and those of others. It was an open airy space, a large studio. In one corner was a king size bed upon which lounged not one, not two, but *three* naked, nubile females, sipping champagne. Roger too held a champagne glass. He took a long swig – the bubbles fizzed in his nose. He walked across to the bed and joined the three women. Life was good. He wasn't worried about the Holden – what did a few hundred quid matter to him now? He had everything he needed. A packet of cigarettes and a lighter sat on the dresser beside the bed. He reached out, withdrew a cigarette, lit it. Roger didn't notice the fleck of ash that flicked from the tip of his cigarette and landed on the top left hand corner of the mattress. So involved was he with his company that he did not notice the slow smouldering that was taking place; and when the mattress finally caught and burst into flame, it was too late for Roger Burton to escape, the three women trapped him, held him down on the bed; and he burned where he lay, the tape-recorder beside him buckling and melting.

Twins

I have two heads. I say "I", I mean we, me and my conjoined twin. She is Trinity, I am Stella. Between us we have two hearts, three lungs, two spines and two heads, as formerly mentioned. Currently, we are learning to drive. We are ever so co-ordinated. People are impressed. Trinity takes control of the wheel, the lights and the indicators, and I take control of the pedals. Off we go, *wheee*, whizzing round traffic islands, ducking and diving through the dirty streets of London, then on to the M4 to Bristol to visit Aunt Margaret. At birth, we had a one in thirty million chance of survival. We beat the odds, we pulled through, survivors. We love life; how grateful we are to be here, how thrilled; each day is a tiny little gift. We make the most of it, get on with it. Wallowing in self pity is not for us. We are battle-hardened. Our parents protected us; said no to the medical men who wanted to make lab specimens of us, poking and prodding and mauling, documenting, labelling, filing away. The world is obsessed by us. We have no desire to be a freak show, though we are one of course. In the street, people stare and take photographs, as if we are Beyonce or J-Lo or Madonna. We hate it. A normal life is what we crave; dignity, composure – heads held high. After all, we are not disabled, not technically. Mentally we are in fine working condition.

At school there has been some cruelty, but also compassion. *Nice girls, those Benson twins*, is what people say, and we *are* nice, we do unto others. Mockery is inevitable, it's typically short-lived and then one of our friends, Evelyn or Kylie or Diana will step in and tell the mocker to shut their fat face or they'll shut it for them. A good group of mates shelters us from storms that might otherwise blow our way. Academically, we excel, Trinity's the mathematical type, I'm more of the arty sort, into poetry and painting, though we're also careful not to try *too* hard in case the other kids get jealous and pick on us even more. Anything to try to blend in. Other people project emotions onto us – hate, fear, pity, love. That's their problem. We shuck it off, off it slides, *whoosh*, water off duck.

There are fights – we are not saints. We bicker in the morning about what clothes to wear; I'm very "street" – hoodies and baggy jeans worn down low with the knickers poking out the top and big chunky, brightly-coloured necklaces. Trinity's more conservative, into neatly pressed slacks and dressy shirts, a classy pearl necklace to top the outfit off. Our mother has told us that we must learn to compromise, to take turns; Trinity dressing us on Mondays, Wednesdays, Fridays and Sundays and me taking the other days, swapping the regime round the following week. We tried it, but we still bicker. There is sometimes conflict between us. *Omigod, I'm not wearing that. That's hideous. What do you think we are? A gangsta?* Or, *Wouldn't be caught dead in that in a month of Sundays. We look like a forty-four year old corporate exec.* People say that Trinity has the dominant personality, that she's very outgoing. – "Bubbly" is the word they use. – I exist primarily in an interior world, a landscape of words; I see everything through the lens of literature, I have been shaped by Keats and Yeats and Wordsworth, by Maurice and Maggie Gee, by Janet Frame and Jeanette Winterson. My mind produces snippets of sentences at random moments, fragments, ill-shaped pearls.

We arrive safely in Bristol. Aunt Margaret is in the kitchen, baking a lemon meringue pie, Trinity's favourite. She hums as she works, *hmmmm*, a pleasant sound like bees swarming around a hive. In the past, Aunt Margaret has been severely depressed, lying in the corridor, weeping and wailing for days on end. Now she takes anti-depressants and lives her life at a slow, manageable pace, just one steady footstep after the other, left, right, left, though she does have relapses, falls into crevasses of the mind. She does gardening and yoga. She's never been married and personally I think that loneliness is one of her big problems, rattling around in that big old house that her father left her when he died, all those empty rooms, too much time on her hands. She doesn't have to work; her father left her a wad of dough. Aunt Margaret is fragile; we pay her these visits to cheer her up. She loves us, throws her arms around us, smothers us with affection. She feels for our plight, people often do, but no, we are not to be pitied. Fate dealt us a certain hand; it could have been better, but it also could have been a whole lot worse. We are expert in making the best of things. We are practical girls. Two heads are better than one.

When she finishes baking the pie, we take Margaret out to the beach; the sea air is good for her, the gulls squawking overhead, their harsh cries piercing the mind. Margaret is our mother's younger sister; a hypersensitive, sickly child, she grew into a hypersensitive, sickly adult. Harsh blows were dealt her in her youth; a boyfriend of seven years upping and leaving her for a waitress from Hull, a miscarriage – life events that a more robust individual would have shrugged off in the course of time, events that were enough to cripple my aunt psychologically. She hobbles along her solitary road. She feels for us and we feel for her. A relationship based on mutual empathy. Margaret fancies a swim, so she tootles across to the shed, changes into her swimming costume and splashes about in the shallows, doing breaststroke and over-arm, a cap covered in rosettes on her head. She looks so happy, all her cares washed away in the water. Simple and free. You would not guess, to look at her, the darkness that lurks within. There is no darkness in the Benson girls! We are lights, shining, pure goodness; we beam golden rays into the world, as if, like Jesus, we have taken humanity's suffering onto ourselves and borne it with good grace, a skip in our step, a smile on our respective dials. Trinity cries sometimes, lamenting our plight; I never do. I am the more stoic of the pair, upright, solid. But neither of us is the type to fall down. We prop each other up.

Our parents have good careers; they are doctors – our father, a paediatrician; our mother, a GP. They are good providers. They helped us build up high self esteem, a buffer zone between ourselves and the world. My aunt's nerve endings are too raw, too exposed – she is uncovered. She walks naked. We will not break like my aunt has broken. Nothing will shatter. We are full of hopes and dreams for the future; Trinity wants to be a vet, I entertain notions of becoming a painter; one of us is going to have to compromise of course, unless she does three days as a vet and I paint for three days, which I suppose is feasible. Teenage *angst* is not for us; some of the other girls weep and wail and flail about, going on silly fad diets, and sobbing because the boy they slept with last Saturday won't call them;

complaining because they're no longer the most popular one in their little group of friends, no longer Number One. We're far more sensible than that. We have crushes, of course, like all girls, but we never let these develop into anything bigger – it would only lead to disappointment and pain. It would take a brave man to date one or both of us, and for the most past, the boys at our school can be divided into two categories; feeble, pale, pasty lads, with gangly limbs; or sports jocks who never leave the gymnasium. There are exceptions, of course. Henry, whom Serena fancies, is a well-built lad with a chunky physique and a maths whiz like her – they compete for top grades. Thomas, whom I have my eye on, hangs around the art room painting gloomy-looking pictures of bats and rats. One day we will secure ourselves one or two men – we will not be denied, we will get our share.

Both of us want to be married, but think of the problems; me shutting my eyes and humming to myself while Trinity is being "serviced". – But whose vagina is it anyway? (It belongs to both of us, of course.) – Trinity blotting out the grunts and groans of my gorgeous husband. Awful. Or both of us conscious and gasping with pleasure, each developing a crush on the other's husband, jealous fights and neither of us able to take ourselves off to the other room in a huff. And a baby, if one is born – who would it belong to? Tests could be done to determine the father, but we have only one womb, so technically it would belong to both of us.

Sometimes Trinity cries at night and I have to comfort her. My mind takes over both arms and I put them around her, tell her that she's safe and that it's going to be alright.

"But what will become of us?" she wails, though never, it should be noted, "Why did this have to happen to us?"

"We'll be alright," I say. "We're just *Different*. We'll make it through somehow."

It's up to me to be strong at these times. The boot, for some reason, is never on the other foot, it's never me howling and her comforting. She is the more delicate one. If it weren't for me, she could fall to bits, like Aunt Margaret. I am the string that binds the pieces of her together, the glue. Sometimes she cries and won't stop crying. It's terrible, it goes on for hours, a caterwaul; and then suddenly she'll burst out laughing, her sobs easing off. She'll mock herself then; imitate her own crying, as a way of making light of the situation, having a laugh. I clown around too, to cheer her up. I say things like *Hey Trinity, maybe we were not born, but were <u>hatched</u>, our mother raped by a swan, like Leda. We came from an egg.* And she'll giggle. The dark clouds leave; the sun comes out. Everything shines.

We have two heads. Hers is blonde, mine brunette. We can nod them in unison, or one at a time. We can turn our heads in opposite directions, away from each other, but we cannot spin to face one another, we are too close together, there is no room. We are a spectacle. We are spectacular. We are special cases. Sometimes we sing, in the shower, or around the house.

"Voices of angels," says my mother. "Heavenly."

She's tone deaf – our singing is terrible, like the squawking of crows, harsh, cacophonous. We continue anyway, just because we can. Turn up the volume, crank up the volume on us, make us louder. We're not going anywhere, we're not going away. We dance too, closing our eyes, swinging our hips in time to the music, heads swaying like Axel Rose whom Trinity loves or Kristen Hersh whose music I adore, side to side. Side by side we set out on life's highway, determined to survive, steely-eyed, we will not become like Margaret with her breakdowns and her relapses and her existence that is not quite a life. Each carries the other; each is the other's burden. Two heads, one body. What will become of us? Nobody knows. We are firmly in the driver's seat. We will make the most of what we have been born with. We are the ones in control.

Sprout

By anybody's standards it was an expensive duvet. It was the best, a leader, a king amongst quilts. It was different from the rest. It was the fluffiest, the warmest, the finest. Fifty percent down and fifty percent large feather, it was not dressed up to the nines, like many of the others, the show-offs, in their gaudy coloured prints and their florals and their tartan covers. It was plain, naked, but it shone with potential. Once inside the cover he had designed, it would knock the competition into a cocked hat. It was a diamond in the rough.

They had come here together to find it. Hand in hand at Benny's For Beds on a Sunday, they'd walked down the duvet aisle, testing and fluffing and plumping, shaking their heads in dismay as candidate after candidate had failed to measure up. And now, just as they had begun to give up hope, here it was, sitting quietly on its own, slightly apart from the others, like a shy pet waiting to be chosen from amongst all the others in the store, overlooked because it didn't bark or turn back-flips. She had a feeling about it. She just knew. Goose bumps on her arms, a shiver down her spine. A strong sense of recognition gripped her, as if she had seen this duvet somewhere before, known it, perhaps intimately, in some other place, in some other life. It was the last one of its kind left on the shelf. She clutched it to her chest like a Linus blanket and gave him *the look*, the look which said *we've found it.* He shrugged, knowing that she was right, averting his eyes from the plastic pricing label tacked to the front of the shelf it had been on. Two small white feathers floated slowly to the ground.

It wasn't cheap. Three day's salary gone in an instant, on a plain cotton cover and some plucked plumage. She shrugged off the expense. It was worth it. It would cover her.

She carried it to the checkout with him trailing just behind, lost in his own little world. She watched protectively as the cashier rang up the purchase and placed her new charge in a large plastic carry bag. She smiled as she handed across her Visa, smiled as they walked across the car park, smiled all the way home, nestled already with her head upon its warmth, smiled as they took it inside, up the stairs where they snuggled together sleepily for a while before falling asleep beneath its cosy warmth.

When they awoke it was night time and the room was filled with a strange light. Groggily, she propped herself up on one elbow and peered through the pane, expecting that perhaps the moon was full tonight, or a few extra stars shone, or the council had erected an extra street lamp outside their house. Nothing outside was shining. The night was dark and cloudy, with a soft rain falling.

He raised himself up beside her, one arm around her waist.

"It's this thing," he said, patting their latest acquisition tentatively. "It's glowing."

Disbelieving, she looked down, and saw that although more a feeble glimmer than a brilliant radiation, the thing was, unmistakably, emitting a dull glow. Its light shone out between the dark seagull shapes he'd designed for its handmade, screen-printed cover.

"Spooky," he whispered, awed.

She picked up one corner of the thing that covered them and fluffed it about, as if the incandescence could be shaken out, as if she suspected that perhaps somebody had planted a few of those awful glow sticks in there amongst the feathers for a joke. Or something electronic and cellular that could be switched on from a distance.

"Maybe it's genetically engineered," he said. "Like those fish with the phosphorescent jellyfish genes."

She laughed, as you would laugh at a child who had discovered some awful truth that, for their own protection, they would have been better off not knowing. Thinking that perhaps to irradiate it with some greater light would stun it into behaving appropriately, she switched on the bedside lamp. Her hunch was right. The duvet flickered, faded and died.

It was not to glow again for several weeks.

There was a more pressing problem with the duvet. It moulted. It had a plumage retention issue. Further, rather than merely confining themselves to the boudoir, the freed feathers saw fit to migrate, and would drift insidiously down the stairs to lodge themselves in strange places. Feathers were found prettily displayed amongst a bouquet of blooms in the living room, neatly curled around a lemon in the fruit bowl, spiked into a pound of butter which had been stored in the door of the fridge.

"How come they're never just on the floor," he asked, when the freed feather fiasco first started. "Why do they always have to *show off?*"

She felt the need to defend the duvet and its offspring.

"They're not doing it on purpose," she said. "It's just coincidence that they come to rest in such strange places."

"It's like they're trying to spite us," he muttered, before going back to picking a scab that had formed on his elbow as a result of a scrape he'd incurred while renovating the bathroom. That was the first sign of resentment he showed towards her precious purchase.

She always found herself taking its side. He wanted to take it back to the store. He thought it was possessed; a demon duvet.

"I wish I'd never made that damned cover," he said. "Then none of this would have happened."

"O don't be so ridiculous," she scoffed, faintly amused by such neurotic notions. "It's as warm as toast. And besides, it's happy here."

He looked at her sideways.

"Happy? How the hell can a duvet be *happy?* You think the little fucker has *feelings?*"

She'd shrugged.

"You know what I mean. It's full and fluffy."

"And that in itself is unnatural," he had countered. "How can it lose so many feathers and still be *fluffy?*"

"It's special," she said. "It's not like the others."

She felt like she was sticking up for some prodigious, bratty child.

"No good can come of it," he muttered and turned his back on her.

She was siding with the enemy; he felt ganged up upon, ostracized in his own home. He formed his own team of one. She heard him banging about in his studio, slapping down paint and kicking in canvases and cursing. She knew not what he was making.

The cupboards that lined the walls of his studio were filled with his creations. In the early days, he'd painted only her, from the side, from the front, from the rear. Nudes, mostly. When they'd lived in different cities she'd flown up to see him one weekend and flown back with one of his versions of herself tucked under her arm. The stewardess had made her put the painting in the overhead locker and something had fallen on it, crushing her right buttock, so that it looked like she'd had a bad dose of liposuction. She'd been his subject for six months and then she had grown tired of posing for him; she told him that he needed new material. As if out of spite, he had started painting other women instead. Bank tellers, mutual friends, a thirteen year old girl he'd paid five bucks to take off her clothes so he could render her immortal. He thought he was doing her a favour.

But she was what he kept returning to. She was the default. Although she had stopped posing for him, he had not stopped attempting to render her in paint. He didn't show his work to anyone, not even her. She was forbidden from his study. Occasionally she would rescue a painting from the garbage and get a glimpse of his interior world. Once, after a fight, he'd painted her as a six headed monster, holding him up in a massive claw, mouth open, ready to devour. In another he had shown her giving a faceless man a blow job in a seedy bar. He signed and dated nothing. These pictures could have been made by anybody. Or nobody at all.

They'd had the thing for just over three weeks when he noticed the first sprout. They were lying in bed together and she was (in retrospect somewhat foolishly) lying on her side, facing away from him, when he reached out a hand and prodded her in the middle of her back.

"There's something weird here. Near your spine. Like a pimple, only bigger."

She attempted to roll over onto her back so he couldn't see it, but he propped a hand under her shoulder and hoisted her over, pressing his face up close to her skin.

"It's massive," he said. "Let me squeeze."

After picking, squeezing was his favourite activity. He sat up straight and crouched over her. Craning her neck she could see his brow furrowed in concentration as he placed an index finger on either side of the offending lump and pushed. Nothing. He pushed again, harder, and then gasped, as if some kindly aunt never before prone to violence had just slapped him across the face.

"What?" She questioned innocently. "What is it?"

She knew damned well what it was. Or what it might be.

"It's this *thing*," he said descriptively. "Protruding. Like a weird white stick."

She didn't want to appear too defensive.

"Just leave it alone," she said. "I'll go to the doctor and get it checked out. I had a mole removed there a couple of years before I met you. Maybe it's just... you know. Old mole bits gone funny."

"Hang on," he said. "I think I can yank it out. Where's your tweezers?"

"Don't yank it," she said. "You'll only make it bleed."

She pointed to his weeping elbow as evidence of the evils of picking and yanking.

"It'll be fine," he said, rising to his feet and fossicking about on the dresser. "Just hold still."

Before she could protest he had gripped the thing in the claws of the tweezers and, in one swift movement, like removing a sticking plaster, hauled it out.

"Holy shit," he said, holding the removed object up to the light. "It's over an inch long."

"Maybe it's a thorn," she said, grasping at straws.

Too slender.

He held the thing he had plucked between forefinger and thumb and snapped it neatly in two.

"Brittle," he said accusatorily, and gave her a cold look, as if he had fallen asleep one night next to one person and awoken the next morning next to somebody else entirely.

"It's nothing," she said. "Don't worry about it."

Although they shared most things, there are always secrets that each individual must keep private, even from those closest to them, and these shoots, these *sprouts*, as she had named them in her mind, were something that she had preferred to keep to herself.

She left the room and plodded downstairs to the bathroom. In the shower she applied hair removal cream to her entire body. It was a precaution she took in between the bouts of electrolysis, which for everybody else was permanent, but which, for her, was only a temporary solution. She was spending a fortune and she dreaded the sessions. The electrolysist was beginning to ask questions. She put another red rinse through her hair, stepped out of the steam and dried herself. Her body was covered in small tender red bumps, not unlike the measles. She looked in the mirror and breathed a sigh of relief. Her face, as yet had been spared.

One evening she returned home from work to find him in the lounge, standing above the duvet and beating it with the wooden spoon that she used to stir soups and casseroles.

"What the…?"

He stopped suddenly and swung round to face her. Fire was in his eyes.

"It spat at me," he said, and reached out his right hand to give the thing another whack.

"It spat?"

"*Poisonous* spit," he added, "Venom. Look."

And he pulled down the collar of his shirt to reveal a great red welt that swelled purple around the edges.

"What the hell is *that*?"

"*That* was caused by *this*," he said, and took down from the mantelpiece a jar which contained a single button, a button which she recognized as having come from the cover of the duvet. She noticed that the lid of the jar was firmly on, with breather holes punched through it, as if the button was some rare biological specimen that he had captured.

"Are you trying to tell me that a single tiny button caused that enormous welt?"

"Oh, this ain't no ordinary button," he said. "The little bugger's infused its buttons with *venom*."

"But the cover's separate," she said. "The cover's nothing to do with it."

"It has *become* its cover," he said theatrically, before throwing the wooden spoon down in disgust and stomping upstairs to nurse his wound.

And the poor thing lay in the corner, quivering from the beating it had taken, shaking like a jelly in an earthquake. She picked up the jar that contained the small blue button, and held it up to the light. So small, so harmless! Was it possible that he had cut himself on purpose, set the duvet up, framed it? Or incurred the wound in some other manner, and thought afterwards to blame it on the duvet? She didn't know whom to trust anymore. She found it hard to believe that the duvet had lashed out unprovoked. Even in the unlikely event that he *was* telling the truth and the button *had* been fired at will, he must have done something to cause it to act in such a violent manner. She put down the jar, picked up the duvet and snuggled on the sofa, not wanting to venture upstairs and disrupt the wounded one. It was the first night they had spent apart in three years.

Over the following weeks the duvet became a thing ineffable. To speak of it was to widen the divide between them even further, to do anything other than ignore it was to make the air too thick for even the sharpest knife to slice through. The tension of not mentioning was killing her. Upon entering their formerly happy home, at the end of her day, she felt herself grow pale, felt the blood draining from her body, as if leeched by some invisible vampire. She found herself looking into mirrors in strange rooms at strange times, as if she would see something behind her, something that lurked just beyond her right shoulder, a sinister Spirit of Resentments Past. A thing unbottled. She knew he could feel it too. Never a loquacious man, he now became even more sullen, silent and withdrawn, like a teenager. He had fenced off parts of himself, erected Keep Out signs. Large areas were off limits. He was a closed book. His paintings turned black; he had entered his noir phase. His work became a dark room that could not be lit. Before, he had kept them hidden; now he left them round the house for her to see, these renderings of dead birds and spiders and rats.

Others were noticing the strain of these changes. Kathleen from the office took her out to lunch and, in between the caesar salads and the coffee, asked if everything was alright.

"Things are slipping," Kathleen said. "Standards. We all have our off days, but an agenda for a meeting was sent out with the wrong address, resulting in several senior managers lost in cabs in the vicinity of Fleet Street when they were needed in the inner city. They're busy people. They need accuracy from their support staff. They need you to be present in both body and mind."

Pause. Sip of cappuccino.

"We're not indispensable you know."

Razor-edged words bound up in cotton wool. In response, she smiled and sipped her coffee, pulling her shirt cuffs down to hide her wrists.

"Mind on the job, please," Kathleen continued, flashing her pearly whites like a small shark that has smelt blood. "And if you want to talk, I'm always here."

It was then that Kathleen reached out to pat her knee, before jerking back in alarm. She had hit bristles, stumps.

"Spanish genes," she said eventually, after a long, pregnant pause, and shrugged, her fair hair and pale skin illuminating the lie. "A bit of a curse."

They were poking out through her stockings now. She'd missed an electrolysis appointment last week and had not been plucking. She smiled, paid the bill, and went back to the office a model of efficiency, a secretarial robot, typing and filing and answering the phone like a thing programmed. Every now and then she would stop and run her right hand along her left arm, from the wrist towards the elbow, feel how strange it felt, like stroking velvet against the grain. Then she would run her hand back the other way, smoothing ruffled feathers.

Every day she sprouted a little more, sprouted painfully and unfairly. Every day he said nothing. He had given up, was pretending not to notice. She began skipping work, calling in two or three times a week to say she couldn't come in that day, lying around the house, giving the odd desultory pluck. Fighting a losing battle. She pleaded illness, family crisis, dental appointments, death. She kept a list of relatives whose funerals she'd already given as excuses for not making it in, so that she never gave the same name twice. On the days she did go in, she baked, boiled beneath her long trousers and shirts and feathers. It was like wearing a sleeping bag underneath her clothes. She saw the other girls giving her glances. Kathleen had been talking. Cruelly, somebody printed out a copy of *Metamorphosis* and left it on her desk for her to find.

She thought he might say something, comment, call a doctor. Instead, he simply spent increasing amounts of time away from the house and down at the pub, coming home and passing out on the sofa, where she would inevitably find him the next morning, snoring in a pile of his own puke. When he wasn't drunk he was working, holed up in his studio, producing yet more pictures of creatures that crept or crawled or flew by night. The bat phase she found particularly disturbing, entailing as it did, his endless visits to the zoo, where he would lurk in the nocturnal enclosure for hours, frightening small children with the sketchings of vampires that he would give away for free.

One night he didn't come home at all, didn't call from the pub to say he would be late, didn't stagger home in the early morning hours, bleary and apologetic. He became now simply an absence. He became something missing.

That same night, at four in the morning, as she had snuggled deeper into its warmth, the duvet had begun to glow. This time she didn't try to
stop it, didn't put it in its place, didn't switch on the overhead light in order to dazzle it into submission. This time the light seemed not sinister, but friendly, comforting. She had settled down into its light, bathed in its warmth, as if wallowing in a sun-kissed ocean, floating beneath small golden stars. It had thrown its corners around her and together they had spent a wonderful night, slipping in and out of sleep and caresses. She remembered thinking that she had never felt so loved, so adored, so cherished.

He was there when she awoke, standing at the foot of the bed and looking down at her in disgust.

When she looked down at her arms, she could no longer see the skin beneath the feathers.

"Of all the people"…he began, and then stopped, choking.

She was coated from shoulder to wrist with plumage, with the odd stray tuft of white down sprouting from the backs of her hands. Still struggling to wake, she rose groggily to her feet and stood in her underwear before the full length mirror. The duvet lurked guiltily upon the bed. Complicit.

"I just never thought you'd…" – He couldn't carry on. She had been claimed, taken over. Invaded. It wasn't just her arms; it was her legs, her stomach, her back, her bum, everything white with the odd grey speckle. Nothing on the face, Jehovah be praised, nothing on the face. She could smell the alcohol on his breath. – "…betray me like this. Look at yourself, just look!"

She did look. She saw.

"I can't stand it!" He screamed. "You can't even see what's happening to you. I'm leaving. I'm leaving you to it."

She shrugged. Nothing was sinking in; everything was bouncing off the surface. Water off a duck's back.

"That's it? That's all I get? A shrug? Seven years of my life and you brush it off with a shrug? The love of my life starts turning into a fucking *chicken* and all I get is a shrug?"

The dam gates had burst; he was a man in full flood.

"You start an affair with a duvet, a fucking *quilt* that I willingly allowed into our home and you expect me just to stand by and watch you being taken from me? Spirited away? I can't stand it. I am *OUT OF HERE*!!"

He fumbled briefly, drunkenly, in the wardrobe, shoved whatever pithy bounty he had retrieved into a small backpack, lurched down the stairs, slammed the front door and was gone.

*

She couldn't go to work; she couldn't go anywhere. She reached for her mobile and left a message for Kathleen.

"Can't come in. Won't be in for a while. Sorry."

Then she sunk back onto the bed and it wrapped its left, and then its right hand side around her.

She went out at first. Braved life as a feathered thing. Attempted to adjust to life's strange changes. When she went to the pub, she wore long trousers and a polo neck, left her gloves on as she clutched her pint of beer. The only parties she attended were fancy dress, where she strapped on a beak and went as a chicken, or a goose or some other kind of flightless fowl.

"Love your costume," people would coo. "God, so realistic. Where on earth did you get it?"

"Overseas," she would say, offhand, noncommittal. "In some other country."

Men found themselves inexplicably attracted to her soft covering, would want to stroke and pluck and pull.

"Jesus, these look and feel so real."

And they would turn to her, the expression upon their faces a strange mixture of wonderment and repulsion. It never went further than that. She was not the kind of girl that you could take home to mother.

She got by. There was one terrible incident at the supermarket in which she forgot to keep her gloves on, grew hot and pulled them off absent-mindedly, an incident in which some stupid young checkout chick mistook her feathered right hand for some strange unclassified product from the poultry section and passed it over the scanner. When the hand did not bleep, the checkout girl looked down and saw what she was holding, then started screaming hysterically. Seeing the manager heading towards her, she dropped her groceries and sprinted from the store, ran all the way home, heart beating double time. She cowered beneath her beloved cover and did not leave her room for a week. When she finally did emerge, she took to ordering her groceries online.

The duvet had its own mind. When it grew grey at the edges she attempted to wash it, but the damned thing stubbornly resisted, slithering from the steel interior of the front loader every time she tried to shove it in. In the end she threw her hands up, *okay you win. Be grubby. See if I care.* And to herself she thought, *the battle but not the war.* She snuck up on it one morning as it dozed, lying like a cat in the sun, dragged it into the laundry and turned on the taps. It reared up like a horse and whacked her in the face with a fore corner. She slapped it back, pushed it down in the tub and gave it another good dousing, then shut the door and left it in there to soak. When she returned half an hour later, it lay there dormant, as if all the life had been rinsed out of it. She wrung it with her hands and hung it out to dry. When she brought it back inside it sulked for a week, wouldn't glow, wouldn't snuggle. It would turn itself freezing cold in the middle of the night, so that she would awake shivering. Her feathers started to fall out, leaving small white scars from the places where they had grown. Eventually she gave in and apologized and promised never to wash it again. It acquiesced, but a rift had been created. She was driving everything away.

He still had his keys. She hadn't changed the locks. She could have sworn that he was entering the house when she was gone, sneaking in while she was out. She stood outside his study. This Pandora pushed open the door.

This had always been his private room, his space away from her, and now that he had left she went through his belongings with curiosity, looking for something, some letter, some diary, something that would in some way incriminate him. She ventured into forbidden places – the cupboards.

She began at the beginning, with the pictures of herself seven years ago, poised and smiling, a target of somebody else's imagination. He'd been into bright primaries at the time and she had been rendered in violently bright shades; her eyes like cornflowers, her lips glowing red, her mouth open, like an invitation. Her skin jaundice yellow. Later, with the bank tellers and the thirteen year old, he'd turned to fleshier tones; dusky pink and beige, shades of muted orange. It was like looking through a photograph album; snapshots that his mind had taken. She found the design for the material from which the duvet's cover was made; little seagulls flying across an endless ocean. More pictures of birds. Hawks and vultures and gulls. Birds exotic and extinct; macaws and moas and dodos. On his desk, a copy of *The New Encyclopedia of Birds*. Turning to the relevant pages, she could see that he'd adapted the drawings from this book, enlarged, envisioned, coloured them in. And then the hybrids. Men with sharp claws and beady-eyed women with beaks. Paintings which grew increasingly outlandish, featuring characters which looked like extras from *Alice In Wonderland*. Pictures, which, when put together, told a tale, a story book, something sinister and not for children. She sat down on the floor, surrounded by these things which had been made by her Brother Grim. Pictures of herself with beak and claws. Her own self as winged thing. Some strange voodoo.

Something was tearing at the inside of her skin. Something inside wanted out. She was bursting, transforming, becoming something other. She saw sideways now, and not straight ahead.

The world had become peripheral. She beat one wing against the window, dug her talons into the sill.

In another part of the city, he smiled to himself, removed his jacket, relaxed.

"So," he said, leaning closer to the redhead at the bar. "You don't have a fear of flying, do you?"

Early Responses
to
"The Shingle Bar Sea Monster and Other Stories"

Laura Solomon's stories inhabit the borders between the mundane and the magical. Whether looking for love, or trying to understand a sibling, these stories have a very human heart. Solomon's characters are often looking for answers, and in the process of dealing with their dramas and disappointments they come across those things that can only be glimpsed from the corner of the eye. Sea monsters and angels, head grafts and werewolves, roses blooming from the tip of a blind man's cane.... The fantastic exists, though the miracle can fade with a wrong decision, or an unkind choice. These stories do not provide easy answers: the fantastic does not compensate for foolishness, and there are not always easy explanations. You may be touched by the marvelous, Solomon seems to say, but what happens next is entirely up to you.

—Viki Holmes, Author of *miss moon's class* (Chameleon, 2008), co-editor of *Not A Muse* (Haven 2009).

I first came across this writer in 1996 when I reviewed her first novel *Black Light*. She was only twenty-one years old at the time. Even at her tender age, Solomon was able to deconstruct the boundaries between art and life, tragedy and humour, producing a sophisticated challenge to the more conservative writers amongst us.

Solomon produced another novel in 1997. This book, *Nothing Lasting,* was about a psychopath who created mayhem wherever he went. I read this novel as an allegory of social breakdown and noted that without the redemptive literary skills of Solomon, the book would be almost too painful to bear.

You may wonder why I am bringing these early novels into this review. I am doing this quite deliberately. A novel can survive with just one character. Not so with a collection of short stories. They are sometimes difficult to grasp, given the multiple characters and plots that crowd around calling out, pick me, pick me! I wanted to find out if Solomon could manage this motley queue and in so doing, tease out the dominant themes of this eclectic collection.

Solomon presents each story to us in various ways, some mythological, some scientific, some within the comfort of social realism. Each story presents itself with some form of bodily trauma as the metaphoric centre of the work. Her characters are constantly seeking a meaningful life.

This collection is one to savour, to read and re-read. Solomon writes with passion and is totally dedicated to her art. Sometimes she wins and sometimes she loses, but she is never afraid to let language off the hook to see where it will lead her next.

—Beryl Fletcher, winner of a Commonwealth Writers' Prize (1992) for Best First Book in South East Asia and the Pacific with her novel *The Word Burners*. Four of her books have been translated into German and Korean.

WRITE TO US!

We are interested to read **your** comments on
Laura Solomon's short story collection,
The Shingle Bar Sea Monster and other stories.
Write to our email address, proverse@netvigator.com,
giving us a few sentences,
which you are willing for us to publish,
describing your response to this book.
If your comments are chosen to be included
in our E-Newsletter or website,
we will select another title published by Proverse
and send you a complimentary copy.
Please include your name, email address and mailing address
when you write to us, and state whether or not we may cut or
edit your comments for publication.
We will use your initials to attribute your comments.

Books by Laura Solomon
published by Proverse Hong Kong

Instant Messages (novella). Winner of the inaugural Proverse Prize (2009). (2010).

Hilary and David (epistolary novel). A Proverse Prize Publication. (2011).

The Shingle Bar Sea Monster and Other Stories. (2012)

An Imitation of Life, second edition (novel), first published by Solidus (UK), 2009. (2013)

Vera Magpie. A Proverse Prize Publication. (2013)

University Days. A Proverse Prize Publication.(2014)

In Vitro (poetry collection), first published by HeadworX (Wellington, New Zealand), 2011. (2014)

Freda Kahlo's Cry and Other Poems. (2015)

Brain Graft (play). Scheduled 2017.

THE PUBLISHERS

Proverse Hong Kong (PVHK), founded by Gillian and Verner Bickley, is based in Hong Kong with long-term and developing regional and international connections.

Proverse has published novels, novellas, non-fiction (including autobiography and biography, history, memoirs, sport, travel narratives), single-author poetry collections, children's, young adult and academic books. Other interests include diaries, and academic works in the humanities, social sciences, cultural studies, linguistics and education. Some Proverse books have accompanying audio texts. Some are translated into Chinese.

We welcome authors who have a story to tell, wisdom, perceptions or information to convey, a person they want to memorialize, a neglect they want to remedy, a record they want to correct, a strong interest that they want to share, skills they want to teach, and who consciously seek to make a contribution to society in an informative, interesting and well-written way. Proverse works with texts by non-native-speaker writers of English as well as by native English-speaking writers.

The name, "Proverse", combines the words "prose" and "verse" and is pronounced accordingly.

THE INTERNATIONAL PROVERSE PRIZE
FOR UNPUBLISHED BOOK-LENGTH FICTION,
NON-FICTION OR POETRY

The Proverse Prize, an annual international competition for an unpublished single-author book-length work of fiction, non-fiction, or poetry, the original work of the entrant, submitted in English (unpublished translations welcomed) was established in January 2008. It is open to all who are at least eighteen on the date they sign the entry form and without restriction of nationality, residence or citizenship.

Founded by Gillian and Verner Bickley, the objectives of the prize are: to encourage excellence and / or excellence and usefulness in publishable written work in the English Language, which can, in varying degrees, "delight and instruct". Entries are invited from anywhere in the world.

The Prize
1) Publication by Proverse Hong Kong, with
2) Cash prize of HKD10,000 (HKD7.80 = approx. USD1.00)

Extent of the Manuscript: within the range of what is usual for the genre of the work submitted. However, it is advisable that novellas be in the range, 30,000 to 45,000 words; other fiction (e.g. novels, short-story collections) and non-fiction (e.g. autobiographies, biographies, diaries, letters, memoirs, essay collections, etc.) should be in the range, 75,000 to 100,000 words. Poetry / poetry collections should be in the range, 5,000 to 25,000 words. Other word-counts and mixed-genre submissions are not ruled out.

International Proverse Prize Annual Entry Deadlines
(subject to confirmation and/or change)

Receipt of Entry Fees / Entry Forms begins	[Variable, no later than] 14 April
Deadline for receipt of Entry Fees / Entry Forms	31 May
Receipt of entered manuscripts begins	1 May
Deadline for receipt of entered manuscripts	30 June

The above information is for guidance only.
More information, updated from time to time, is available on
the Proverse website: proversepublishing.com

WINNERS OF THE PROVERSE PRIZE WHOSE ENTERED WORK HAS ALREADY BEEN PUBLISHED BY PROVERSE HONG KONG

Rebecca Tomasis
Laura Solomon
Gillian Jones
David Diskin
Peter Gregoire
Sophronia Liu
Birgit Linder
James Mccarthy
Philip Chatting
Celia Claase
Gustav Preller
Lawrence Gray

WINNERS OF SUPPLEMENTARY (PUBLICATION) PRIZES

Victor Edward Apps · Rupert Kwan Yun Chan ·
Sally Dellow · Patricia Glinton-Meicholas ·
Lawrence Gray · Patricia W. Grey ·
Andrew Simpson Guthrie · Emily Ho · Henrik Hoeg · L.W.
(Lawrence) Illsley · Jupy James ·
Akin Jeje (Akinsola Olufemi Jeje) ·
Lelawattee Manoo-Rahming · James Norcliffe ·
Jan Pearson · Jason S Polley · Shahilla Shariff ·
Laura Solomon · James Tam · Dennis Wong

THE INTERNATIONAL PROVERSE POETRY PRIZE
(SINGLE POEMS)

An annual international Proverse Poetry Prize (for single poems) was established in 2016. The international Proverse Poetry Prize is open to all who are at least eighteen years old whatever their residence, nationality or citizenship.

Single poems, submitted in English, are invited on (a) <u>any subject or theme, chosen by the writer</u> OR (b) <u>on a subject or theme selected by the organizers.</u>

Poems may be in any form, style or genre. Each poem should be no more than 30 lines.

Entries should previously be unpublished in any way (except in the case of unpublished translations into English of the entrant's own work already published in another language, providing the entrant holds the copyright).

In 2016
cash prizes were offered as follows:
1st prize; USD100.00; 2nd prize: USD45.00;
3rd prizes (up to four winners): USD20.00.

If there are enough good entries in any year, an anthology of prize-winners and selected other entries will be published.

In 2016, judging took place at the same time as the judging for the Proverse Prize for unpublished book-length fiction, non-fiction or poetry.

Judges: anonymous (as for the Proverse Prize for an unpublished book-length work).

Max number of entries per person: No maximum.
No poet may win more than one prize.

The above information is for guidance only.
More information, updated from time to time, is available on the Proverse website: proversepublishing.com

FICTION PUBLISHED BY PROVERSE

Those who enjoy **Curveball** may also enjoy the following novels, novellas and short story collections (listed separately).

A Misted Mirror, by Gillian Jones. 2011.

A Painted Moment, by Jennifer Ching. 2010.

Adam's Franchise, by Lawrence Gray. November 2016.

An Imitation of Life. 2nd ed, by Laura Solomon. 2013.

Article 109, by Peter Gregoire. 2012.

Bao Bao's odyssey: from Mao's Shanghai to capitalist Hong Kong, by Paul Ting. 2012.

Black Tortoise Winter, by Jan Pearson. 2016.

Bright Lights and White Nights, by Andrew Carter. 2015.

cemetery – miss you, by Jason S Polley. 2011.

Cop Show Heaven, by Lawrence Gray. 2015.

Curveball: Life Never Comes At You Straight, by Gustav Preller. 2016.

Death Has a Thousand Doors, by Patricia W. Grey. 2011.

Hilary and David, by Laura Solomon. 2011.

HK Hollow, by Dragoş Ilca. Scheduled 2016/2017

Instant messages, by Laura Solomon. 2010.

Man's Last Song, by James Tam. 2013.

Mila the Magician by Zhang Jian (Catherine Chin). 2014 (English/Chinese bilingual edition).

Mishpacha – family, by Rebecca Tomasis. 2010.

Paranoia (the walk and talk with Angela), by Caleb Kavon. 2012.

Red Bird Summer, by Jan Pearson. 2014.

Revenge From Beyond, by Dennis Wong. 2011.

The Day They Came, by Gérard Louis Breissan. 2012.

The Devil You Know, by Peter Gregoire. 2014.

The Perilous Passage of Princess Petunia Peasant, by Victor E. Apps. 2014. (Young adult)

The Village in the Mountains, by David Diskin. 2012.

The Monkey in Me: Confusion, Love and Hope Under a Chinese Sky, by Caleb Kavon. 2009.

The Reluctant Terrorist: in Search of the Jizo, by Caleb Kavon. 2011.

Tiger Autumn, by Jan Pearson. 2015.

Tightrope!: a Bohemian tale, by Olga Walló.
Translated from Czech by Johanna Pokorny, Veronika Revická & others. Poetry translated by Justin Quinn, Veronika Revická. Edited by Gillian Bickley & Olga Walló, with Verner Bickley. 2010.

University Days, by Laura Solomon. 2014.

Vera Magpie, by Laura Solomon. 2013.

SHORT STORY COLLECTIONS

Beyond Brightness, by Sanja Särman. November 2016.

The Snow Bridge and other Stories, by Philip Chatting. 2015.

Odds and Sods, by Lawrence Gray. 2013.

The Shingle Bar Sea Monster and other stories, by Laura Solomon. 2012.

FICTION – CHINESE LANGUAGE

The Monkey in Me, by Caleb Kavon. Translated by Chapman Chen. 2010.

Tightrope! A Bohemian Tale, by Olga Walló. Translated by Chapman Chen. 2011. Chinese translation supported by the Ministry of Culture of the Czech Republic.

~~~

FIND OUT MORE ABOUT OUR AUTHORS BOOKS AND EVENTS

Visit our website:
http://www.proversepublishing.com

Visit our distributor's website: <www.chineseupress.com>

Follow us on Twitter
Follow news and conversation: twitter.com/Proversebooks>
OR
Copy and paste the following to your browser window and
follow the instructions:
https://twitter.com/#!/ProverseBooks
"Like" us on www.facebook.com/ProversePress

Request our free E-Newsletter
Send your request to info@proversepublishing.com.

Availability
Most books are available in Hong Kong and world-wide
from our Hong Kong based Distributor,
The Chinese University Press of Hong Kong,
The Chinese University of Hong Kong, Shatin, NT,
Hong Kong SAR, China.
Email: cup-bus@cuhk.edu.hk
Website: <www.chineseupress.com>.
All titles are available from Proverse Hong Kong
http://www.proversepublishing.com
and the Proverse Hong Kong UK-based Distributor.

We have **stock-holding retailers** in Hong Kong,
Singapore (Select Books),
Canada (Elizabeth Campbell Books),
Andorra (Llibreria La Puça, La Llibreria).
Orders can be made from bookshops in the UK and elsewhere.

Ebooks
Most of our titles are available also as Ebooks.